Alexandra Deen

Alexandra Deen

A Harrington Family Story

Tamara Martin

The Henry Mayberry Group

First published in Australia 2017 by The Henry Mayberry Group

www.thehenrymayberrygroup.com

National Library of Australia Cataloguing-In-Publication data:

Martin,Tamara, 1973-

Alexandra Deen / Tamara Martin

1st ed.

ISBN: 978-0-6480250-0-9 (pbk.)

Cover Design: Kristyn McGuiggan, Drop Dead Designs

*For Mum who knew I was a writer before I knew
what a writer was xx*

Chapter 1

Beside me, the River Seine bubbled like a witch's brew. Fat raindrops soaked my clothes, chilling me right through to the bone. Tears streaked what remained of my make up and I was glad I couldn't see my own face. I'd become a version of myself I no longer recognised. Not just in the last couple of hours, but the last few years if I were honest. If I were brave enough to face the reality of who I'd become, who I'd allowed myself to become because it would be easier. It was expected.

The streets of the most romantic city in the world were suspiciously quiet, as though it were ashamed it hadn't lived up to the hype. My feet hurt, from the cold, from the wet, from poorly chosen pretty ballet flats. I shivered, unable to stop the quivering of my lip.

A car horn blared, my heart near leapt from my chest.

I stepped back onto the kerb. 'Pay attention, Lexi,' I scolded myself. Billy bloody McCrae certainly wasn't worth getting run down on a dark Parisian street. So my life was officially in the gutter, it wasn't reason enough to die. Or worse, end up in a Parisian hospital all alone and having to call my mother to come and get me.

Catching my breath, I wiped my tear-stained face, checked the street for traffic and trundled across the road towards the music, the laughter, the dry roof of the hostel matching the map on the now bedraggled pamphlet in my hand.

I was angry and sad and so disappointed the weight of it crushed my lungs, stealing my breath as I stood before the big blue doors, the rain falling in sheets around me, my clothes soaked and heavy. I watched a piece of peeling paint flapping in the breeze, resisting the urge to pull at it and wondered if I should I knock on the door or should I just walk in? I'd never stayed in such a place before, somewhere without a doorman to direct me. Was there an etiquette I should have been aware of? The paint chipped doors suggested etiquette didn't rule this little corner of Paris.

Looking for guidance, for something, I spotted a girl with wild black curls sitting on the balustrade of a small verandah heaving with jovial young people, drinking beer from bottles, unaware the world was full of misery and cheating bastard boyfriends. She laughed, her whole body shaking from the happiness. I wondered if it would feel as good as it looked, to laugh that way, to be that happy. I wondered if I'd ever been that happy. If I'd ever laughed that freely. I couldn't remember.

The girl looked over her sun-kissed shoulder, smiled and nodded towards the door. I turned away, embarrassed. What was wrong with me? I don't stand on streets in the middle of the night, lurking, staring at strangers. I was losing my bloody mind.

I sucked in a deep, fortifying breath. It wasn't a palatial hotel with marble floors, but it would do until I could get the hell out of Paris, I reminded myself and pulled open the door.

The foyer was sparse but clean and dry. A worn timber chair sat beneath a phone attached to the wall. A staircase opposite wound its way up into the hidden heart of the hostel. The well-worn reception desk was directly in front. Behind the desk, sat a girl with red hair so bright it almost glowed, framing a face as perfect as porcelain. The girl chuckled at something Homer Simpson said in French on the television beside her, completely oblivious or perhaps purposely ignoring the fact that I'd just stumbled in and was dripping all over the streaked timber floor.

I walked towards the desk, my shoes squelching loudly in the quiet, my insides cringing from embarrassment. She finally looked up from the television as I reached the counter, raising her eyebrows, trying not to smile at the makeup streaked all over my face and hair stuck to my head like paint and dripping all over her counter.

'Dorm or single, hon?' she asked with a poetic French accent.

'Whatever's cheapest?' I stammered, tears choking my vocal chords as I pulled scrunched, damp euros from my handbag.

'Dorm it is, then. Room two, bunk three.' She put a key attached to a block of wood atop a pile of linen and a towel and handed the pile over the counter as though I were an army recruit reporting for duty. She sent me up the stairs with no further question, as though I'd stood before her in a sundress in the middle of the afternoon instead of a drowned, miserable version of a person in the middle of the night. But maybe that's what happened in places like this? Vagrants, society's misfits and those spat out by the world, appeared at all hours so often, it was accepted as the norm?

Four bunk beds had been crammed into the room she sent me to, each flanked at the foot with a metal locker. Flimsy curtains covered the long, short, rectangular windows that were too high up to see out of. The dull light from the bulb hidden under the white plastic shade on the ceiling wasn't dull enough to hide the worn timber floor covered with the debris of the room's missing inhabitants; a discarded towel, a pair of thongs, backpacks, socks and a navy blue hoodie.

They had squeezed the tiniest bathroom I'd ever seen into the far corner, just big enough for a toilet, basin and shower. It was a far cry from the fancy hotel I'd woken in with its giant bathtub and shiny white tiles and luxury complimentary bath products, but it didn't matter. Not much mattered right now other than getting through the night and thinking about tomorrow when tomorrow showed up.

As I organised my things, my mind flashed to the morning when I'd strolled the streets of Paris, the bridges that arched over the Seine, hand in hand, happy, in love. I'd seen the Eiffel Tower rising above the trees in the distance, wondered if it would be there that Billy would sink to one knee on the grass and ask me to be his wife. I'd have said yes, too. I'd been a fool. Of course I'd been a fool. I'd been a fool for years. Now I had to find the strength to go home and face my family, my friends. What friends? They'd all known, I'd seen it on their faces in the fancy Parisian restaurant where we were dining, when my life had unravelled at my feet. They'd eaten dinner in my home, eaten my food and drunk my wine laughing in my face, laughing behind my back.

No, they were Billy's friends and he could keep them. I didn't want them. Friends don't allow you to be blindsided in foreign countries. Friends save you, they protect you, they look out for you. They don't just sit back and watch your life crumble. No, I had no friends. I didn't have much of anything now. Perhaps just the scrap of dignity I'd held onto when I'd told Billy to go to hell and walked out of the fancy restaurant where he'd sat with that woman draped across his lap and the revelations had unfolded, piece by piece in seconds but what had felt like hours. I'd walked out with nothing, no friends, no savings, nowhere to go, nothing.

I dug around in my suitcase for something to wear to bed but almost everything was damp. I knew I should have bought the one with the hard shell case, I thought to myself as I began pulling things out. After hanging my wet clothes over the edges of my bed, over my suitcase, from the open locker door, I squeezed between the bunks to the bathroom. The cubicle was small but the water was hot and I thawed, movement returning to my fingertips and toes. I leant on the wall, letting the hot water beat on my body, glad to be feeling something other than devastation or misery or self hatred.

Careful not to overuse the hot water, I reluctantly stepped out of the shower, my bones finally warmed, my skin red, raw, and shiny new. I threw on an almost dry t-shirt and undies, already imagining the sweet perfection of the warm bed and the desperate bout of indulgent wallowing that waited.

With my towel and wet clothes gathered in my arms, I

squeezed between the bunks and found the girl with the wild black curls sitting on my bed, absently picking at a hang nail and swinging her leg as though to a tune only she could hear.

She looked up as I dropped my loot onto my suitcase.

'Hey,' she said in an Australian accent, holding out a bottle of beer.

'Hello,' I replied as though in question, but taking the beer she offered anyway.

'You alright?' she asked.

I shrugged.

'Wanna talk about it?' she asked.

'Not really.'

'That means you really should. It'd be better than wallowing or letting it eat you up all night. It might help you sleep at least,' she offered.

I shrugged. She had some good points and really, what did I have to lose? Pride? I couldn't lose much more and maybe once I hit bottom I could start building myself back up. Somehow.

'I got duped, that's all. Utterly blindsided. The man I loved wasn't who I thought he was. My friends let me down, let me fall. I just, I don't know, my head's still spinning.'

'Are there actual details in there? Come on, sit, spit them out, otherwise you'll keep seeing them every time you close your eyes.'

'I sure as hell don't need that,' I laughed, surprising myself. 'We came for a wedding. We were at dinner with some of our friends. I went to the toilet, stopped to take a phone call from mum. I'd called her earlier but forgot the time difference. Anyway, we only talked for a few minutes. When I came back into the restaurant, there was this girl, I'd seen her a couple of times at the footy, never paid her any attention, knew she knew some of our friends but had no idea her and Billy knew each other as anything more than passing acquaintances. I'll never forget her, tall, lanky, all arms and legs, Kardashian hair and a laugh like a strangled hyena. She was draped all over my boyfriend. His hands were all over her and his face was buried in her hair. I don't know what he was doing, kissing her neck, whispering something. I don't know. I just froze and when he saw me he just laughed. He was drunk I guess, just enough to not care what I saw or what he said. Suggested a ménage a trois. Said it'd be very French of us.'

'What did your friends do?'

'They just sat there. Fuckers,' I laughed, taking a long sip of cold beer.

'Fuckers,' agreed my new friend, tapping her bottle to mine.

'She wasn't the only one. She laughed when I thought she was. Then it all began falling into place, the late nights, the 2am showers, the unanswered calls and I asked the questions. Turns out he's been all over the place with anyone who'd take him for years. None of it was real. We weren't real and I just don't know who I am now without him. Everything has been him. Everything I'd planned for the rest of my life had been with him. Now it's just me and I don't know what to do. He chose everything, decided everything and I let him because he was usually right and it was easier than hearing I told you so. So I let him and now I feel so stupid and lost.'

'Did you notice you never said you loved him or that your

heart was broken? You've just been humiliated and horribly inconvenienced,' she smiled.

'Really? Huh,' I mumbled, realising she was exactly right. I was pissed off. I was annoyed. I was afraid and utterly humiliated. But I wasn't sad. I wasn't brokenhearted. How was that possible? I'd loved him, didn't I? We shared a home, a bed, a future. I'd planned babies and old age with him. I had to have loved him. But this bringer of beer and kind shoulders was right, my heart didn't feel broken. I wanted to wallow but I didn't feel the need to cry for him. I'd cried from the surprise, the devastation, for who I'd become, but the thought of never seeing Billy again, never having to listen to his obnoxious lectures or be bossed around, left me with nothing but relief.

As I finished my beer, my new friend said, 'Come on, plenty more of those downstairs. Your new life starts now. A new life where you're in charge,' she smiled.

I liked the sound of that.

'We'll be gentle, I promise,' she offered, holding her hand out to me.

I took her hand and let her pull me up.

'I'm Lydia,' she said, finally introducing herself.

'Alexandra.'

'Come on Alex, let's go see if you're in there somewhere.'

I laughed, forgiving her for the choice of nickname. I hated Alex, it was a boy's name. My friends and family call me Lexi, but for one night, what did it matter? For one night I could be anyone and at that moment I was pretty done with Lexi the lovely doormat.

I followed Lydia onto the verandah and into the throng of

people still enjoying the night and thanked my beer buzz when she called everyone to attention, commanding the spotlight.

'Alex, this is everyone. Everyone, this is Alex. She needs beer and kindness and it's our duty as fellow travelers, to provide her with both,' she insisted as I tried smiling.

Mumbles of agreement followed sympathetic nods. Beers were passed forward through the crowd of people with words of sympathy and welcome. Lydia draped a kind, friendly, comforting arm around me and led me to the balustrade she'd occupied earlier.

'What a bastard. Forget him,' Lydia said. 'Everything will be better now you've left him, you'll see. You'll pick yourself back up and find a new way now you've found the strength to stand up for yourself.'

'He has to be a real asshole to bring you all this way and then do that,' claimed a bright, bubbly girl with blonde dreadlocks when Lydia told her my boyfriend had turned out to be an ass. She was another Aussie. In fact, they mostly seemed to be Aussies, like the hostel was a magnet for lost Aussie souls, although I seemed to be the only one truly lost.

'Thanks,' I said, taking deep breaths, waiting for the tears welling in my eyes to evaporate. It would take some getting used to, figuring out who I was without him, thinking of how I would move forward alone, it had all happened so suddenly it was a lot to comprehend. Six years with the same man was a long time. He's all I knew, we'd been together my entire adult life.

A few beers in and I couldn't believe the world I'd landed in. These people spoke of adventures and places that sounded too good to be true, surfing in places I'd never heard of, finding treasure in small European towns where no one spoke English, cycling along the coastline in remote villages, the sun kissing their skin, falling in love, eating incredible food. They laughed loud, they wore simple cotton summer dresses and crazy board shorts, the men with permanent five o'clock shadows, living in a world so far removed from my grey cubicle and suburban life back home that I could hardly comprehend any of it and now here they were, welcoming me into their fold, commiserating with me over beers as though we were old friends.

I leant on the balustrade, looking out over the dark road, slick and wet under the moon's bright rays now the clouds had moved on. Had I really stood out there on the footpath in the rain? Now I was dry and warm and comforted, sipping cold beer amongst the laughter and camaraderie, I couldn't believe that had been me. Who was that person? In fact, who was that person I'd become over the last six years? Not someone I recognised. Not someone I particularly liked and I hadn't even realised it was happening. Somewhere it'd just been easier to give me up and go with the flow, abide by everyone else's expectations, my boss, my mother, Billy. I didn't even know which bits were me and which were Billy. All I knew was Lydia was right. It was time to find out who I was.

'What's with all the thinking?' asked Lydia, twisting the top off another beer.

'Oh, nothing,' I half smiled. 'Just thinking how different the day's ended to how I'd expected.'

'Yeah, life does that,' she smiled.

'I've been here one bloody day and my life's been turned

upside down. How does that even happen? This trip was not supposed to go this way.'

'Maybe it was and you just didn't realise it. The universe has a way of kicking us up the behind when we don't pay attention.'

I laughed a huffy laugh because she was probably right. 'It was easy to ignore it all.'

'Isn't it always,' she grinned. 'Until the kicking comes and you have no choice.'

'So, what are your plans from here?' a man asked, joining us at the balustrade.

I turned away from the rain soaked street, looked up and our eyes locked. It was him. My knight, my saviour who'd given me the pamphlet that had led me here. The waiter with the sun bleached shaggy hair, broad shoulders, wide smile and laughing grey green eyes that knew things, that loved things, that loved life. He wore a loose fitting, faded yellow tank top with bright, multi-coloured board shorts and blue thongs on his sun drenched feet.

The sun had soaked his body, from his biceps to his beautiful broad shoulders. I tried not to look but my eyes wanted to linger, to drink him in. Where did men that beautiful even come from? What was I even doing noticing? I was supposed to be crying into my beer not admiring handsome strangers that help damsels in distress find refuge. But for just one second, everything stood still and my breath caught in my chest.

'You?' I asked softly.

He smiled.

'You know each other?' Lydia asked.

I wanted to laugh, as if I know men that look like him. Billy was alright, handsome enough, a good catch even, so everyone kept telling me, but Billy had nothing on this bloke. This bloke was tall, slightly rugged, his strong jaw covered lightly in stubble, everything about him was strong, then there was his lovely mouth and puppy dog eyes that smiled without trying. I mentally shook my head clear to stop from staring.

'It was my restaurant she was at earlier,' he told Lydia. 'Well not mine,' he said to me, 'the one where I was working. Just filling in actually, not really my thing waiting tables, prefer pouring beers, but a mate needed a favour, they were short and needed a hand.'

'Well, thanks,' I said. 'I've no idea where I'd have gone without the pamphlet you gave me.'

'Oh a regular knight, huh,' joked Lydia.

'I'm Tom by the way,' he smiled, his whole face lighting up as though lit from the inside by his own personal sun. Then, his right bicep flexed beautifully as he stretched his arm around Lydia's shoulders, draping it there casually, as though he'd done it a thousand times. I felt my heart sink all the way down to my toes.

Don't be ridiculous, I told myself. Of course he has a girlfriend. What was wrong with me? What was wrong with my brain? I'd just left Billy, the supposed love of my life, the man I'd shared intimate moments with, cared for when he was sick, gone to birthday parties with, hosted barbeques with, told all my deepest secrets and wishes to, the man I'd expected a bloody proposal from under the Eiffel Tower. My head was still spinning with everything that had happened, where I'd ended up, what lay ahead. I couldn't fancy someone else already. My traumatised brain was just confused, that was all.

'Um, I'll see if I can get a flight home in the morning, I suppose,' I said, answering Tom's question

'Home? No!' cried Lydia. 'You're in Paris, Alex. You've only been here a day. You can't go yet. This is one of the most beautiful cities you'll ever see.'

I shrugged. She was right. But I was short on funds now I had a life to rebuild and really, no inclination to wander the streets alone.

'You know what you should do,' Tom said, looking at Lydia as though he'd solved the most intricate puzzles of the universe.

'Absolutely!' she cried, reading his mind.

I watched them, waiting for an explanation.

'Come down the coast with us, Alex. Oh you have to. It's just what you need, a bit of sun and sand, the ocean will heal all those wounds and you'll be good as new in no time. France is incredible, you can't miss out now that you're here. Please. Please say *oui*,' Lydia begged, gripping my arm in anticipation.

'What? No, no. We just met. You don't want me imposing on your trip,' I insisted, despite how nice the prospect of forgetting my life and laying on a beach in a foreign country sounded.

'Don't be ridiculous, the more the merrier. We'd love you to come with us. I promise, we're relatively normal, non murdering types, you have to come and balance out all the testosterone,' she insisted with a smile that left me both nervous and more excited than I could remember ever being.

'We have a car,' Tom added proudly.

'That's so nice, really it is but I don't think my failing funds will allow me to stay much longer than tonight anyway, I'm afraid. This was Billy's trip. He paid for the flights, the accommodation. I've just got a little spending money for bits and bobs, souvenirs, snacks, maybe a dinner or two, that sort of thing,' I admitted sadly.

'That doesn't matter,' Lydia said, waving my worries away. 'None of us have any money, but we get by, that's half the fun.'

'Really?' I couldn't believe it. They were all so happy. They didn't look hungry and the travel stories they'd shared in the last hour were so mind blowing they didn't even seem real; how could they all have no money? Living the life they lived cost money, surely? Billy and I had spent nights planning and budgeting for this trip. But what if all this time I'd had it backwards? 'But how?' I had to ask.

'Ah, you have to come for us to share all our secrets,' Lydia winked, laughing.

'C'mon, Alex, it'll be fun. You need some fun. We leave first thing tomorrow and it's just for a few days. It will cost next to nothing, I promise. We have a spare bed in the villa, and I am pretty sure it has your name on it,' Tom insisted.

'You can't go home yet, you have to come,' begged Lydia.

All the usual thoughts ran through my head again as though on repeat. Blah, blah, blah. What I really wanted to do was blow off my life and go to the bloody beach with this group of the coolest, most amazing people I'd ever met. To have the much needed fun Tom spoke of. To lay in the sun and pretend none of it had happened, that I hadn't been so humiliated I was afraid to look people in the eye. Forget it all and laugh. It'd been so long since I'd just let go and laughed, I'd forgotten what it felt like.

These people were reminding me and I wasn't ready to let it go, to go back.

So, after taking a long sip of beer for courage, I ignored that annoying voice in my head, the one that had led me down this path in the first place. 'Fine, fine, okay, *oui*,' I agreed, panicking as soon as the words were out despite my newfound courage and resolution.

I couldn't drive to some French coast with these people. I'd just met them. It was crazy. Lydia was crazy. Tom was crazy. They were all crazy. But it did seem silly to waste the airfare Billy had paid for and they were right, I was in Paris, anything was possible in Paris, right?

Chapter 2

I opened my eyes, closing them again as the bunk bed above me spun like a carnival ride. My head throbbed as I quelled the building nausea, vomit and bile churning in my stomach, rising higher and higher. I needed sleep, hours, days of it and water, litres of water but Lydia had taken to banging on the wooden bed surround, the thumping reverberating and echoing like thunder inside my head. Why couldn't she just speak like a normal person?

'I can hear your brain ticking over Newbie, just get up and let's go,' Lydia called, way too amused by my pain.

'Fine,' I groaned, forcing myself out of the bed. People were waiting on me and in the light of day, I'm not sure I even cared if they did steal all my stuff and leave me on the side of the road . It was better than facing home, the humiliation of explaining to my mum and everyone else what had happened to their perfect Billy and seeing the looks of disappointment on their faces, the pity in their eyes. '*Lexi, how could you mess that up,*' Mum would say in that know all voice that always made me feel guilty for letting her down. She'd always thought the sun shone out of Billy's rear end. Everyone did. The perfect man with the perfect job, successful, smart, well dressed and charming. He'd charmed us all until we couldn't see straight.

Ambling to the shower I felt nothing, not the cool morning air, not the pain of my insides, only my throbbing head, regretting the night before with every step and every drop of water. I blame everything on the beer. Nothing good ever comes from drinking beer. I'd only had a few, but after the day I'd had, they'd gone straight to my head and I was vulnerable and in desperate need of friendship, that kind of emotional trauma should never be mixed with beer. Stupid, stupid me.

What was I even doing, I thought as the water warmed up? I don't go to foreign beaches with people I don't know. I don't willy-nilly wander off to goodness knows where with strangers. But I wanted to go, despite how terrified I was. For just a minute I wanted to know what it was like to be them, to laugh like I'd seen Lydia laugh the night before. For just a minute I wanted to forget the fool I'd become. I wanted to know who I was without everyone else sticking their noses in and deciding for me. I knew these few days could be the key. If not, it would be a few days where I could forget about my humiliation and that was something.

As Lydia hurried me again, her voice laced with far too much humour, I wondered why she was so chirpy anyway? She'd drunk buckets of beer. Conditioning, I decided. She probably does it every day. While I sit in my cold grey cubicle typing inane memos to people who don't read them, she's off somewhere sunny, warm and fabulous drinking beer and having wild adventures with hot surfer guys like Tom.

The heaviness of indulgence filled every cell of my body but I was clean and managed to dress without succumbing to the nausea or falling down to sleep. I wore the only thing in my suitcase not still damp because it had been zipped in it's own garment bag. It was the blue and white-striped strapless number I'd planned to wear to the stupid wedding Billy had made me come here for. His old uni buddy and some ultra beautiful doctor. I don't know why they couldn't have just gotten married in Australia. If they'd just gone to the wine region or the beach like everyone else, maybe none of this would ever have happened? I'd be none the wiser and living my miserable life in ignorant bliss. Now I was probably overdressed but my head pounded far too much to care. Exiting the shower I found my bed stripped and my suitcase zipped.

Lydia handed me a banana and a coffee. 'Our chariot awaits, Newbie, let's go,' she said, pulling my arm, almost tipping the precious coffee before I'd even had a sip.

We dumped our used linen in the trolley at the bottom of the stairs, then I pushed my sunglasses onto my face and followed Lydia into the bright morning sun. Idling at the kerb puffing out wafts of black smoke was a blue van that should have been destined for the scrap heap, not ferrying a group of nomads to the beach.

'That's it?' I asked.

Lydia only smirked.

'It looks like a death-trap,' I told her as the ancient, faded people mover before us groaned and polluted the perfect blue sky.

'Ah, it'll be fine,' she laughed, instilling no confidence whatsoever.

Tom looked up from loading backpacks into the boot and gave my enormous suitcase a confused once over.

'What?' I asked. 'I didn't know I'd be going to some beach with a bunch of crazy backpackers, did I?'

He laughed, shaking his head.

'You remember everyone,' Lydia interrupted as way of introductions.

I nodded although I only remembered a couple of faces, few essential details. But I didn't say so, my brain was too busy racing through its, *what the hell are you doing?* dance while everyone began piling in. Tom whipped my bag into the back of the minibus, minivan or whatever they called the death trap on wheels so fast I could only assume that's where it had vanished to.

Everything with these people happened too fast. They did things when they decided to do them, they didn't dally about procrastinating. I should have been terrified, I should have been a lot of things, but I wasn't. I should have been mourning for a start, for my life, for what could have been, for Billy. But in the light of day, I didn't care about any of it. The hopeless devastation I'd expected to rip me apart was still evading me. Instead I felt a lightness I couldn't ever remember feeling. I sucked in great big lungfuls of air and it tasted cleaner and sweeter than I ever remembered it tasting. The weight on my chest from the night before was gone. The weight I'd carried every day, that was gone too. I felt a smile tugging at my mouth as I noticed the beauty of a bird soaring across the clear blue sky, the smell of morning, the warming sun on my arms. What kind of person did that make me? That I was smiling? That I wasn't curled in a corner, a broken shell? I didn't care. Other than the seediness from the night before's overindulgence, I felt better than I could remember feeling in a really long time. How could that be a bad thing?

I was about to follow the others aboard the van when a chill ran over my spine a second before I heard Billy's voice and everything inside me flinched.

'Lexi?' Billy called, freezing the blood in my veins.

'Ooh fancy,' Lydia cried at the use of my name, raising her eyebrows a few times in jest from the top of the van's steps before disappearing aboard, leaving me to deal with Billy alone.

I turned, my hand gripping the door rail of the van for stability. Billy stood on the steps of the hostel looking the wannabe preppy he was in his freshly pressed shirt and pants that I'd diligently ironed and hung when we'd arrived while he'd attacked the mini bar and flipped through channels on the television.

'What, Billy?'

'What are you doing? Where are you going?' he asked, baffled. Good, about time things were reversed, I thought, not even caring how he'd found me considering all the hostels in Paris.

'None of your business,' I said, turning to climb into the van.

'Lexi, don't be ridiculous,' he called, his voice becoming slightly shrill. 'Who are these people?'

Turning to him blank faced, I answered with a sigh, as if the answer was so obvious only a moron wouldn't know, 'They're my friends.'

'Friends? Don't be absurd. You've only been here a matter of hours. How can you have a busload of friends?'

'Well, it seems I am a very likeable person, Billy. Who knew! Now, the van is running and everyone is waiting for me. Have a lovely stay in Paris,' I said, promptly turning and climbing aboard the van before he tried to change my mind. I was determined not to fall to the ground and cry like a baby on the Parisian footpath. Billy had always had that power and I wasn't sure how strong this new Alex was. I wasn't sure how much testing she could take at this point and I wasn't ready to find out.

I took the seat Lydia offered me by the window and exhaled. I hadn't even realised I'd been holding my breath. That's what Billy did to me. That's what my life had been doing to me and I hadn't even realised. Yesterday I'd arrived in Paris with my lovely boyfriend on my first ever overseas trip, expecting a stupid proposal under the stupid Eiffel Tower, now here I was, no boyfriend and a bus load of strangers, on my way to a foreign beach goodness knows where only just realising I'd been holding my breath for years.

It was no doubt an episode of SVU waiting to happen but this life worked for my new friends, what would happen if I embraced it, too? I wondered as we drove away leaving Billy standing alone in front of the hostel, his hands shoved deep into his pockets, his brow furrowed like an old gnome. Billy had been my man for so long, we'd shared a bed all of my adult life, now I watched him shrink away in the distance as I left behind the only life I'd ever known.

Andrea, the hostel receptionist, unmistakable with her short, bright red hair, was driving and weaving the van further and further away from who I was, who I'd been, from Lexi the lovely doormat. I imagined her, my former self, standing beside Billy and I was glad to be done with the both of them.

It was time to find a new me, find out who she was and what she loved and how she wanted to live. I knew being with these people was going to help me find her.

I looked around the van, surveying, trying to figure out how all these people fit together, how I fit. There was Tom across the aisle, taking up more space than was naturally possible. Behind him, the girl with blonde dreadlocks whose head rested on the shoulder of a handsome, boy next door type of man with shaggy hair like Tom's. As for the others, some faces I recognised from the night before, some I didn't recognise at all but they were all here, together, relaxed and comfortable, staring out the window at the passing scenery or catching up on missed sleep.

'Don't look so worried,' Lydia laughed. 'We're not going to cook you, you know.'

I laughed, suddenly feeling silly. 'How are you all together?' I asked.

'I dunno,' she shrugged. 'We've all been hanging out so long now we're like a little family. Well, Michael and Moe up the front,' she said, indicating two guys in front of Tom with black drill pants and black t-shirts playing gaming devices, 'they've been on the run with us since the start.'

'On the run?'

She laughed. 'Yeah, you know, from family and stuff. We fig-ure if we don't stay still for long they'll never find us,' she said, giving a fake evil laugh but there was something in her tone that told me it wasn't entirely a joke.

'They that bad?'

'Yeah, they're that bad.'

I wondered what a family could possibly do to make their children run to the other side of the world and live like gypsies but it was only day one, I didn't want to pry any further if Lydia didn't want to elaborate, so I let her finish detailing our travelling companions.

'You know Tom. Behind him is Bex and her Merry Men.'

'Her Merry Men?' I asked a smile creeping across my face.

'She's like Maid Marion. They all dote on her and the four of them are inseparable. Johnno, the guy beside her, that's her boyfriend and one of Tom's best mates. The other two, Harry and Chris, they picked them up along the way, now, when we're not all hanging out like this, they travel the world, Europe, South America, Bali, anywhere there's surf to be found as a happy foursome . Behind us is Daz and Damo, good guys. Stoners though. But they live to surf. Hard core. They'll go down the coast tomorrow, hunt for the big, untouched waves. Like I said, hard core.'

I nodded like I had some idea what she was talking about. Waves were all the same to me.

'And those two?' I asked quietly, nodding towards two Japanese girls sitting in front of us.

'Just hitching a ride,' she shrugged. 'We only met them yesterday.'

'They're all Aussies?'

'Yep, all Aussies, bar those two,' she said indicating the Japanese girls.

I didn't see how I fitted in with this motley group of people with my plain, boring hair, my ordinary office job and my ordinary suburban life. My legs weren't suntanned, my hair wasn't sun-kissed and I regularly had dark circles under my eyes from holding everything together. I had nothing interesting to say compared to the stories they told. I'd never been anywhere or done anything anyone would care two hoots about. I wore cardigans and ballet flats. I was predictable and responsible. I smiled politely, followed the rules, went to the gym a few times a week, cooked meat and three veg four nights a week, a roast one night a week, takeout on Fridays, had a restaurant dinner on Saturdays and barbeques with friends on occasional Sundays. All things none of these people did or, I suspected, would even consider doing. They lived in a whole other universe to boring, plain Jane me and I wondered what would make them want to befriend me at all. Did they just pity me?

No, I looked around, these people didn't pity, they didn't judge, they liked who they liked and did what they did and went where they went, all as they pleased. None of that social climbing or the image concerns I was so used to. It was nice. I liked it. None the less, I prayed these people didn't steal all my stuff or murder me and leave me in a French ditch. I prayed I didn't embarrass myself and I prayed for clean toilets.

A castle popped up on a hill in the distance, big stone walls and turrets and everything, just sitting there basking in the sun as it had for centuries. I thought of all the people in history that had passed that castle, driven along this road, ridden horses into battle along those hills and suddenly my woes seemed inconsequential. Who were Billy and I in comparison? Nothing, not even a blimp in history. There'd be no mention of our relationship implosion in the pages of stories and historic tales. We didn't matter. Our troubles were insignificant. All that mattered was here and now, soaking in the beauty and being alive.

I took a deep breath and released him with the exhale. Nothing was ever as easy as that. I still felt like the stupidest person on the planet for not seeing who he really was, but it was a start.

'Okay, Newbie, we need to eat, it's your pick,' Lydia said, as we approached another cute town that looked like it belonged in a storybook.

My heart beat a little faster and the first thing I thought was what if where I choose is the worst in the town. It had been a while since I'd gotten to choose where we ate. Billy always chose, he didn't even ask me anymore. Sure, I chose a sandwich from the shop at the bottom of my office building, bought groceries according to the list we kept on the fridge and added things I knew he'd like but that was it. How had I allowed myself to become this person who was afraid to choose somewhere to eat for fear of getting it wrong? Can you even get it wrong? Billy had always thought so, I always picked the wrong one, the food was always bad or cold, the service always crap. He always picked the hippest, coolest places, the ones you bragged about to everyone on Monday. The food was always reviewed in the newspapers, five stars on online and Facebook. After a while, it was easier to give up and let him choose. How had that alone not been a shining beacon of trouble in paradise? I shook Billy's bullying ways from my head and pointed to a cute looking café.

Lydia shook her head. 'Geez, what'd that bloke do to you?' she laughed kindly.

I just shrugged, I'd done it to myself. I'd allowed it to happen. It was my own fault.

As we climbed out of the van, Tom linked his arm through mine. 'Gorgeous day, isn't it?'

'Yeah, it really is,' I agreed, looking up at the clear blue sky.

'So, how you doin' today?' he asked.

'Better. Much better,' I smiled.

'Good, because you know, life's too short to spend it crying in a corner over a tosser like that bloke,' he smiled. 'And when you're in France and the day is this gorgeous, it would be a crime to be sad,' he added.

'Well, that sounds pretty true to me,' I agreed, thinking how right he was.

'You wait, a few more days like this, because I promise you,' he said conspiratorially, 'it's always like this.'

'Always?'

'Yep, even when it rains, it's gorgeous out here. Not as good as home, but still, pretty bloody amazing,'

'Well, so far I have to agree,' I smiled. I liked his way of thinking, his energy. Tom had a goodness about him, something I couldn't quite put my finger on, but it came from within, from the way he thought, the way he lived, who he was and I wanted to soak it up, feel what it'd be like to have that goodness inside me.

We walked into the cute, picture perfect café I chose with its lovely Parisian wicker bistro chairs and paintings of beautiful streetscapes hanging on the stone walls. The inside of the café looked almost as old as the castle I'd seen, with its stone walls and old but loved stone floors and I felt as though the fabric of history was drawing me in, weaving me into its tapestry. For the first time in as long as I could remember I felt a part of something, of somewhere, connected.

We all took our bathroom breaks and when I returned to the table and took the last remaining seat, I found myself opposite Lydia and next to Tom. Tom smiled widely and winked at me before returning to his conversation with the boys on his other side leaving me a little giddy.

Perhaps that's what I needed? A fling? Isn't that what people did in my situation? Shagged themselves silly before returning to the real world cleansed and fresh, ready to start over. It wouldn't be hard to fall into bed with someone like Tom. Flings and one night stands had never been my thing, probably because I'd started dating Billy at eighteen but I'd heard from the girls in the office the therapeutic benefits of such things. It was a shame Tom was out of bounds. I wondered about the stoners on the other side of the table or one of Bex's Merry Men. But none had shown any interest at all in me. The stoners hadn't even looked at me other than to pass me an uninterested absent nod when we passed getting out of the van.

I pushed the thought to the side as my crepe arrived. I let the creamy goodness of the spinach, mushrooms and whatever the delicious cheese was flow through me, let it fill me. I raised my eyebrows at Andrea in an attempt to thank her for ordering for me.

As I filled my tummy, my head felt clearer. Perhaps I'd just enjoy some sun over the next few days and go to a club or something at home and have that rebound fling. One of the girls from work might come with me. They were the only friends I had left now. We had never socialised outside of work, so it would be a long shot to change the parameters after all this time. Or maybe, I needed a new job to go with the new flat I'd have to find and the new single me? That was something to think about.

'Good?' Tom asked, dragging me out of my thoughts.

'Yeah, it's amazing,' I said.

'Good choice,' he said, complementing my choice of eatery and making my tummy flutter, again. 'So if you haven't been overseas before, what is it you do with your time off and all the money you earn from the day job?' he asked.

I shrugged. 'I don't really know. We go to Queensland once a year with some friends, rent a house in Noosa. But there's not a lot of money left over after I pay my share of Billy's mortgage and bills. I just finished paying off my car, that'll free up some money, so that will be nice,' I told him.

'So you like your job?'

'Not really,' I smiled. 'But it pays my way.'

He watched me curiously before shaking his head, 'Have you ever wondered if there's more to life?'

'Not before now but since last night, yes but I've no idea how to change it. I've been me for so long, this has been all I've known since I was eighteen,' I said, sipping my glass of water.

'Well, perhaps you'll find some inspiration on this trip,' he smiled. 'There's a big world out there and you can do anything you want to. People change their lives every day, there's no reason you can't be one of them. Just think, how many people have walked down that cobblestone street.' He pointed out the window. 'Imagine the lives they led and the things they saw and how much has changed since they stood there looking through that very window,' he said before someone called his name from further down the table.

I wanted to hug him, I wanted to curl up beside him and draw on his positivity and beautiful spirit. I wondered where it came from, if he'd always been that way and how to get some for myself because I liked the idea of being anyone and doing anything I wanted. I just had to figure out who that someone might be and what she might want to do. I hoped he was right and I'd find all that out on this trip, but it was a lot to ask for in just a few days. I put it aside for the moment and instead joined the conversation between Lydia and Bex about groceries. 'Breadsticks, cheese, ham, coffee, tea, milk, snacks,' Lydia said, her brain clearly ticking over as she spoke. 'Anything in particular you want, Alex?' she asked me.

I shook my head, 'That all sounds fine to me,' I said, not knowing what else we'd need, anyway.

As if on autopilot, everyone threw their scrunched Euros onto the table to pay for our food and gathered their things so I followed suit, looking longingly around the quaint and lovely café as I followed everyone out.

I felt lighter as we walked down the street to the small supermarket. Tom had filled me with hope that I could be someone. That place, this place, it had a magic to it, an age old feeling, something that took away all the Billy, all the Lexi the lovely doormat and left me feeling light and clean and ready for something else, to be someone else.

As we walked through the electronic doors and entered the

chill of the little supermarket, Lydia hooked her arm through mine as everyone scattered to do what they needed. 'Stick with me, Alex, I'll look after you.'

'So, how did you figure all this out?' I asked as Lydia went about filling her basket with hams and cheeses and milk.

'I don't know really. I guess it just comes from a need to survive as best you can. We've been doing this a long time now. We met some people early on, perpetual travellers like us, they shared some tips and tricks like how to eat and sleep cheap, how to get the good jobs with the best value. But it's been a habit now for so long,' she said thoughtfully.

'How long exactly have you been doing this?'

'Years,' she laughed theatrically. 'Two, nearly three I guess.'

'How?'

'Dual visas,' she smiled proudly. 'Mum was born in the UK. She's been in Australia since she was five and has no accent or anything but she kept dual citizenship and passed that onto us.'

'But why?'

'Why not? There's always something more to see or do or experience. It's better than being tied down to a nine to five. No offense, but that'd just seem a waste of time when there's a whole world to explore. We live cheap, stay in hostels, get jobs that include room and board, serve beers, that sort of thing. We have a little stash of savings if we get stuck. It hasn't all be smooth sailing. We all have our own issues but for the most part, it's pretty awesome.'

'Don't you miss home? Family? Friends?'

'Sometimes. I miss my mum and my sister, maybe my

brother. But not enough to go home, nothing could make me go home,' she said, smiling tightly.

I nodded as though I understood, as though it made any sense at all. But the way she lived, they all lived, made no sense to my well-trained brain. Society told us to be responsible, finish school, go to university or get a trade, work hard, get married, have children, buy a home and pay a mortgage. Nowhere in any of the rules, in any of the wildest of dreamings did anyone ever suggest you could live like a gypsy, live however you please, make the world your oyster. If I hadn't seen it for myself, I'd have thought it was made up. But I was standing in a supermarket not unlike the small supermarket I visited on occasion an ocean away, but I was somewhere in France, selecting ham and assorted snacks with my new friend the gypsy wanderer with her lovely sun kissed, glowing skin and one of the lightest hearts I'd ever known.

Lydia paid for our communal groceries with the money we'd all pooled together and I bought some chocolate, chips, nuts, water and a magazine for myself, then we headed back down the street to the van.

I was lagging behind the group, thinking about what Lydia had said, what Tom had said back in the café, when Tom sidled up next to me. 'Hey, you okay?' he asked.

'Ahuh,' I mumbled.

'Right, so you're always this quiet?' he asked.

I laughed. 'I am actually. Habit,' I said as though it'd make sense to him.

'Hmmm...' he mumbled thoughtfully, his eyes catching mine, my heart skipping a beat as my breath caught in my chest.

Shit, what was that? I mentally shook myself free of the feeling. Tom didn't flinch, instead he smiled so wide, his whole face lit up, his green eyes glistening as they wrinkled in the corners, then he winked and turned away.

We were almost at the van. The others were already inside when a man started shouting.

'Monsieur, monsieur,' he called.

Tom froze. His whole body went rigid as he all but pushed me behind him to face the man who turned out to be about four feet tall, his head, chin and jaw covered in white curly hair. Tom appeared to exhale and relax his muscles as the man said something to him in French and handed him some coins. Tom had forgotten his change.

'Are you alright?' I asked.

He smiled tightly, 'Sure, everything's fine,' he said quietly and climbed into the van.

Chapter 3

We left the Japanese girls behind at the last stop where they met waiting friends. As we drove the final few kilometres to the villa, people starting changing out of their clothes and pulling on wetsuits and rashies over their swimmers.

The van stopped in front of an old stone, two-storey villa nestled between cliffs and overlooking its own, private piece of ocean. As they exited the van, everyone grabbed a board from the pile one of the cargo pant gamers took from the roof and ran for the ocean. I stood outside looking at the villa, looking at the crumbling stone, dead flowers and chipped tile roof, wondering what the hell I'd done.

We were a million miles from anywhere. I'd thought we'd be going to a tourist spot of some sort. That there'd be others, nightlife, something. But there was nothing. We were in the middle of nowhere and I was standing in front of a forgotten, sad, two story villa with a wrap around verandah. It was right on the beach, hidden amongst rocky cliffs. No road or walkway lay between its protected perch and the sand that stretched all the way to the bright blue ocean that glistened as far as I could see, meeting with the perfect blue sky. The view was incredible, worth a million dollars. The villa itself though, with its wonky verandah and weather worn window frames, looked like it should be demolished and replaced with a glittering mansion worthy of the view.

I supposed this was what living with limited funds bought. But who cares if the house is falling down, I told myself as I looked out over the ocean. It was one of the most incredible views I'd ever seen. This was the perfect place for me to heal and renew myself. Besides, I hadn't seen much of an escape route on the road to the middle of nowhere. I had no choice but to stay.

The others surfed while I put away the groceries we'd bought at the last stop and made a coffee. I took my coffee out onto the sand to sit in the sunshine and watch my friends and try to make some sense of everything and find some peace in my head. I should be crying rivers of tears, heaving sobs of devastation. I kept waiting for it to come but I had nothing. If I was going to cry, I suspected it would only be for the lost dreams, for having to start over. I had no tears for Billy, no matter how mad I was at him. I had nothing left for him but contempt and pity.

I think I'd suspected Billy's true nature, on those late nights where he'd come home in the wee hours stinking of booze. I'd always expected more from love but everyone gushed about what a great catch Billy was, he was successful and handsome enough, after all and I just thought maybe I'd read too many romance novels in my teens and set up too many unrealistic expectations. But maybe it was everyone else who was wrong?

Mostly though, I was disappointed in myself. The pitiful excuse of who I'd become flashed before me and I didn't like what I saw. Well no more. Never again. It changed now. Right here on this French beach in the middle of nowhere it changes. From now on I live my life. No more tip toeing around someone else's sensibilities and expectations. No more desperately trying to please, contorting myself, forgetting myself to keep other people happy. From now on, I please myself. I stand up, do something that counts, something of value, something worthy, something worthy of a story to tell.

I sipped my coffee as I scrunched my toes into the sand, watching my new friends bobbing in the ocean, carefree and happy, how people should be. Far out in the ocean the water began swelling with white wispy tips. One of my bobbing friends began fiercely paddling on their board and as the wave rose to a small, clean curve, the person jumped onto their board. The curving wave grew, the person on the board gliding across the top of the watery arc like an angel or some biblical God, smoothly turning their board left and right until the wave propelled them towards the sand.

The water had tamed Lydia's wild black curls, but I could see it was her by her wide smile that beamed as she sailed across the water into the shore and why wouldn't she beam? What she'd done was incredible, the thing of dreams and mystical storytelling. She leapt off her board into the shallows, sweeping her board under her arm so effortlessly it was as though the board was an extension of her own body and ran towards me.

'Hey Newbie, what you doin' out here?'

'Just watching. You were amazing.'

'Ah, thanks, but I'm not really that good. You should see Tom. Ah look, here he goes,' she said, pointing as another person began paddling to catch a growing wave.

The wave was bigger than Lydia's, it curved high and Tom swept his board over the face of the wave, kicking it out at the top, flying over the wave, the board stuck to his feet as though with super glue. He came back down from the sky, skimming over the water, gliding over the face, flipping his board left and right, riding across the whitening tip until it began merging back into the ocean. He rode effortlessly on top of the water until he hit sand.

'Show off,' Lydia laughed.

I'd never seen anything like it. I live in Australia; I should be a surfing expert. But I'm a suburbs girl. Not by choice, just by circumstance. If I went to the beach, it was the swimming beach populated by the masses, not the beaches of magical waves and handsome men that glide over them. I couldn't say why not, there were plenty of them up and down the coast, I just hadn't, I hadn't thought to. Now I wondered if I'd missed a whole untapped resource in my youth. Perhaps I should have been there, at the surf beaches, rather than the local football games where you ran into people like Billy bloody McRae.

'Nice wave!' Lydia declared when Tom reached us. Water dripped from his body, his bare chest glistening in the sunlight, a shiny wetsuit covering his bottom half but leaving nothing at all to the imagination. Like mine needed any help with the details, he was a far cry from Billy McCrae. Billy was fit, gym fit mostly but he was shorter, wirier that Tom, no amount of gym could change that, it's just how he was built. But Tom, he was the thing of storytellers and wishful women everywhere, fit and muscled from life, tanned by the sun and he was standing before me, smiling at me, with that neoprene hugging every single perfect curve.

Lydia didn't even seem to notice the perfection standing in front of us. Perhaps that's what happened when girls dated guys like Tom? When they spent their days, their lives, around surfer guys on their beaches, they become oblivious to the most perfect of God's creations; blinded to their rippling torsos, their jubilant, addictive love for life that showed every time their face lit with a smile.

'So, Alex, you going in?' Tom asked.

I laughed, 'Ah, no!'

'Why not?' he asked, smiling big and kind and far too interested, sending my stomach into somersaults.

I caught my breath and declared, 'No bathers,' thinking that would surely keep me safe from making a fool of myself.

'You don't need bathers,' Lydia told me.

I gave her a look of 'are you seriously mad?' Of course you needed bathers to go into the ocean.

'You've got underwear on, right?' she asked.

'Yeah,' I whispered, wishing away the warmth creeping up my neck at the mere thought of discussing my underwear in front of handsome Tom. It seemed I'd regressed to a ten year old in his presence.

'Well then, that's all you need. I'll loan you my wettie and you'll be all set,' she smiled.

'That's great. Thanks. Thanks. But, I can't surf.'

'You've never surfed?' Tom asked surprised, as though the

mere thought of someone never having surfed was incomprehensible to him.

'Dull suburbanite, I'm afraid.'

'I'll teach you then,' Tom said as Lydia reached behind her, pulling on the cord that unzipped her wetsuit.

'C'mon,' Lydia said, indicating my shorts.

I had two choices, to be a party pooping prude in front of my new friends or throw caution to the wind. Lydia told Tom to turn around but it didn't stop me from being horrified, just having a man so handsome, so enigmatic standing so close while I stripped to my underwear was too much for my pounding heart. I had to work fast, I decided. I unzipped my dress and let it fall to the sand as I quickly stepped into Lydia's wetsuit, covering myself as quickly as humanly possible. She helped me pull up the zip, then with a wink and a wish of good luck, she was gone. Lydia disappeared into the ocean, leaving me alone with Tom who was now watching me far too intently. Tom's eyes were suddenly dark as they scanned the tight neoprene hugging my body, his mouth turning up at the corners as though holding onto a smile.

I should have been mad, mortified, embarrassed, uncomfortable, something but I wasn't. Turns out I didn't mind him looking. I particularly liked that slight twitch of a smile as though he liked what he saw. I was sinking into a hole that was going to cause me nothing but pain, I just knew it. I looked out to where Lydia now bobbed in the water with the others. Nothing but pain lay in store for me. Even without a girlfriend like Lydia, there was no way a guy like Tom would fancy boring old suburban me. I tried putting it all out of my head, pushing away the explosion of butterflies that erupted whenever he looked at me and paying attention. I was here to have fun and forget about Billy, not cause myself a whole new kerfuffle.

Tom placed his board on the sand and began his instruction. I concentrated on what he was saying, not him, not his shirtless body or his flexing muscles and straddled the board as I was told to, jumping to my feet when I was commanded, falling and swaying each time, showing just how clumsy I really was and both of us laughed too much.

'You never mentioned you were this uncoordinated,' Tom laughed.

'You never asked. You can give up, you know,' I told him.

'No way. I love a challenge,' he winked. 'Now come on, pay attention.'

Winking and smiling and butterflies mean nothing, Lexi, I told myself. I decided it was just my broken soul begging for comfort, for someone to put it back together. Tom was just being nice to me. That's all it is. I couldn't go reading more into it. Besides, he has a girlfriend, a fabulous girlfriend and I'm on the rebound, so I told myself to pay attention, learn to surf, have some fun.

With the safety of the sand beneath me, I practiced over and over, desperate to be better, to impress Tom, however fruitless that was, I still had a little pride left. I pretended to paddle in the sand, the grit scraping the tips of my uncoordinated fingers as they accidentally brushed too deep into the sand, then jumping to my feet as Tom told me to engage my core, to put all my balance in my thighs, bend my knees just right, hold my arms up just right. We kept going until I got it, until I could feel the back of my neck starting to burn.

'I think you're ready,' Tom finally said.

'Really?' I asked. I'd been sticking pop ups as he called them for ages but I'd hoped I'd never have to actually go in the water.

'Yep, nothing more dry land can do for you, it's time to get wet,' he smiled.

My insides liquefied.

He raced up to the villa, returning with another board. Together we paddled out to where the others were straddling their boards, bobbing up and down in the calm water waiting for waves to come.

The others cheered when we finally reached them, my arms aching from the paddling, my pride refusing to admit it and my ego soaking up the camaraderie.

'You ready to feel invincible?' Tom asked, the excitement in his voice showing how much he loved it. It was contagious and had my stomach fluttering in anticipation. I hoped it was anticipation for the riding of waves and had nothing to do with his lovely smile.

I bobbed in the ocean with the others, thinking this isn't so bad. Until Tom decided it was time for action.

'Okay, here comes a baby one, Alex, this one's yours,' Tom insisted.

'Now? Me?' Shit! I wasn't ready. Why was it my turn anyway? They'd all been waiting longer. Wasn't there some honourable hierarchy to all this or something?

'It's a good beginner's wave,' Tom insisted. He must have

seen the fear in my eyes. 'Come on, I'll ride it with you,' he said. 'Start paddling.'

I did as Tom said and started paddling in rhythm beside him, the group behind us yahooing as my body lay flat and rigid on the hard board, my arms turning like propellers in the water, every nerve ending at the ready to pop up like he'd taught me. I could feel the wave growing beneath me and tensed, completely forgetting everything Tom had said on dry land. I just kept paddling my arms through the water, watching Tom beside me, hoping he'd tell me what to do.

Just when it was time, he shouted, 'Now!'

Together we both popped up to our feet, his switch more nimble, smooth and sure than mine. I swayed a minute, bending my knees and letting my thighs take my weight as panic and adrenalin surged through my body. I had no idea how I'd even done what I did. I tried ignoring the shouts and cheers behind us, focussing instead on keeping my feet on the board and staying upright.

'Balance yourself, use your centre of gravity,' Tom called.

I followed each of his instructions, focus, centre, take the weight in your thighs and before I knew it, the sand was coming towards me.

I'd done it. I couldn't believe it. Then I wobbled. I couldn't regain my balance no matter how many instructions he called over to me, and my legs fell out from underneath me. The water caught me as I sank, the board, still strapped to my ankle, pulled and tugged, water rushing in and around my ears and up my nose. I flapped my arms and kicked my legs until I rose to the surface, water racing into my mouth as I sucked in air too early.

I coughed and spluttered out half the ocean and wiped stinging salt water from eyes.

Tom waited patiently, straddling his board, the beads of water on his tanned skin glistening like diamonds under the sun, a smile stretched across his face. 'You okay?' he asked, laughing kindly.

I swept my hair away from my face, coughed out some more of the sea water I'd swallowed and nodded.

Climbing off his board and jumping into the water, he reached down, unstrapping the board from my ankle and walked to shore with them both, one under each arm, me splashing along like a baby elephant behind him.

I fell to the sand as I got out of the water. Lying on my back, my arms outstretched I declared, 'That was amazing, bloody amazing!'

He laughed knowingly, standing the boards in the sand. 'You did great,' he commended. 'Ready to go again?' He stretched his hand towards me.

'No way!' I laughed.

'Come on, you're a natural,' he insisted.

'That was totally beginner's luck,' I laughed. 'I don't want to ruin it.'

He laughed. 'That sounds fair. You want me to sit with you?' he offered.

'No, it's okay,' I smiled. 'Thanks though. Thanks for all of it.'

'No problem,' he smiled. 'See you in a bit, then,' he said, winking before paddling back out as another tiny person boarded a wave.

Once I'd been dried by the sun, I put my dress back on and

stayed on the beach watching them come and go, completely amazed I'd done it, skidded across a wave, risen above ordinary, joined with the ocean to create magic and achieve the impossible. I'd been more alive in those seconds than my whole entire life. Alexandra Deen, surfer. I liked the sound of that. Way better than Alexandra Deen, Billy McRae's doormat. Life had definitely taken an unexpected and liberating turn. France was fast becoming my favourite place ever.

One by one, they all rode the final waves of the day to shore and made their way into the villa to shower and change. Then, one by one, they all returned to sit beside me on the verandah to watch the colours of sunset dance across the sky as Lydia brought out a big platter of baguettes.

Chapter 4

Tom sat next to me on the edge of the verandah as we ate our baguettes. 'So Alex, what do you think?' he asked, indicating the villa with his head.

'Lovely,' I smiled politely. There was no need to insult him after all he'd done for me.

'Come on, you can be honest. It's a bit of a dump,' he laughed. 'But it serves its purpose. And who can argue with that?' he asked, nodding to the last of the colours in the sky.

'Well, you have a point there,' I smiled, my breath catching in my chest as I accidentally looked into his eyes and forgot all the words and questions on the tip of my tongue. Our eyes locked together and the whole universe beyond him and me faded to nothing.

He smiled as if knowing every thought and skipped heartbeat I was suffering. He watched me intently, for a moment before winking and turning back to the ocean and watching the last of the colours leave the sky in silence.

I didn't know what to do. He looked at me like I was something but I couldn't be something to him. Every story Lydia told involved Tom. They joked and laughed and finished each other's sentences like an old married couple. I was so confused. I wanted to hide.

Perhaps I was just making more out of it than there was. I was fragile and emotional after the whole Billy business, so it would be a reasonable assumption. I'd just stay out of his way and surely whatever this was, would dissipate back to nothing and I'd get a handle on my stupid, overactive imagination.

Once the sun was gone, everyone disappeared to do their own thing. After helping Lydia wash the dishes and tidy the kitchen, I went to hunt out somewhere quiet to think. I was hiding in the living room, sitting on the sagging couch watching Michael and Moe wave their arms at a television game console. Tom came in and sat beside me igniting every stupid neuron in my body at once.

'You alright?' he asked.

'Sure,' I nodded, but I couldn't breathe. The villa's walls were closing in. The villa wasn't big enough for Tom and me. I couldn't be fancying my new best friend's man. I couldn't. 'I think I just need some air,' I told him. What I needed was for it all to stop, the breathlessness, the butterflies, the way he looked at me.

Ignoring the disappointment in Tom's eyes when I walked away, I pushed open the flimsy screen door, stepping into the warm night air. The faint smell of something sweet like Jasmine hung in the air like soft webs, it floated on the gentle breeze mixing with the salt spray from the waves crashing on the beach.

I sat on the bench under the window and inhaled. Breathe in, breathe out, I told myself over and over until the knots in my stomach began to loosen.

Watching the waves in the fading light as they came in and crashed and receded again under the shimmering white glow of the rising moon unknotted my stomach and settled my swirling head. From the corner of my eye I saw a shadow move and quickly turned my head to see. I walked over to the verandah ledge to get a better look, praying I wasn't about to get mugged on some beach in France.

Lydia walked out of the bushes and I sighed with relief. Walking barefoot in the sand, the moonlight glowing around her, she looked like an angel. Andrea walked beside her carrying a bottle of wine or champagne, sipping from the bottle and laughing. I was about to wave when they stopped, looked into each other's eyes a moment too long then kissed, their mouths eager, their bodies responding familiarly to each other.

Who were these people? I couldn't believe it. First Tom winking and smiling his lovely flirty eyes at me and now Lydia was kissing Andrea; none of it made any sense. Whatever relationship Tom and Lydia had going on, I wanted no part of it. It was sick and indecent to mess with people that way.

As if sensing me staring, they looked around. *Shit!* I hurried backwards trying to blend with the shadows but my feet caught on the pebbles and shells littering the deck. They walked back into the bushes as I stumbled over something hard, I tried to rebalance, then something else sliced my foot and I lost my balance altogether, falling, crumpling to the timber decking. My body shook and an eerie, horrible cracking echoed around me. *Oh great, I've broken something!*

I ached and hurt and once my head stopped spinning, I tried pushing up from the rough deck but the stupid rotten wood gave way, opening up like a vortex to another world and before I could even comprehend what was happening, scream or call for help in anything other than a last minute whisper, I fell straight down to the hard dirt ground of the cellar a floor below.

Everything hurt, my shoulder, my elbow, thigh, knee, ribs, head. I reached up to touch my cheek to find it was slick and sticky with blood. My stomach convulsed at the thought of a giant gaping hole in the side of my head but fear beat down shock as something scratched around in the darkness.

'Alex?' Tom called from above.

'Tom!' I called back, never so relieved to see Tom or in fact, anyone.

'*Thank you,*' I whispered into the darkness as Tom's handsome face peered over the edge.

'I can't even see you down there. You okay?' he called.

'I hurt, but I don't think anything's broken. Does that count?'

'Yeah, that counts.'

'Can you get me out?'

'I'll see if I can find something for you to grab hold of.'

'Be careful, Tom, the floor's rotten,' I called back as his face disappeared into the darkness.

Tom stepped away from the opening I'd created in the floor and the familiar cracking of the rotten wood giving way followed his step and the deck exploded. There was nothing I could do but watch his beautiful body fall. In only a second he was beside me on the ground, his face millimetres from mine groaning from the pain of connecting with the solid dirt floor.

'What are you doin' down here?' he asked, the hint of a smile in his voice.

The warmth of his shirtless body and the sweet smell of the ocean on his skin sent my insides into a frenzy. *Oh crap!* There was no escape. I was stuck in a basement somewhere in France with flirty Tom who has a girlfriend who's kissing another girl on the beach. Sweat formed on my brow, butterflies swam in my stomach and *holy crap,* something ran over my foot.

Drawing my knees to my chest I pushed back against the stone wall. There was no way out. My body shook involuntarily. I dared to look at Tom. His amused, beaming face looked back at me. Even in the half-light dripping down from the bulb way up on the porch, his tanned face glowed.

Stop, stop, stop, Lexi, what are you doing? I chastised myself. This wasn't good. I couldn't fancy Tom and his lovely green eyes. I couldn't do that to Lydia.

I felt his hand slide over mine, it was warm and strong and butterflies took flight in my stomach. I ignored how good it felt and looked at him, waiting for the punch line. He had to know this was wrong. Any way you looked at it, it was depraved.

'What?' he asked, his eyes big and surprised and sad when I gave him a look of daggers.

'What, what? What are you doing?'

'I'm holding your hand, Alex. What's the problem? I know you like me. I thought you felt... whatever this is, too? Is it too soon? Shit, sorry, I thought you were doing okay,' he said, chastising himself

I exhaled, relieved, it wasn't just my imagination. 'I am okay, surprisingly, better than I would have thought I'd be. And I do like you. Whatever this is, I feel it. But what about Lydia? I won't do that to her.'

'Lydia?' he asked, his eyes squinting into each other in confusion.

'Yes, Lydia! Remember her?'

'How could I forget her?' he asked, smiling.

'Look Tom, I don't know what you two have going on; her and Andrea, her and you, whatever, it's your business. But I don't think I should get involved.'

He gave an infuriating little laugh, 'What business is that, Alex?' His smile was tight, curling up in the corners. *Is he mocking me?*

Keeping a hold of my hand, he stroked the side of my face with his other hand, sending goose bumps across my skin. 'Tom!' I cried.

'Alex, come on!'

'No, Tom. Lydia has been kind to me, I'm not doing this to her.'

'Seriously, Alex, I don't think my sister will care one bit what we're doing.' His tight smile stretched into a full mocking beam.

'Sister?' I whispered. I'd gone an assumed their intimacy was a couple thing and I'd been too busy trying to make sense of the whole Billy drama, so blinded by trying not to fancy Tom, I'd been too stupid to ask any questions. It just hadn't even seemed necessary. The answer seemed clear as day. I'd tormented myself for nothing. That was such a me thing to do and here I was thinking I'd become this whole new person, but I wasn't. I was the same old stupid me. *Fool!* I mentally chastised myself.

Tom nodded, his green eyes darkening, filling with all things sinful and improper and before I could consider him or the situation any further, he drew me to his mouth and I melted like the fool I am, letting my hands stray over his beautifully rippled body. His lips were soft and delicious, his mouth warm and desperate as though he'd been waiting for this. A jolt of intense desire raced through my veins as my mouth pulsed and begged beneath his.

My body burned, my heart pounded so hard I thought it might explode or crumble. I melted into him, fitting against his body in perfect symmetry, like two pieces of a puzzle finally reunited. His hand cupped my face tenderly, his other hand stretching around me pulling me closer, but then he groaned, and I felt his face scrunch in pain a second before he pulled away.

We both sat a moment, wordless, breathless, panting, desperate for air, the lust inside still surging, searching, with nowhere to go.

'You okay?' I eventually stammered once I was able to breathe, to speak.

'Yeah,' he groaned, forcing a smile. 'Damned shoulder,' He said, leaning against the wall, draping his good arm across my shoulders and pulling me to his chest. 'How 'bout you? You okay?' he asked.

'Yeah, mostly.'

It wouldn't have mattered if my bones had been shattered.

All that mattered in that moment was committing everything to memory, his smell, the feel of him, his arms around me, his body beneath me, the sound of his heart beating too fast, his mouth on mine, the memory of his mouth making all my lady bits tingle. Remembering the most incredible minutes of my life just in case that's all I ever got, in case he realised he was way out of my league and I never again got to feel what I just felt.

Tom's defeated eyes scrunched tight, his mouth stretching into a tight line as he suppressed whatever pain he was feeling. I wish I knew what to do, how to fix him. He didn't strike me as the wimpy type so I tried not to think of how much damage he'd done. Instead, I touched his face, running my fingers over the stubble growing on his jaw. Bravely, I touched his lips with mine; kissing him softly, savouring the warmth of his mouth, tasting the sweetness of him, happy to be trapped forever as my whole body tingled.

'Hello?' Lydia called down from the deck.

He pulled away, smiling. 'Lydia!' He called, almost regretfully. 'Lydia, get Moe or Michael will you and get away from the edge, it's not safe,' Tom instructed.

Lydia's feet softly tapped across the boards on the verandah above us. The screen door opened then slammed closed. Leaning against the wall we waited. The intensity that had sizzled between us only moments before had now vanished and was floating somewhere into the night sky.

There was a rattling in the dark void to our left but it was too dark to see anything beyond each other. I happily snuggled into Tom as he pulled me close, I didn't want to contend with any more furry creatures in the dark. Then light flooded in as a door opened and Michael grumbled a slew of words I couldn't quite make out. *Of course, a cellar usually leads to a house!*

Michael helped Tom up, draping an arm around him and helped him hobble out. Moe expertly scooped me up, carrying me past a smirking Lydia, dropping me onto the couch with a bounce. The debris of the game playing had been shoved into the corner creating a snake pit of wires. I tossed a remote stuck between my butt and the couch into the mix.

Moe fussed with the hole in my head. 'I'm fine, I'm fine,' I insisted. 'Tom's shoulder's buggered though,' I said while trying desperately not to look at Tom's naked chest all too visible under the bright house lights. A blush crept over my skin as I remembered his warmth and smell and how perfect his skin had felt beneath my hands.

Tom insisted it was my head that needed looking at and that his shoulder would be fine. Lydia shook her head, 'Come on, there's a late night doctor in town,' she said, shuffling us into the van while Moe grabbed the keys off the bench.

'Hey Lids,' Tom said when we were on our way. 'Did you know Alex thought we were a couple?'

'What?' she asked, turning around her eyes wide, horrified. 'What would give you that idea?' she demanded.

I shrugged. 'All your stories were together. You finish each other's sentences and you have an intimacy that you only get from knowing someone really well, like that first night I met you and Tom draped his arm around you as though he'd done it a thousand times.'

'He probably has,' she smiled. 'Do we act that much like an old married couple all the time?' Lydia asked.

I shrugged, nodding, smirking.

'Really? We've definitely spent way too much time together,' she laughed.

'And it's not like you look anything alike,' I said, trying to make her feel better.

'Lids looks like Mum,' Tom said. 'Sadly, I look like Dad.'

'Lucky you got mum's temperament,' Lydia added. 'Mostly,' she giggled to herself.

'Lucky indeed,' he smiled as Moe parked the car.

I followed the others into a plain, brightly lit room with a reception desk and a few plastic chairs to wait in.

While we waited for the doctor, with only inches between us, Tom's body still shirtless, I remembered the amazing, incredible kiss and my toes tingled.

'What are you smiling at?' Lydia demanded.

'Me? Nothing,' I insisted, shaking my head. I couldn't help sneaking a look at Tom and he smiled at me with his darkening, flirty eyes. I blushed beetroot, well it felt beetroot and we giggled like schoolchildren.

'Hey!' Lydia interrupted. 'What did you two get up to down there?' she asked, frowning.

'Nothing, Lydia,' Tom said rolling his eyes. 'Perhaps what you were doing on the beach would be more interesting?'

'Shut up, Tom!' said Lydia, looking out the window with a scowl, Tom smirking with brotherly victory.

The doctor saw us one at a time, clearly unimpressed with being on the late shift, him and his grouchy receptionist. But we got what we needed. Tom's dislocated shoulder got put back in, apparently an old, recurring injury and my not so giant gaping hole in my head got a Band-Aid and the cut on my foot got glued back together and we were sent on our way, grateful for travel insurance.

'Does it hurt?' I asked Tom as Lydia helped him and his ice pack into the van.

'Nah, not so bad,' he said.

'You got drugs, didn't you?'

He laughed, 'I did, but I'm sure I'll be fine by morning. What about you?'

'Just bruised mostly.'

He put his arm around my shoulders and I leant against him while Moe drove us home.

When we returned, it was late, the downstairs empty.

'Well, I'm done. You coming up, Alex?' Lydia asked when we were inside.

'In a minute, you go, I just need to take some painkillers,' I said.

''K. See you in a bit. Goodnight,' she said, going upstairs.

'Night,' we echoed.

'I'm done too. Will you be right getting upstairs?' Moe asked Tom, dropping a friendly hand onto his shoulder.

'Yeah man, go,' Tom insisted.

'Right. Night then,' he said, leaving us to it.

Then it was just Tom and me, and as my palms began to sweat, I started rethinking my decision to stay behind. There was water in the bathroom I could have used to take my pills.

'Hell of a night, hey?' Tom smiled. 'You sure you're okay?' he asked as I filled a glass with water and hunted in my bag for the pills.

'Yeah, yeah, I'm fine,' I nodded. Suddenly, with his face so close, I'd lost all my words.

'Do I make you nervous, Alex?' he asked, smirking.

'Maybe,' I smiled shyly.

He took my hand, kissed it. 'Take your pills. I'm going to have a cuppa. Join me?'

'Sure,' I smiled, thinking it was just what I needed, some quiet, pressure free time together. He really did crazy things to my insides and as nervous as it made me, it was addictive.

We both took pain pills while we waited for the kettle to boil, then I let Tom lead me outside, past the precarious deck and onto the beach.

It was so perfectly quiet with just the sounds of the ocean. Not another soul was anywhere on the beach. There were no lights, no people, no sound, just Tom and me, and it was perfect.

It was still warm enough to not need to have changed and as he draped his arm across my shoulders and pulled me into the nook of his body, I went willingly.

'The stars are really pretty, aren't they?' he said. 'I miss seeing them at home. Out in the bush where it's quiet like this, no lights, no noise, no pollution.'

'How long has it been?'

'Long. Too long,' he smiled.

'You never go back?'

He shook his head. 'Look, did you see that one shoot across the sky?' he asked with a child-like wonder.

I smiled. 'Yeah, I did.'

'Did you make a wish?' he asked.

'Maybe,' I smiled. 'You?' I asked, looking up at him.

He nodded. 'Although I'm kind of afraid to ask for anything with you sitting beside me.'

'Why's that?' I asked, worried he was wishing for someone else, worried he was more like Billy after all.

'It feels greedy,' he winked, his finger trailing a line across my jaw, then reaching under my chin, gently tipping my face so my mouth met his and we kissed, under the stars, the wishing stars and the moon and I couldn't imagine anything more perfect. Until his hands begin to roam, until our breath became heavy, as he ignited something in me, a fiery, desperate need I had never felt before.

His hand went under my dress and I arched to him, groaning, craving, wanting.

His mouth left mine, left me gasping, his hand stopping still, leaving me needy. 'Not here,' he whispered, breathless.

'Why not?' I begged.

He leant up on his elbow, tucked stray hairs off my face and smiled. 'Not tonight, not like this. Not sore and drugged up. You and me...argh,' he groaned. 'The anticipation is going to kill me but not here in the damp sand, which let me assure you, is not nearly as romantic as movies would have you believe. No, you deserve romance and a bed and nothing short of amazing. Tonight is not a night for amazing. Tonight is a night for looking at the stars with my girl and making out like teenagers.' He smiled before his mouth met mine and he kissed me like no teenage boy I'd ever known. No man either for that matter.

So we made out under the stars until our lips were swollen and sore, until I was in serious danger of beard rash and the sand became damp and the cold began to seep into our bones.

Tom watched me intently, like no one ever had. It was unnerving and exhilarating at the same time. He trailed his forefinger along my collarbone, over the rise of my breasts.

I watched his face, his naughty smile, the way his bright green eyes darkened like the forest and I liked what I saw. I liked how it made me feel.

'I cannot wait to have my way with you,' he grinned. 'But now, it's getting late and cold, we should go inside.'

'I could lay here all night with you, even with the cold.'

He kissed me, long, deep. 'Me too, but I can't have you getting sick,' he grinned. 'You're going to need your strength.' He smiled and my toes tingled.

This was it. I knew he was it. Everything; the world, the universe, my place in it, all made sense. I don't know how and I don't know why. We were from different planets and I had no idea how any of it could even work, but in that moment, I knew. I knew I was ruined from that moment on. He made me wonder what I'd been doing wasting my life accepting okay all this time. It was like finally, for the first time in my whole life, I felt alive.

Inside, he helped me readjust my dress with a wink and held my hand as we climbed the stairs.

Standing on the landing, between our bedrooms, he kissed me one last time, then said, 'Goodnight,' but it was a second before he moved, a second where he just stood, looking into my eyes, holding my face close to his, as though he could see into my soul, as though as lost in all the magic as I was.

He smiled as he released me from his hold and suddenly, as he took a step back, all the space around me felt empty and cold.

I looked at him one last time. 'See you tomorrow.' It was

almost a question more than a statement because something so perfect couldn't possibly still be mine tomorrow.

He nodded, 'I will see you in the morning.'

Lydia and Andrea were sitting on the single bed talking quietly when I opened the door. They stood as I walked in, Lydia moving to her bag on the other side of the room.

'It's cool, you guys, I saw you on the beach,' I smiled nonchalantly, well as best as I could manage with the stiffness from the fall finally starting to kick in. I doubted my make out session on the beach helped. Really, I probably pulled a face similar to a demented version of the Joker.

'Saw what?' Lydia asked.

'Seriously, it doesn't make any difference to me,' I said, wondering why it was even a secret. I didn't imagine their gypsy free living friends would care anymore than I did.

They seemed to breathe a sigh of relief but still, Lydia climbed up to the top bunk.

Whatever, I thought. I suddenly had no strength left to care about their issues. My body ached. I felt as though I'd been hit by a truck and I just wanted to sleep and my lips were still swollen and tingly with the memory of Tom. There was no space left for Lydia's sexuality. Even though I'd just now happily have spent the night rolling about on the beach with Tom, I hurt too much to bend down and rummage through my suitcase for anything resembling pyjamas, so I carefully unzipped my dress, letting it fall to the floor and grabbed the black and silver Oooh La La tank top I'd bought my sister as a gift, slipped it on and climbed into bed.

'You don't care but you got into bed pretty quick.' Lydia stated.

'You think I was worried you'd be laying their ogling me in the dark? Don't be ridiculous. Go to sleep Lydia, I'm too tired for nonsense.'

I snuggled deep into the cool sheets, closing my eyes, letting the memory of Tom fill my mind. Remembering how it had felt to be in his arms, his warmth in the cold, dark basement, his strength and how safe and protected I'd felt there and how he'd felt like home when we snuggled on the beach. How images of us as old people snuggling on faraway beaches had filled my mind. How every neuron in my body had bubbled and tingled when he'd kissed me; the urge I'd had to kiss him back, and more. Desperate urges I couldn't remember ever having for Billy.

What did that mean? Is this what a fling felt like? I didn't want a fling, not any more. I'd changed my mind. Circumstances had changed. Kissing Tom had changed me. All I knew though is I'd do anything to feel that heat surge through my body again, to feel so alive my insides might explode. I was already addicted to the way he made me feel. *That can't be good*, I thought as I drifted off to sleep.

Chapter 5

'Good morning, sleepyhead,' Lydia joked as I walked into the kitchen. 'Coffee?'

'Please,' I said in desperate need of just that.

'How do you feel?' she asked.

'Stiff, sore, like I went one on one with a truck.'

'Well, just take it easy, yeah?'

'I think I can manage that,' I said, accepting the cup of coffee she handed me.

She raised her eyebrows as though disbelieving me. Then I felt him. It was like there was an elastic band or a magnet that joined us and I could feel every step he took that brought him closer.

'Morning, Tom,' Lydia said with a smile.

'Morning,' he said, far less cheerful.

'Coffee?' she asked, holding the pot aloft again.

He nodded to her, kissed me on the top of my head and

smiled for the first time. 'Morning,' he said, only to me, softer and with one of his heart stopping smiles.

'Morning,' I said, blushing as I could feel every person in the room stop what they were doing and stare at us.

Tom accepted his coffee and everyone went back to their conversations.

'Damo and Daz already gone?' Tom asked no one in particular.

'Yeah, at first light,' Johnno said. 'You missed some great surf this morning, man,' he told Tom.

'Bet I did,' Tom groaned as he sat at the table talking surf conditions with the boys.

Lydia set Tom and I up on the verandah – after testing it's stability – with coffee, water, pillows and snacks before racing across the sand and into the water with her surf board.

Tom looked on longingly. I couldn't help but smile. 'You look at the water like it's a part of you.'

He laughed, short, gruff, sexy. 'It sometimes feels like it is. I get twitchy if we're apart for too long,' he said, looking at me with something in his eye I'd never seen directed at me before. 'I have a feeling it's going to get some competition,' he added wryly.

I wasn't quite sure what to make of it. Being the object of someone's blatant desire was strange, exposing, it left me feeling vulnerable and excited. Sure, I'd felt as though Billy fancied me sometimes. When I looked particularly nice, he'd looked me up and down appreciatively. In the bedroom he'd put on a good show, having me believe I was the source of his randiness where in fact he was just randy and I was handy. Billy had certainly never looked at me the way Tom looked at me. Not even in the early days and I hadn't even noticed. He'd said all the right things, done all the right things and I'd thought that was enough, how it was supposed to be. He kept calling, he took me to fancy restaurants and moved me in not too long after we started dating so I thought it meant things. But the way Tom looked at me on that verandah on a French beach in the middle of nowhere after only a day said more than anything Billy had ever said, verbally or physically. My skin tingled with possibility.

'So whose house is this, anyway?' I asked in an attempt to change the subject, or at least extinguish that twinkle in his eye.

He smirked knowingly and I wasn't sure if that excited me more or frustrated me that he knew the affect he had on me. Was he that sure of himself? Was it because, like Billy, he had women all over the place or was I just that obvious?

'It belongs to Andrea's Grand-Mere's best friend. She doesn't come out here anymore, she's in a home watching old movies with Grand-Mère, she likes that we come out to check on the place now and then because her daughter is in New York and doesn't get to visit as often as she'd like. It works out well for all of us.'

'Well that's handy indeed. Thanks to Grand'Mere's friend,' I said, toasting her with my coffee cup as I watched Lydia, her wet hair glistening under the bright sun as she rode a wave towards the shore.

Lydia ran up the sand, laughing with a freedom, an abandon that made you want to be just like her. 'You two okay up here?' he asked, shielding her eyes from the sun.

'I'd rather be out there but otherwise, just fine, Lids.'

She laughed. 'I bet. The water's perfect and the waves are unbelievable. You're really missing out,' she giggled.

'Thanks. How's that for sisterly compassion,' Tom asked me smiling too much to really be cross.

As Lydia ran back to the ocean, I had to know how they got here, how to get some of what they had for myself. Surely their family couldn't be so bad when they were... well, them.

'How did you and Lydia really end up here because looking at you two, I can't imagine your family being that bad.'

He chuckled, that deep, sexy, manly way of his. 'We weren't always this happy. Don't get me wrong, we've always made the best of every situation and really, it's not that hard when Lydia's around. But growing up, life, especially for me was tough. My life was planned out, all of it from birth. The schools, the subjects I'd take, the roles I'd play in the company when I graduated until my Dad thought I was ready to be in charge. He tried guiding me towards the girls he thought it appropriate for me to date, the friends he thought I should have. I led a double life but eventually it was too much. Johnno joked about joining the Army one afternoon. He went to a different school than me, copped grief from the footballers, didn't always see eye to eye with his dad for the same reason and I guess the idea appealed. We drank a few beers and as the night wore on the more the idea appealed. Joined up the next morning and had to keep it a secret until we ran off one night to go to Wagga for training. Dad couldn't exactly complain about his son being a noble patriot. Anyway, near the end of my initial service, I was hearing about his health troubles, he used passive aggressive bullshit he'd perfected over the years and I felt bad for mum so I left and joined the business thinking it was the right thing to do. I'd forgotten how bad he was though and planned an alternate life not long after I returned and here we are,' he smiled. 'Now, how did a girl like you end up with a guy like Billy?'

'Much the same really. Escape. My mother didn't have the power your dad seems to have but she was the master of the passive aggressive guilt trip with a theory on how I should live and behave despite who I was. My sister was much better at following the rules than I was, well, I thought so but she did get knocked up at 17,' I smiled, thinking of my niece. 'Anyway, I felt like I was in prison, and Billy, well, Billy swept me off my feet. Took me to fancy restaurants, bought me lovely gifts, desperately wanted me to move in with him after only a couple of months and I couldn't resist. He was handsome, well, handsome enough and smart and successful. He owned his own home by twenty one, that's impressive in my world,' I added, not sure why I was defending Billy. Maybe I was just defending myself.

'And now here we are, free as birds soaking up the sun on a faraway French beach together,' he grinned.

'Here we are indeed,' I grinned stupidly, still unsure how I'd gone from one life to the other in the blink of an eye.

'Have you always surfed?' I asked, curious.

'I learnt on holiday in Hawaii when I was about seven. It was one of those things that just felt so natural and easy. It wasn't until much later, when I was older that I realised it wasn't that easy for everyone. As soon as I could, Johnno and I were escaping up the beach surfing all day as often as we could, being bums, meeting girls,' he confessed sheepishly as though I couldn't have guessed someone as handsome and as charming as him would be surrounded by them everywhere he went.

'So what is it this tyrannical father of yours does?'

He shrugged. 'Family business. Property. Boring stuff. What do you do for fun?'

It was my turn to shrug nonchalantly. 'I didn't really have much time for fun. I have a job...'

'Doing what?' he interrupted.

'Boring admin. I support a sales team. I'm their lackey really, their gofer. I sit next to this fat balding guy who thinks he's hilarious but is the most disgusting, insulting pig I've ever met but I have to laugh at his foul jokes and nod politely when he tries to tell everyone he once dated a Swedish supermodel or he makes my life hell.'

'Sounds inspired,' he joked.

I giggled. 'I never meant to do this. Although I don't know what else I wanted. This was supposed to be the stop gap while I figured it out but well, here I am, twenty four and I've been doing this job for six years. I started dating Billy just after I got the job and well, life happened, I guess. Slowly he became my life. I stopped hanging out with my friends and hanging out with his coupled friends instead, throwing complicated dinner parties that had me stuck in the kitchen for days at a time. He played football so I spent a lot of Saturdays on the sidelines with the other wives and girlfriends watching.'

'You know how miserable that all sounds, right?'

I couldn't help laughing. 'It sounds worse than miserable. Is there something worse than miserable? Pitiful maybe? I'd pity me if I was looking in from the outside.'

'That's not fair.'

'Isn't it? I let it happen. I let Billy become my entire world. I stayed in a miserable job because the company impressed people. Because I thought as soon as Billy and I got married in the next year or two, I'd have babies and leave anyway. How pathetic is that? I'd let myself become nothing but shadows of other people.'

'You stood up for yourself when it counted.'

'Did I really have a choice? Standing there in that restaurant being utterly humiliated in front of everyone?'

'He begged for your forgiveness. Hunted you down at the hostel. But still, you held strong. You should be proud of yourself for that. Now you get to choose. You get to choose what happens next.'

'Can't I just stay here with you guys?' I asked without thinking.

He looked at me curiously.

'I didn't mean to impose myself on you like that,' I added sheepishly, realising how stalkerish I sounded after only one night of kissing.

'Don't be sorry. Regardless of what happens with me and you, you're welcome here. Our door is open. You get to choose. But there's consequences for this life too. They need to be considered before you choose. No hurry,' he said, pulling his cap down over his eyes and leaning back into the pillows for a nap.

What a concept. Choice. I just had to figure out what it was I wanted. Men aside. Tom aside. We'd just met, after all. But the life he and Lydia led, they were so damn happy who wouldn't want that for themselves? But leaving my niece for who knows how long? My sister? Where would I get money? How would I live? Could I do the menial work they did to get by? There was a lot to think about as I nestled back into my own pillows to nap, the sun high, the squeals of laughter ringing out from the middle of the ocean as our friends jostled for waves.

The sun drenched surfers had returned when I woke and milled around in the sun telling stories, drinking, eating. I listened, I laughed. The more they shared, the more I wanted what they had but I had to find my own version of it. I had to find my own path. Tom was right, there were consequences for their life. They all had their reasons for living the way they did but it couldn't be the only version. It was their freedom and their happiness I envied. What was it that would make me that happy, give me that kind of freedom?

I spent the rest of the evening trying to think of things that made me happy, things I'd wanted to be when I was a child. But the only thing that had ever truly made me happy was reading. Books had always been my saviour, my escape, my happiness. In books I found a version of myself I could never be anywhere else, I could go to far away places and meet interesting people from the comfort and safety of my bedroom, between studies and dinner parties, from the warmth of the car when I was supposed to be watching Billy play football in the rain. I'd read and I'd find happiness. I'd love to be able to write but I knew I couldn't, just like I knew I couldn't sing and I couldn't dance with the grace of a ballerina but it didn't mean I couldn't love it. I thought of the little bookstore in the strip of shops around the corner from home. It had been owned by a quirky older couple for as long as I'd lived there and they looked happy. How could they not when they talked of books all day. I went to bed that night with an option, a choice. How I would make it happen, who knew, but I had an idea and that was more than I'd had in a long while.

The next day was much the same but with more mobility. Tom and I walked along the beach, his hand reaching for mine. I connected with Tom in a way I couldn't remember connecting with another person. We laughed. We sizzled when we looked at each other. I was happy in his company when we were quiet and it felt like for the first time in my life I didn't have to pretend. I didn't have to be anyone else's version of me but mine. He was interested in my stories, in what foods I liked to cook for the dinner parties I hosted, he laughed at my cooking disasters which were many because I really wasn't that good but could mostly follow a recipe and make something simple look fancy enough to pass Billy's judgement. We laughed when I told him how I'd completely messed up one day but had enough time to nip over to the local shops and pick up leftovers from the food court and passed them off as homemade. Billy would have had a fit if he'd known he'd been eating food court food, let alone end of the day food. It didn't compare with Tom's travel stories but he was as interested as if they did.

As the sun set the others headed off for a night of pizza at a local favourite promising to bring us some back. Neither of us felt up to the outing, instead we sat in front of the television, snuggled on the sagging couch until we gave into the heat of a kiss that led way past teenagers making out.

'How do you feel?' Tom asked in the electrified quiet.

'What do you mean how do I feel?'

He grinned. 'How's your mobility?'

I looked at him confused.

'I want to take you to bed, Alex, I'm asking how injured you are and if you're up to it?'

'Oh,' I stumbled. 'Well, my foots still a bit iffy but I doubt I'll need my foot too much, right?'

He laughed. 'No, I don't think you're foot will be an issue.'

'How's your shoulder?' I asked.

'Stiff but I'm sure a little activity will be good for it.'

'Well, okay then,' I agreed cautiously.

'Well hasn't this turned into a romantic affair,' he joked.

'Sorry, I'm not that good at any of this,' I confessed. Billy had never asked, we'd never discussed things. Sex was just something we did a couple of times a week as part of our routine with no more thought than taking a vitamin.

'Oh, I think you're doing just fine,' Tom insisted, edging me down onto the couch as he stroked his thumb over my lips before his mouth followed, slow, soft before he turned up the heat and I ripped off his shirt.

His hands did things that should be illegal, elicited groans that should have come from an animal not my throat. My tank top somehow found its way to the floor before I realised he'd taken it off. His mouth, hot and perfect, worked its way over my breasts then down my body. He angled me just right before his mouth did unexpected and glorious things and I arched into him, begging in the most unladylike way as I felt him smile against the most delicate parts of me.

I rocked from the most exquisite orgasm just as the distant laughter of our friends echoed through the open front door.

'Shit,' grumbled Tom, replacing my panties before getting up and rubbing his hand through his unruly hair in frustration.

He handed me my tank top with a smirk as he pulled his own t-shirt on, reaching for a pillow to cover what must have been an almost painful erection, while feigning nonchalance as he stared at the television. My body still twitched and tingled as the others walked in, handing us our pizza without paying us any further attention before heading into the kitchen, the sound of water filling the kettle following right after.

'You okay?' Tom asked quietly, his finger leaving a trail of goose bumps down my arm.

'Ahuh,' I mumbled, not quite able to speak.

He gave one of those deep, sexy, laughs of his before reaching for a slice of pizza.

'Its not quite what I need right now but looks like it'll have to do,' he grumbled as he took a bite. 'Lucky it's damn good pizza,' he grinned.

I could only wonder what would have happened if they hadn't returned when they did. If he was that good with his mouth and his hands, how good was he at the rest of it? I was suddenly really worried I was way out of my league.

Chapter 6

I was eating toast at the counter, sipping my hot coffee when Tom walked in looking sexier than he should have been allowed to first thing in the morning. His hair was damp from his shower and had taken on a life of its own. He wore board shorts but hadn't yet got around to a shirt. His eyes were still sleepy and he grinned lazily at me before tapping me on the nose instead of doing what he clearly wished he could. Damn morals and self respect, I don't think I'd have complained if he'd taken me right there on the floor in front of everyone. Well I might have, just, if I'd managed any cognitive thought.

A phone rang, interrupting the animated talk of surfing conditions that had been going around the dining table and Moe pulled it from the pocket of his board shorts and answered. His face grew serious, his mouth tightening and the entire room went silent. An eerie silence that hung thick in the room as Moe grunted a few words, 'yep, yep, sure, 'k,' that sort of thing as he shared knowing looks with Michael and Tom. He hung up, put his phone in his pocket, glanced in my direction and began talking about surf conditions like they hadn't already done that, like there hadn't been any weird call at all.

The room was suddenly tense, awkward and uncomfortable. I looked around, waiting for an explanation, for something, but suddenly I felt like one puppy in the litter too many and had been pushed out of the circle while everyone forced pleasantries between themselves.

I sculled the rest of my coffee and went outside to get some air. Carefully avoiding the area of rotten wood someone had thoughtfully patched up, I sat on a step and watched the ocean coming in and out. Inside, the room had turned to ice and I wasn't wanted. What had the call been about? Suddenly I didn't feel so good. Suddenly I ached all over. Suddenly I wanted to be somewhere else, anywhere else.

I went back inside and headed for the stairs. I could hear everyone whispering in the kitchen as I passed. *Whatever*, I thought. Clearly I was still the newbie. Why did I even care? Of course they had secrets, everyone had secrets and we'd only just met. But that weird feeling was more than just a few closeted secrets. Moe had looked at me like he wished I were gone. My heart hung heavy somewhere around my toes. I'd gotten my hopes up, thought I'd fit, somewhere, finally but it was too soon. I'd been too hopeful. I wasn't really one of them. I'd never be one of them. I took my disappointment up the stairs and went back to bed.

The room was dark when I woke. There was scuffling in the corner. I rolled over to see Lydia rummaging through her bag and finally pulling free a jumper.

'Hey,' she called. 'You okay?'

'Sure, fine,' I mumbled, rolling over to face the wall.

'You don't seem okay,' she said, sitting on the side of my bed.

I sat up. I had to ask. 'What's going on? What was all that about this morning?'

'That? That was nothing. Don't worry about it. Don't give it any thought,' she said with a horribly fake smile.

'Did I do something to upset someone?'

'No, no, don't be silly. It was just...stuff.'

'Fine,' I declared, flopping back down onto my pillow and pulling the sheets over my face.

'Alex, c'mon! Seriously, I promise, it was nothing. Don't worry about it.'

'Promise?' I asked, pulling the sheet down like a sulking child.

She smiled, clearly amused. 'Promise. Come on. Come down and have something to eat,' she said.

'Fine,' I conceded, climbing out of bed and reaching for my shorts before realising I'd slept the day away and the evening had brought with it a chill and put on cotton drill pants and a long sleeved t-shirt instead.

Gingerly, I slowly followed Lydia down the stairs, it seemed the more I slept, the stiffer I became. We joined the others gathering outside around a makeshift barbeque where they talked and laughed, the smell of sausages filling the air. My stomach grumbled loudly from the smell.

Everyone seemed to have gone back to normal while I'd slept, there was no more tension or unspoken words, just laughter. Lydia handed me a sausage in a slice of thick crusty bread, holding a jar of tomato relish aloft. I nodded and she spooned the red lumpy sauce along the length of sausage and then got one for herself. I looked around, everyone was happy, laughing, sipping beer, stuffing their faces, but Tom was missing.

'He's upstairs resting. Go up and see him,' Lydia whispered into my ear.

'What? No, it's okay, I'll leave him be.'

'Go. He was asking for you earlier, he was worried. He checked on you like a hundred times,' she grinned.

I felt my face redden, the heat creeping up my neck.

Laughing, Lydia nudged me playfully in the ribs.

Shoving the last of the sausage and bread into my mouth, I licked the relish off my fingers, and hurried inside, suddenly energised. I wanted to race back up the stairs but my aching body protested with every step but I went up as fast as it would let me.

I wasn't sure which room he was in. I checked the first door at the top of the stairs. It had two bunks. Both bottom bunks were unmade with heaving packs at the foot of the beds. A guitar case covered in Anime stickers leant against the wall. Michael and Moe's room, I guessed.

I opened the next one and it was like mine: one bunk and a single. The bunks were empty, the bedding folded neatly at the end of each bed. I guessed this was where Damo and Daz had slept before going further down the coast. Lying on the single, his long body taking up all the space was Tom. His face was soft in sleep, the stubble from the previous night longer. My insides leapt, aching to touch him. I wanted to go to him, to touch his face, breathe in his essence, let that feeling of life and heat explode inside of me.

'Go away!' he mumbled.

I froze, my heart sinking to my toes as my brain slowly comprehended he'd asked me to leave. Finally regaining function of my brain and body, I quietly closed the door and went back to bed.

I rolled over feeling the wetness of my tears on the pillow. I'd find a way out in the morning. How had I been so stupid? Of course he didn't want me to stay. A super-hot, free gypsy like Tom couldn't possibly be interested in boring old me. He needed someone beautiful, free and adventurous like him, someone who knew this crazy gypsy life, not plain Jane, boring me and my suburban life. I'd have to go back to that other life eventually anyway, whatever form it took on. Tom needed to be free. I'd leave tomorrow and he would be free to roam and live as he pleased without me hanging around like a rock tied to his ankle. I was an idiot to even think anything else could be possible.

Lydia shouted in the hallway. How was I supposed to indulge in a little self-loathing with all the noise? I just wanted to sleep and find a way home. If I was going to be a humiliated fool, I was better off doing it on my mother's couch. No one responded to Lydia's shouting. There was a lot of 'how could you,' from Lydia, but nothing else. Then a door slammed and Lydia stomped down the stairs.

I looked out the window, it was still dark. *The longest night in history!*

I rolled over to face the wall, wishing I were at home in my own bed. Home? I had no home anymore. My bed was Billy's bed and I wasn't going back there. I had nowhere to go, I'd have to hope my mother or sister would take pity on me until I could get back on my feet. I'd have to go back to the office and laugh at Stan's jokes until I had enough money to do something else. How had I found myself here? Again. Had I learnt nothing from Billy?

I couldn't stop the avalanche of tears. Finally everything from the last few days came crashing down on me at once and my horrible life wouldn't let them stop.

'Hey,' Tom soothed.

I hadn't heard him enter, but his deep smooth voice was like a comforting blanket. He sat on the edge of the bed, wiping the pool of tears from my cheek before his lips brushed my skin, the tingling, searing heat burning itself into my memory.

I opened my eyes, looking at him confused. He'd asked me to leave. What was he even doing in here? He kissed my other cheekbone, my whole body cringing as he tasted my pathetic tears.

Then our eyes locked, my heart pumping, my blood bubbling its way through my body. God it felt so good.

Stop it, stop it, I told myself. I couldn't want to feel this. He'd asked me to leave so that's what I was going to do. What he was doing now was just mean.

It took all my strength but I moved away from him and leant against the wall. 'I'll go in the morning,' I stated, not looking at him. I couldn't look at him again without my heart breaking into a billion pieces.

'Why?'

I chanced a glance. His handsome face was worn, his beautiful green eyes sad, as though the world was falling in a heap at his feet.

'You told me to get out, so I will,' I told him.

He scrunched himself under the bunk, leaning against the wall beside me, his long legs stretched out, hanging over the edge. 'Sorry, I thought you were Lydia with another lecture,' he explained.

It was a reasonable explanation but too convenient. 'I swear,' he said, holding up Boy Scout hands. 'She's been on at me all day about some stuff.'

'*Stuff*! Yes, everyone's been on about some *stuff*!'

'Hey, trust me, you don't want to know.'

His eyes pleaded. I couldn't walk away from him. I had to, but at that moment, I couldn't even move to the other side of the bed. I froze under his gaze, his eyes, his handsome face looking at me so intently, held me captive.

All I wanted to do was reach up and touch his face, to make sure he was real. I didn't realise I was doing it until I felt his stubble. He smiled, his face lighting up, his hand cupping my face as he kissed me, hard and rough, his tongue eagerly searching as his hand gripped tighter, pulling me closer. Every part of me caught fire, the need for him surging through my veins, a desperation taking over my very core. My hands made their way over his naked chest, his muscles rippling beneath with every movement he made, only making me crave more.

I felt the beautiful weight of him as we inched back onto the bed. Our groins met, the hardness of him pressing against me, a fresh wave of searing, heat and passion filled my body. His mouth left mine, moving to my neck and I groaned involuntarily, my body so alive I thought I'd explode.

'Ahem... Sorry, don't mean to interrupt,' Lydia said from the doorway, Andrea beside her. Andrea reached for a jacket. I felt Tom's hardness disappear as he caught hold of his breathing, slowing it to manageable.

'Tom you might want to be invisible for a bit, eh!' Lydia instructed, her face serious as a rumbling of motorbikes, shook the house.

Tom nodded, kissed my forehead, got up and left the room. I looked at Lydia hoping for an explanation. But she gave me nothing, just said, 'You should just stay in here, Alex, yeah? Just be asleep.'

Then they were gone. Something was going on. I didn't like it and if I had to be asleep, why couldn't Tom be here? *Oh God, why couldn't he be in here?* The heat from him still surrounded me but I felt empty when he was gone. What was happening to me? I'd become an addict, Tom was my drug. I needed more. I craved him like my body craved air.

I flopped onto the bed. There was no way I'd be able to sleep. I was way too wound up. I heard heavy footsteps echo on the floorboards at the base of the stairs and then Lydia shouting. The heavy footsteps moved towards the kitchen. Pots crashed and then more shouting. I sat up, listening intently, worried as the shouting grew louder.

I stood by the door, opening it a crack, listening to the scuffling below. And then a bang so loud the house rattled and the windows shook. I held my breath. *What was that? Was it...was it a gunshot? No! Why would there be a gunshot?* My blood froze and deep inside I knew it was. *Oh shit! Crap, crap, crap!* Who was shooting? At whom? Why? *Shit, shit, shit.*

More shouting, doors slamming and Lydia yelling filled the house. I wondered what on earth was going on out there. Sneaking a glance towards Tom's room, I saw him, barely a shadow, in his doorway. Putting his finger to his mouth, looking towards the stairs, which were empty, he waved me over. Barefoot in a tank top and the only decent, non-frilly, non-lacy undies I'd brought with me, I quietly scurried across the hallway to him.

Softly closing the door, Tom wrapped his arms around me, holding me tight, the warmth of his body enveloping me like a shroud. He put his finger to his mouth, pushing me behind him while he went back to listening to the commotion downstairs through the small crack of the door.

Motorbikes rumbled and gurgled all around, shaking the air and putting the foundations of the old villa to the test. I put my hand on Tom's naked back, wishing for once he was wearing a shirt I could grab a hold of as the bikes echoed off into the distance.

Tom breathed a sigh of relief, his whole body relaxing with the exhale, but then there were footsteps stomping up the stairs. He carefully closed the door and we flattened ourselves against the wall.

'Just me!' Lydia announced.

Tom opened the door as my heart moved from my mouth back to my chest where it belonged.

Lydia came in, a purple bruise forming on her cheekbone. 'What are you doing in here? I told you to sleep,' she said, her eyes narrowing at me with fury.

'Stop it, Lids,' commanded Tom. He touched the horrible bruise on Lydia's cheek.

'It's nothing, Tom, leave it,' Lydia shouted, storming down the stairs, Tom following right behind her.

Almost tripping over myself, I hurried to follow. There was no way I was being left behind after all that had just happened.

At the bottom of the stairs Lydia whipped around, her face full of rage. 'I said leave it, Tom. Shit,' she spat, storming into the kitchen and Andrea's arms.

Tom went to follow but Andrea held up a hand. He slumped onto a step instead. I flopped down beside him. 'What's going on, Tom?'

'Nothing.'

'It's clearly not nothing. There were gunshots, Tom. Gunshots! It's something!'

'Nothing you should worry about. Nothing you want to be involved in. I'm sorry we probably shouldn't be doing this. I should have known better. It's all my fault. I'm so sorry,' He said, his eyes glistening as he looked longingly, wishful, apologetically into mine.

He kissed the top of my head, holding on a moment too long before getting up and walking out the front door, leaving me feeling empty, airless, surrounded by a dark, cold bubble of nothingness.

Chapter 7

I sat on the step alone, a black and white vortex swirling all around me, my insides frozen as I watched the door Tom had walked out of, my heart heavy, my body numb. What did he mean we shouldn't be doing this?

Shadows moved in the corners of my eyes but I didn't move. I couldn't move. I stared at the door waiting. Waiting for Tom to come back. He had to come back. He had to.

Goose pimples raced up my arms. He'd left without his shirt. He'd be back soon, he'd be cold, he'd need a shirt. Sombre sounds drifted in from where everyone was talking in the kitchen. They sounded far away, almost another place altogether. The smell of sausages still hung in the air. My own stomach churned, horrified with the thought of food. But Tom hadn't eaten any of the sausages. He'd be hungry. He'd be back soon. He had to eat. He had to sleep. He couldn't stay out all night.

I needed to speak to Lydia, find out what was going on but I couldn't seem to make myself move.

I waited.

And I waited.

One by one Bex and her Merry Men, Michael and Moe stepped over me as they went up the stairs to bed. Plates and glasses clattered in the kitchen as Lydia and Andrea cleaned up. He'd have to be home soon.

Andrea mumbled something as she stepped over me. Her voice sounded blurry and so far away I barely noticed the sounds she made at all. I could only think of how cold Tom must be on the beach with no shirt.

Nothing made any sense. The hiding and bullets flying, the motorbikes and Tom's leaving. My brain was doing somersaults. I needed to check everyone was okay but I couldn't get past Tom, I couldn't get past my own disappointment, my worry for him. I thought we were sharing something a bit more than just a passing flirtation but now there were all these secrets. Who were these people?

All I knew was I couldn't go back to before. I couldn't go back to Billy bloody McRae. I couldn't go back to a black and white life. I needed to be the person I was with him. These people had shown me a whole world of possibility, I didn't want to walk away but how could I stay? It seems I didn't even know them at all. I didn't know Tom. He'd shown me a world I'd never known existed, never knew I wanted and now I wanted it more than anything but did any of it even really exist? I had to know what was going on. I had to at least know he was okay. Why wasn't he back?

It was still dark when I woke with a start, my head against the staircase rungs as the front door slammed, my heart skipping a beat, my lungs freezing, but it was just Lydia. Her mouth moved but I couldn't take my eyes off the door. I could only watch it, waiting for Tom to walk through it.

Lydia tugged on my arm until I looked at her. 'Alex, he's gone.'

'What?' The question sounded like it came from somewhere else, someone else far away. 'How? Where? He didn't even have a shirt. He can't have gone.'

'His board's gone. If his board's gone, he's gone. Sorry, hon. Come on, come have a cuppa,' she said, helping my stiff body off the step.

Lydia led me, dazed and confused, into the kitchen. Nothing made any sense. The last 48 hours made no sense. This entire trip made no sense. Nothing had made sense since before I'd boarded the plane in Australia, my whole world had gone topsy turvy the minute I landed.

I slumped at the table, which was in desperate need of a good sand and stain, staring at Lydia as she placed a steaming cup of tea in front of me, waiting for answers, hoping for something. He was her brother; surely she knew where he was?

'I'm sorry Alex,' she started, softly. 'He promised this was different, you were different.'

'I don't understand. What does that mean?'

'There are things about Tom you don't know, about both of us. I usually slide through undetected, but not Tom and when trouble finds him, he runs. That's about all you want to know about yesterday, it was trouble looking for Tom. That's why

Damo called yesterday morning. He and Daz, they'd heard things, people asking about us which is never good. Tom promised he wouldn't run this time. He said he couldn't. He was supposed to just stay in his room until they left and we could get on the road back to Paris.'

'I still don't understand. What happened yesterday?' I asked, shaking my head, struggling to comprehend anything she said. It just didn't make sense.

'It'd take too long to explain everything, and I promise, it's long and boring and you're better off not knowing.'

'That's it?' I asked, frustrated.

'Trust me, it's all you want to know. Just hold onto the nice memories and move on, forget you ever met us.'

'I can't forget that, I can't forget you,' I told her, still waiting for everything to make sense.

'It'll be easier if you do. None of us will forget you either if that helps.'

'No, it doesn't help,' I said, getting cross. 'Its ridiculous, Lydia, all of it. I just don't understand.'

'I know. I know and I'm really sorry you got caught up in any of it. We all are and if I could change it, I would. If we could go back to Paris I'd offer you a beer, pat you on the shoulder and walk away.'

'You'd wish we never met?' I asked horrified.

'I don't wish it, Alex, but I'd do it, I'd do it for you.'

'I wouldn't. You saved me. All of you. You showed me I'd been living a life no one should live and there's so much more I could be doing. This, right now is shit and stupid but I wouldn't change meeting you, I wouldn't change coming here, I wouldn't change the last three days. I'd change right now and have you tell me what's going on. I'd put Tom in the chair beside you and demand answers, I'd ask why he made me think he liked me more than he clearly does and tell him he's an ass for doing it but I wouldn't change any of it. I'm worried for you though.'

She nodded. 'I'm sorry, it's all I can say,' she said, reaching for my hand. 'We'll get you back to Paris as quick as we can. You'll be safe there.'

I nodded but it just wouldn't sink in. 'So he's gone?' I asked, needing confirmation, unable to believe it was true, that he could just leave like that after everything that had happened.

'Looks that way.'

'Will he be back?'

'Probably not.'

'But you're his sister, he can't just leave you in the middle of nowhere.'

'I have the others, I'll be fine. We'll all go back to Paris and Tom and I will hook up again before too long. He'll hide out somewhere for a while and when he thinks it's safe enough he'll come and find me. That's the way it always works. The fool thinks he's protecting everyone when he disappears,' she said, shaking her head.

'Protecting who?'

'Me. You. Everyone?'

'From what? From who?'

'Trouble. Those guys yesterday, they were trouble looking for Tom. But they'll be back as soon as they realise I lied and sent them on a goosechase. So we have to go,' she said.

'What? Leave? We can't leave without Tom.'

'Yes, we can. We have to. He'll resurface eventually, when he thinks it's safe.'

'But by then I'll be gone,' I mumbled, almost to myself.

'I'm sorry. Really, I am,' she said, her hand on mine. 'I know it's an awful time to ask, but I need you to do us a favour. We're out of food and Dre can't drive all the way back to Paris with no food and no water. You're the only one they don't know, won't recognise. There's a bakery in town. I'll give you money. We just need croissants, water, whatever they have as snacks.'

'Okay,' I mumbled, wondering how on earth I would find my way when I wasn't sure I could even stand up without falling apart, the last week had just been too much. The gun wielding bikers were too much. Tom leaving was too much. Lydia and her secrets, all of it. My life had crumbled around me and I'd thought I'd at least had them, thought I'd at least had something with Tom. Who knew yet what it might be but I'd thought it was something, going somewhere, even if it was only for as long as it took for me to get to Charles De Guille for my flight home. At least there'd have been a conclusive ending, not him walking out in the middle of the night with no shirt leaving me hanging like a fool. He was gone. Trouble. What did that even mean? I was torn between worrying for him and wanting to punch him in the face.

'Alex,' Lydia said, bringing me back to the present. 'You need to go now. We don't have time for you to fall apart. Michael will walk with you but he'll have to stay out of sight. It's just a little walk down the beach,' she told me.

I nodded as though it made sense, as though anything made sense.

I heard footsteps behind me moments before Michael put a comforting hand on my shoulder. 'You ready?' he asked.

No, I wasn't ready, I wanted to tell him. I wanted to crawl into bed and never wake up. I didn't want to go grocery shopping. My heart had shattered into a billion irreparable pieces and they wanted me to buy croissants. I couldn't breathe. I couldn't eat. I didn't care about croissants. But I knew it was necessary.

'Hey,' I said, suddenly remembering the shots from yesterday. I'd been a selfish cow, totally focussed on my stupid man trouble. 'Shit Lydia, I didn't even ask, is everyone okay? Who got shot at?'

'Don't worry about it, we're all fine.'

'Who got shot?'

'No one, they missed.'

'Who did they try and shoot?' I asked annoyed. She was dodging my question. The bruise Tom had touched now wiggled as she scrunched her face annoyed at my probing.

'Me, okay. They tried to shoot me. I wouldn't give them Tom. Michael did what Michael does and they missed but one got a good left hook to my cheekbone,' she said, rubbing the purple bruise.

I nodded as though it all made perfect sense. But none of it made any sense at all. What on earth had I gotten myself into? They were all lovely, kind people. Why were crazy blokes on motorbikes coming and shooting at Lydia and scaring Tom so much he disappeared into the night without so much as a shirt or a see ya later.

'Come on, worry about it later,' Michael said, taking my hand and leading me to my feet before sharing a worried look with Lydia. I didn't blame him. I was sitting at the dining table in my underwear, almost catatonic over a man I'd known five minutes when I'd barely skipped a heartbeat after walking away from the man I'd thought I'd marry. I'd lost my mind. So I didn't blame them.

Andrea passed me some pants with that same concerned look on her face. It seemed emotions and facial expressions were a global language.

'You ready?' Michael asked doubtfully after Lydia and Andrea had helped me put on my pants.

I nodded and he led me outside on to the beach.

Michael draped his arm across my shoulders as we walked. I let my head fall onto him as tears pressed against the back of my eyes. But I was too numb, too dumbstruck, to actually cry.

I looked out at the surf, the cresting waves, empty and alone. I'd half expected him to be there, riding a wave with a jubilant smile on his face as though he were conquering the world, but he wasn't there. He wasn't anywhere and I was here, walking on the beach, Michael the only thing holding me upright as I concentrated all my effort to put one foot in front of the other. Again and again.

Finally we stopped. Michael turned me to face him, putting his hands on my shoulders to keep me grounded, focussed, whole.

'Okay Alex, this is as far as I can go. The bakery's just across the road. Are you okay?'

No. But I nodded. Everyone was relying on me so I nodded, took the money he handed me and tried not to get myself killed as I crossed the road.

I didn't even have the presence of mind to admire the beautiful display of cakes and other baked goods filling the window displays. I just wanted it all over, to get out of this place and be somewhere else, I couldn't say where, just somewhere my friends weren't shot at. I weaved my way around the rattan Parisian bistro chairs and into the little shop.

'*Bonjour*,' the young baker greeted cheerily.

I smiled tightly and mumbled a sad little *bonjour* in return before ordering. There were only eight of us now but I ordered ten croissants, just in case Tom returned and a spare in case someone was extra hungry. It was always good to have a spare. I ordered ten cakes, I didn't know which ones, I didn't care, I just kind of waved at some and took ten bottles of water out of the fridge.

I paid and the kind man who'd politely ignored my fallen face, tear filled eyes and shaky voice, helped me load everything into the reusable bags Lydia had sent with me.

I left with a half smile of thanks and a complimentary coffee he clearly thought I needed, which, it turned out, I did.

I sipped gratefully as I crossed the street, back to Michael who was waiting in the shadows of a grove of trees.

'All done?' he asked sympathetically.

I nodded, taking a long sip of the coffee for strength.

He took the bags from me and draped his spare arm across my shoulders and led me down the street.

It was quiet except for the sounds of a nearby carousel gearing up for the day.

'There's a market in the town square,' Michael explained.

'That's where we'd planned to go this morning,' he told me sadly. 'He'll be okay Alex,' he added, referring to Tom.

I nodded but I didn't know if I could believe it. I didn't know much of anything anymore. All I knew was my chest hurt and I couldn't breathe. I wanted to be mad, to be angry, to hate him, but I couldn't. Perhaps when I didn't hurt so much, the anger and the fury would come. Perhaps when something finally made sense again, I would be able to yell and scream, cry and hate but I couldn't do any of those things. I still wished he'd come back. That he hadn't left me at all. That maybe, just maybe, he liked me enough to come back and see us through properly.

We lost ourselves in the sand dunes as we headed home. My calves burned, but Michael insisted it was safest not to take the same route both ways.

I wanted to ask, safe from whom or what but I suspected as soon as I opened my mouth, the giant lump that resided in my throat would burst and the avalanche that would come would never stop and now was not the time. I needed to hold it together, until we left, until I returned to my other horrible life. The sooner I got back to Paris and forgot about France altogether, the better. The sooner I got home and got on with my life, the better. I suspected I'd never again be the same, not the girl who'd flown to Paris with Billy and not the girl Tom had brought out in me. I wondered who I'd be once the dust settled and I found a way forward. But I'd gotten to like being Alex, living this life. Finding Alex had been a gift but now I had find a new me. How many versions could there be before I went completely mad and did I want another version? No. I wanted Alex. I wanted Tom. But it seemed, as always, I wasn't going to get what I wanted.

As we were coming out of the dunes, into the open space, we heard the sounds of people. French words, angry words. Michael pushed me behind him as we slowed, as we carefully looked around the dune.

'Shit,' Michael mumbled. 'Tom!' he muttered. 'Stay here, don't move,' he demanded before disappearing.

I looked around the dune to see Tom taking on two burly attackers that looked more like human bulldogs. It was two on one but he was holding his own. I couldn't pick his fighting style, there was boxing and kicking and probably just plain survival.

One of the bulldog's fists connected with Tom's face and I was sure I could hear bone crunching from my hiding place. But before I could worry further Michael snuck into the fray and made it a fair fight. They had one down but the other disappeared in a blink and before I knew it I was being pulled up by my arm pit and dragged into their makeshift fighting ring.

Tom's eyes went wide, steam almost spurting out of his ears.

The bulldog with the iron grip on my arm smirked as he put a gun to my head. 'Who is winning now? Huh?' he challenged as his friend laughed, pointing a gun at Tom who was now staring at me in fear.

Tom was going to do something stupid, I could see it in his eyes. Give himself over to protect me, something. I looked to Michael, begging through the tears and snot streaming down my face now frozen in fear. I could hardly feel anything, it took all my energy to hold onto my bladder.

Michael and Tom shared one of their silent communications

and before I could comprehend what was happening, Tom had broken the jaw of his captor with his elbow and sent him to the ground clutching at his crown jewels while Michael took the opportunity to similarly disarm my captor while he was too shocked to see Michael coming.

'Who sent you?' Tom demanded, a gun trained on one while Michael held the other down with a booted foot to his throat and a gun in his face.

Michael screamed the question when no one answered.

'We don't know, okay,' stumbled Michael's captive. 'No one tells us that, we just do what we are told,' he insisted.

They asked a few more questions but I was squatting in the dunes, trying to get a hold of myself, trying not to vomit now the realisation of what almost happened hit.

'If I see either one of you again, I swear it, you won't be walking away, do you understand me?' Tom shouted at the men in a voice that frightened me.

They must have agreed because they scuttered away like bugs in the sand and it was quiet.

'Alex...' Tom begged, crouching in front of me. 'Are you okay?'

'Don't. Don't touch me,' I cried, pulling away from him.

'Alex, please...' Tom begged through his constricted throat. 'I'm so sorry.'

'Sorry for what? For leaving me here or for this, for having a gun held to my head? Why Tom? Who the hell are you people?' I sobbed.

'Now's not the time, Alex,' Michael insisted kindly beside me. 'We need to get out of here and get somewhere safe.'

'Why? Because there might be more?'

'Yes. That's exactly why,' he said bluntly.

'Well, I'm not going anywhere with you people. I'm going back to Paris and back to my miserable life. At least no one holds a gun to my head there,' I said, getting up onto my wobbly legs.

'Alex, I'm sorry,' Michael said, steadying me. 'But you can't leave.'

I pulled my arm free. 'The hell I can't,' I insisted.

'No, you can't,' begged Tom. 'They know your face now.'

'So what? They're after me now, too?'

'Probably,' he said, sadly. 'I'm so sorry.'

'Sorry? You're sorry? I'm a freaking target for crazy gun wielding meatheads and I have no idea why and you're freaking sorry?' I stormed off, not wanting to hear anything else he had to say. This was crazy. I didn't know what was going on with these people or who they were but it was time I left. Somehow I was getting back to Paris and going home and they could get back to living whatever messed up life they had going on.

'Wait!' Called Michael as I was about to go into the house. 'Please, Alex, it's not safe.'

I stood in front of the open door and waited but didn't turn around.

'The door shouldn't be open,' Michael said. I don't know who he was informing, Tom, himself, maybe me but I no longer cared. 'Wait here,' he said, pulling a gun from his waistband.

Tom put his hand on the small of my back but I shrugged him off. 'Don't touch me.'

'Alex, please, I'm so sorry. You can't know how much. I'm so sorry,' he begged.

I looked at him then, took in the purple bruise on his cheek bone, the cuts on his eyebrow and lip and I just wanted to fix him, to make sure he was okay. What was wrong with me?

'It's clear,' Michael called back to us.

'Stay behind me, anyway,' Tom demanded as we entered the house.

I peeked over his shoulder, gripping onto his shirt as we walked over the threshold. No one was there. The room was empty, except for a body lying on the floor. Bex's Johnno.

'Shit,' Tom grumbled.

'Alex, can you shoot a gun?' Michael asked.

'What?' I stumbled. 'Me? No, no, no,' I said, shaking my head.

'Yes, you, you have to, we have to check the rest of the house. Here, take this,' he said, handing me a small gun and setting it so it was ready to fire. 'In the corner. You shoot first, ask questions later, understand?'

I nodded mutely, the gun shaking in my hands.

'Okay. Go. Sit. We have to find Lydia and the others.'

I nodded again and went and sat in the corner, holding the gun up, ready.

Michael and Tom disappeared up the stairs and I waited. It seemed an age that I waited then I heard unfamiliar voices talking softly and swivelled so my gun was pointed at the two unfamiliar men who'd just walked in from the kitchen shoving leftover, cold sausages in their stupid mouths.

'Well, well, lookey here,' one smirked, his mouth full of sausage. 'I told you there were more, that they'd be back,' he grinned.

My hands shook. I had to pull the trigger. Shoot first, ask questions later, Michael said.

'Get lost, or I'll shoot,' I told them, my voice strangled.

'Sure you will, girlie,' said the other man, another bulldog of a man with a head like a watermelon.

'I will. I'll shoot,' I told them, even though I could barely hold the gun straight.

They laughed at me.

'Where's your boyfriend?' the first asked, his mouth now empty.

'I don't have a boyfriend,' I said.

'Now we know you're lying. We know the others. We don't know you.'

'So. That doesn't mean anything.'

'Where is he?' he demanded.

I saw Bex's Johnno moving out of the corner of my eye. Thank God he wasn't dead. But I couldn't let them have another go at him so I had to step up before anyone else came back. I had to stop being such a sissy. I closed my eyes and squeezed the trigger.

Watermelon head squealed like a little girl. Then Michael walked up behind his mate, holding his gun against the guy's temple. 'Are we really going to do this, fellas?' he asked.

'Alright, alright,' surrendered the guy with the gun to his head while his mate continued to groan in pain holding the hand I'd shot. Then they walked out the front door.

Michael fired his gun at their feet, 'Next time I won't miss,' he told them as they ran.

'Are you okay?' he asked, checking me over.

I nodded, unable to stop the shaking or the fresh wave tears streaming down my face.

Michael pushed some stray hairs, covered in tears and goo and who knows what else off my face. 'Come on, sit down,' he said, leading me to the couch.

'Hey,' Tom said, turning my face to his with his finger. 'Alex, I'm so sorry. I thought you'd be safer if I left. I'm so sorry,' he said, pulling me to him and I no longer had the strength to push him away as the avalanche of tears almost overwhelmed me. I finally breathed, sucking in gulps of air that made my head spin. But I'd thought for sure I'd never again feel his arms around me again.

He kissed my forehead, holding my folded body to him until eventually the sobbing and the shaking stopped. His arms wrapped around me, squashing me close enough for me to breathe in his scent, the smell that made everything better, already imprinted in my memory as safety and warmth.

I didn't want to move. Even after I'd stopped crying, I didn't want to move. I was afraid if I were okay, he'd leave. I couldn't be apart from him again. Not now. I'd shot a man and I didn't know what that meant, what would happen to me. I didn't even know why. All I knew was I'd had a gun held to my head and if I hadn't shot him, he would have hurt me or Johnno and Johnno was in no state to protect himself. Tom smelled of soap and salt and man. He was warm and clammy. I could feel his heart beating under his skin. He was my person. I couldn't let go. I needed him to tell me it was okay, that I'd be okay. Just for now, just until I could breathe again then I was getting the hell out of this messed up place.

Tom pried me from his body, looking deep into my eyes, trying to smile while wiping away my tears. 'It's okay now. I'm here now. I won't leave you again.'

'Promise?'

'Promise,' he said, kissing me softly.

Johnno finally sat up, rubbing his head.

'Hey, man, what happened?' Johnno asked.

'They came back,' Michael said. 'You alright, Johnno?'

'Yeah, nothing a few painkillers won't fix. Everyone else?' he asked ignoring his own well being.

Michael shook his head with a knowing smirk. No doubt knowing Johnno was far from alright and probably had a concussion and seriously bruised ego but he wasn't admitting it, not while there were still things to do and people to protect. 'I think so. They were upstairs in the attic following the protocol they should have followed the other day. But I can't find Moe.'

'I think they took him,' Johnno said, rubbing his head.

'But we just kicked them out,' Michael said, confused.

'There were more. Five or six of them. I tried to stop them but...well, you can see the result, two against six, we had no chance,' he said, leaning against the wall for support looking pale.

'Shit. I should have shot that bastard properly then,' he huffed. 'Alright, we gotta get out of here,' he said, pulling his phone out of his pocket.

'Alex?' Lydia said softly, suddenly kneeling before me. I hadn't even heard them come down the stairs. 'Are you okay?' she asked.

I nodded, numb. 'No,' I admitted. 'I shot someone. None of this makes any sense.'

'It was only his hand,' Michael quipped as though it were nothing.

I hadn't cared where I shot him, it was only dumb luck it was his hand. But they'd both had guns dangling from their hands. 'I didn't want to die,' I whispered.

'Come on, it's okay, you're safe now and it was just his hand. Won't do the bastard any harm, trust me,' she consoled. 'Here,' she said, holding a cup of hot, sweet tea to my mouth.

I sipped and waited to feel better. I took the cup and continued sipping and slowly I stopped shaking, stopped quivering, stopped crying.

'Come on, we have to go,' she said.

I nodded. 'I just want to go home,' I whispered.

'Sorry, hon, but that's not going to happen. Not right now, anyway.'

'Where are we going then?' I asked, resolved for the moment that they knew more about this than me. Which wasn't particularly comforting considering the world I'd landed in but it was true, I didn't want to die and if they could keep me safe for a day or two until I could go home then fine, I'd deal with it for a day or two.

'To a safe house. Michael just called his people. There's a safe house not far from here. We'll have to lay low for a few days, at least, until we find Moe, find a way to sneak back into Paris unnoticed,' she said.

'It'll be okay,' Tom insisted beside me. 'We'll be okay,' he added, leaning his forehead to mine. 'I promise.'

Chapter 8

'Come on people, get your things, we gotta get outta here,' hollered Michael as he walked down the hallway like an army general.

I shoved everything into my suitcase and zipped it up. I had to get Michael to carry it down the stairs where Bex was putting a small plaster on Tom's split eyebrow.

'Our resident medic,' Lydia said from behind me. 'She used to be a lifeguard and is a pro at patch ups. That's how her and Johnno met. He'd been smacked in the head with his board and she'd been charged with checking him over before calling in the ambos. She's very handy to have around,' she quipped with a laugh.

It was good for Tom I supposed but still, the fact they needed a person with medical capabilities at all was unnerving. All of it was way more than unnerving and I just wanted to get moving, get out, get home, forget it all.

'Are you okay?' I asked Tom, checking his face over when

Bex was finished. I was still mixed with mad and needing to protect and care for him. It was an odd combination.

'I'm fine, just some bruises. Took a good kick to the head. But I'm fine,' he insisted.

I looked to Bex for clarification and she nodded. 'He's got a tough head, he'll be fine.'

I nodded and headed out to the sad blue van.

'Are you ever going to forgive me?' Tom asked, taking the seat next to me.

I shrugged.

He sighed.

After weaving her way through the country roads, Andrea stopped the van in front of a pair of large, imposing, black iron gates. 'Well, this is the address,' she said to Michael. 'Are you sure this is it?'

'That's the address I was given,' he said, clearly as surprised as the rest of us.

We all stared dumbly out the windows. The gates said we were in the right place, but the house that sat atop a small hill beyond the gates, was so much more than a house. The stone building was more sprawling chalet or chateau than house. A sprawling, beautiful stone structure topped with a couple of turrets and surrounded by bright green grass and grape vines stretching over the undulating hills. We looked around the van at each other in wide-eyed confusion.

Andrea stretched her pale arm out the window and pressed the intercom button on the stone wall. There was no response from the intercom but the giant iron gates slid open and we drove through, following the curved driveway to the front of the house.

A silver lion's head was perched in the centre of the door; Lydia knocked it against its equally shiny silver base and we waited.

We stood, fidgeting, waiting. Finally, the door was opened by a handsome man with thick black hair with the slight kink of a 1940's movie star. He wore an immaculate suit and smelled divine.

'I am Henri Carcassone,' he said, introducing himself. 'Come, come,' he said, opening the door for us.

We followed him down the long stone hallway, his expensive cologne trailing faintly behind him. Henri led us into a large room filled with books on all the walls, dark antique timber furniture with rich tapestry cushions and a small fire burning on one side fighting off the chill creeping in through the stone walls.

'Sit, sit, please,' insisted Henri. 'You are safe here, I promise,' he said as we took our seats in the settees and armchairs, all beautifully upholstered in rich red brocade coverings.

I slowly relaxed as the fire warmed my bones and I finally stopped shaking. I was far from okay but glad my bones had stopped rattling.

A thick set man with dark grey hair and a pink face silently moved into the room producing large, fine cut crystal wine glasses, almost goblets. Wine. Yes, I needed wine. I thanked the man when it was my turn to have my glass filled and took a long, therapeutic sip.

Once the man left, we quietly sipped the light fruity red

wine, fidgeting, forcing smiles, but completely lost for words. I had nothing to say, I'd been rendered mute and wasn't even sure I wanted to speak to any of them. I doubted anything they could say could make up for a gun being held to my head or being forced to shoot a man. The tension radiated through the group, was it coming from me or were they just taken aback by the finery we found ourselves in?

'How do you find the wine?' Henri asked, breaking the uncomfortable silence.

A lot of nodding and mumbling ensued. 'It's delicious, Henri,' Lydia said, covering for all our ineptitude and unintended rudeness.

'It's one of my most prized vintages,' he smiled.

'This is one of yours?' Lydia asked.

'Of course,' he nodded, proudly.

'It really is a fine wine, Mr Carcassone,' Andrea agreed as we all nodded.

'Oh, Henri, please,' Henri insisted.

'Oh, of course, Henri,' agreed Lydia.

The old man appeared in the doorway and Henri added, 'Why don't we eat something?'

Michael and Tom nodded and we all followed Henri and the butler to the dining room.

At one end of the dining room hung long red velvet drapes. A large marble fireplace had the room toasty warm and dancing in a romantic glow. A happy couple and their small boy were encased in a gold gilt frame above the mantel and kept watch over the long mahogany dining table stretching down the centre of the room between rows of exquisitely carved high back chairs with rich, red velvet upholstery.

Large crystal vases of giant white flowers with bright green decorative foliage sprung from the middle of the table and set before each of us were more crystal wine glasses and regal white china with gold edging waiting to be filled with the food we could smell wafting in from somewhere.

The butler filled each bowl with smooth bisque, the colour of caramel that smelled so rich, so good, my mouth began watering instantly. With each spoonful the soup warmed away the horribleness of the day. If any dark shadows remained, the rich beef stew filled with potatoes and carrots that followed chased them far away as though it had been cooked with magical healing properties.

Henri tried making small talk, asking where we were from, where we'd been but we were a group of incredibly rude and hungry travellers, too busy nodding and grunting between slurps and groaning like animals that all he managed to elicit for his efforts were monosyllabic answers. I knew I should have been ashamed, embarrassed but I wasn't. I was as bad as the others, this meal was the best food I'd tasted in what seemed a really long time but in actual fact was only a few days. I blamed it on my horrible day. I needed the comfort of home cooking, so I, too, was a perpetrator of bad manners. Lucky for us our host appeared more amused than insulted.

As the sugar of the crème brulée that completed the feast hit people's blood streams, conversation resumed with the relaxed, excitement and joviality of full, grateful bellies as though the day hadn't happened at all.

'That was amazing, Henri,' Lydia told him.

'Thank you,' he smiled. 'I don't get to eat so well all the time, it is very nice to have guests, and I think Marguerite enjoyed the chance to cook,' he smiled.

Tom asked Henri about his winery and Henri came alive as he spoke of the work he was doing, his grapes and vines, his plans for the winery, expansion and exportation.

The more he talked, the more alive Henri became as though it had been forever since he'd had company and laughter in his home. Perhaps it had been. Although he was a handsome man, strong, sure features, everything in proportion. He dressed well, he looked fit, had impeccable manners, that suave moustache and perfectly groomed hair. Surely there was a lady somewhere who had her eye on him, if not a queue of them waiting their turn.

'So Henri, why is there no lucky lady sharing this place with you?' Andrea boldly asked.

He smiled. 'I have not had time for a lady. I have come home from the Special Forces when I got shot and then my papa died and I was left with the winery and the house and everything. There has not been time and I do not get out so much now. Work is very busy here. There is a lady who works in the winery, she makes sure everything runs on schedule but she has a son and is shy. Perhaps someday I will ask her to the house for dinner,' he suggested as though the thought of doing so had only just occurred to him.

'Oh you really should,' Andrea said. 'This is all very impressive.'

He laughed.

The butler returned and began gathering the plates. Henri nodded to Michael who nodded in return.

'We should go now, and bring in your things, yes?' asked Henri as the butler left with our plates.

'Yes, that's a great idea,' agreed Michael.

The boys followed Henri, who followed the path of the butler to collect our things from the van. I didn't expect they'd encounter much trouble out on Henri's lovely curving drive but who was I to argue with the extra precautions. I was still waiting for my chance to find out what was going on in the first place, why Moe had been taken, what trouble could possibly be following Tom and Lydia? They could be anyone, now I thought about it. They could have done anything before they came here. But something inside me said they were not the problem. That I could trust them. I guessed Henri felt that same thing or he wouldn't have invited us all into his home.

I was about to broach the subject while it was just us girls, but the room seemed too cavernous, too quiet without the others. Before I could decide, a tiny lady with white curls brought in a tray of coffee. I wondered if this was Marguerite, the cooker of the amazing meal we'd just eaten. She pointed to the doorway so we followed her back to the room with the books. Marguerite placed the tray of coffee onto the table, indicated the milk and sugar and left.

'Can you believe this place?' Bex asked softly.

'I know, it's like we've time warped into a forgotten renaissance painting,' Lydia said, looking around.

She was right, it was perfect and beautiful, the kind of place you could forget your troubles, forget you'd had a gun held to your head or that you'd shot someone.

'So, are we really going to stay here?' Bex asked incredulously.

'Looks that way,' Lydia smiled. 'If Tom and Michael say so, who are we to argue?' She leant back in the chair, crossing one leg over the other, sipping her coffee like a royal lady of leisure. 'I hate that Henri and his people have been dragged into all of this though, I know it's a safe house and it's what they do, but still...' Lydia said more seriously, Bex and Andrea nodding in agreement. Seeing as I still had no idea what *this* was, I just watched them blankly, not even sure I wanted to know anymore. 'You too, for that matter,' Lydia nodded at me.

'Me?'

'Yes, you, Newbie. Everyone else has been around long enough to know what they might be getting themselves into when they travel with us, but you, you've no idea and it's probably not fair that we dragged you into all of this. But I swear we had no idea any of this trouble was coming. We've had no sign of it for like a year, I promise. If we'd known, we'd never have suggested you come. Forgive us?'

'I can't forgive you if I don't know what's going on,' I grumbled, unable to hide my annoyance.

'You don't want to know, trust me.'

'Yeah, you keep saying that but you didn't shoot a man, you were safe and protected in the attic.'

'I'm so sorry. Alex, you have to believe me. I promise, in the morning Tom and Michael will tell you everything. It's better if they do, they'll explain it better than me. But I promise, you're safe now and we're not the bad guys.'

Her green eyes were so similar to Tom's, but somehow brighter, perhaps it was her rich black curls that made them glow, but they begged my forgiveness and I couldn't help but laugh at her expectant face. 'I'm not even sure I want to know. I had a shotgun aimed at my head today; I shot a man; I think that is enough drama for one day,' I said, waving my hand as though the whole sorry mess was forgotten. But it was far from forgotten. Now I had a tummy full of food and was sitting by the nice warm fire, I was just too tired, too shocked and worn out by the day. I just wanted to pretend none of it had happened, stay the hell out of their crazy drama until I could get home. I didn't want to be a part of any of it.

The sound of the heavy wooden door closing echoed down the long hallway. Henri came in and announced, 'That is all done. You must all be exhausted. Shall I show you to your rooms?'

'Yes, thank you,' Tom said, as we all followed Henri out of the room.

'What's he smiling at?' Lydia whispered as she wedged herself between Tom and me.

'How am I to know?' I asked, wondering myself why he was smiling to himself.

'He's up to something,' she grinned as she fell back next to Andrea.

Suddenly I was afraid. What was Tom up to? He'd said we wouldn't be apart again. Was he planning on coming through with his promise of getting me alone? I wasn't sure I wanted to be alone with Tom, anymore. I was too mad at him.

'Okay,' Henri called us to attention at the top of the stairs. 'You,' he said pointing to Andrea, 'in here.' He pointed to the first door.

Shrugging, way beyond caring about rooming arrangements, Andrea went into her room.

'Mademoiselle,' Henri continued gesturing kindly to Lydia, then a door.

Next was Harry and Chris then Bex and Johnno and then it was just Tom and me left standing beside Henri in front of the last door along the hallway. Henri had roomed Tom and me as a couple. No wonder Tom was smiling. My stomach flipped, the blood in my veins stopped flowing, my brain died, becoming incapable of thinking anything beyond the fact I had to share a bed with Tom and suddenly I wasn't sure if I could. Suddenly, the enormity of the last few days came crashing down on me, waves of self-doubt paralysing me. I wondered if Lydia would mind some company?

Tom politely thanked Henri and led me, his hand on the small of my back, into our room. My suitcase sat happily beside Tom's bulging backpack at the end of a big four-poster bed. Thankfully, there was none of the netting of worlds gone by; it would have been more than I could take. An armoire sat in one corner, two winged chairs rested in front of the fireplace in front of the bed and an enormous bay window, which I'm sure over-looked something amazing in the daytime was beside the bed, complete with padded window seat.

I stood in the middle of the room, frozen to the spot.

'Are you ever going to forgive me?' Tom whispered from behind me.

I shrugged. 'Nothing to forgive, I suppose. It is what it is.'

'Alex, come on, I'm sorry.'

'For what exactly?'

'For walking out, for leaving you, for getting you caught up in our mess.'

'A mess I'm better off knowing nothing about.'

He sighed heavily. 'Do you really want to get into it now?'

'No. I'm tired, Tom and I want to go to sleep.'

'I'm not going to bed until I know you're okay.'

'Then you'll be weary at sun up because I'm not sure I'm ever going to be okay.'

He pulled me to him and I couldn't help falling into him despite being mad. I sobbed into his chest and revelled in his arms holding me tight. I never wanted that moment to end. I wanted everything to go back twenty four hours when Tom's arms around me and his mouth on mine was all that mattered in my world.

'I promise you'll be okay. I'll get you home and you can forget all about us.'

'Is it that easy for you to move on?'

'I live with it every day, Alex, I never move on.'

'From me?'

'From you? No, that won't be easy. It won't be easy at all. I've never been in love Alex, but I have a feeling that this is what falling in love feels like. But I'll let you go to keep you safe. I couldn't bear it if anything happened to you,' he declared, holding me tighter.

Love? Could that even happen in three days? Outside of movies and Nanna's romance novels? I looked up into his eyes and my world tumbled a little as it always did and if the circumstances were a little different then maybe I'd happily fall right along with him because nothing had ever made me feel so excited, so whole, so at home as I felt when I looked into his eyes.

Before I could stop him, before I could think about it or what it meant for my mental health or my heart, before I could remember how mad I was, his mouth crashed down onto mine in a rough, hard, heated kiss that curled my toes.

'When I saw you in the dunes, when he put that gun to your head, I swear I thought I might die. I've never been so afraid, Alex, never. I was terrified I might lose you. I would have done anything to protect you, anything, I swear.'

I nodded, wanting so much to believe him.

'We're the good guys, Alex, I promise. I'll explain everything in the morning but tonight, I just need to hold you, one more time, to know you're safe, for everything to be okay, to be as it was yesterday one more time. I know I don't deserve it after leaving you,' he added, losing the rest of his words.

Stupidly, I needed it too. He had to be the good guy. I couldn't imagine him as anything else but I was too tired for anymore what ifs and I was too tired for a full explanation, I just wanted to sleep.

Tom's arms snaked around my waist and beads of sweat formed all over my body as the air electrified with possibilities I wasn't sure I was capable of after everything that had happened.

'It's okay, Alex,' Tom whispered into my ear with a hint of a smile, 'no funny business tonight, I promise, I just need to hold you close.'

My whole body exhaled with the relief.

Tom laughed softly. 'Do I still make you nervous, Alex?'

I turned to look at him. The corners of his mouth were tight, trying not to explode into a grin, mischievous thoughts racing behind his darkening green eyes. I had no words. I searched for the right words but they wouldn't come. I didn't want him to think I was pathetic. I didn't want to admit that every time he looked at me my blood raced through my veins and that a heater switched on in my toes, firing up every cell of my overwrought, overexcited body.

He saved me from myself, his lips softly brushing mine, his breath warm and sweet from the wine. His hands moved over my back, pulling me closer and closer. I softened into him, needing this one night, this one moment, as much as him. As his mouth pressed harder, his tongue searching for mine, I gave into him, holding on tight. My knees weakening, I melted into his body, the lusciousness and perfection of his touch.

Then it was over. He pulled away, searching my eyes for a moment as I caught my breath. Then he repeated, 'No funny business, I promised.' He smiled, unbuttoning his shirt and throwing it to the floor before letting his pants fall to the floor beside his shirt and climbing naked into the enormous, inviting bed, made perfectly for funny business.

I stood, staring for a moment unsure what to do next, frozen to the spot unable to move. I had to share a bed with Tom, who was beautiful and naked under the covers. I couldn't breathe. I couldn't move, but I knew I had to. I needed to be cool and calm.

'*You can do this,*' I told myself. '*It's no big deal. He's just a man.*' Wasn't he? But what would I wear?

Under my tank top and pants I still had the only non frilly, non lacy underwear I had. It was all the equivalent of Nanna beige. I couldn't climb into bed with beautiful, naked Tom wearing those, although they were better than everything else I had, all the frilly bits of nothing. I had nighties but they were just teensy slips of satin and lace themselves. I'd packed for a romantic getaway with Billy, I'd expected a proposal under the Eiffel Tower, I'd packed to please. It all seemed so silly now. I wished for my ordinary black knickers back home, my ordinary jammies, tank top, shorts. I didn't even like these teensy slips of nothing.

I opened my suitcase and found a clean, plain tank top, that'd have to do. 'I need to shower,' I declared, needing a minute of space to gather myself, to wash the stench of the bulldogs from my skin.

I returned, feeling a little less disgusting but unable to look at him as he lay propped up on one elbow watching me. I knew he was in there completely naked but I was putting it out of my mind. My body was heavy with need for sleep and I was still too mad to have sex with him. I quickly climbed under the covers, facing the opposite direction.

I could feel the warmth of him all the way across the bed. The sensation of his naked body only centimetres from my own had mine buzzing. The electricity and invisible connection we shared stretched across the bed and I couldn't think, I couldn't breathe. I scrunched my eyes shut, trying to block him out. I couldn't think about him. I had to pretend he wasn't there.

I felt the sheets move and hoped to goodness he was just rolling over but he wasn't, his arms laced around my stomach pulling me close, his mouth moving against my hot skin, kissing the divot under my earlobe. His warm tantalising breath hovered over my neck, the wetness of his tongue sent every ounce of my resolve dissipating to nothing. Maybe one night wouldn't be so bad? My skin exploded beneath his touch, my heart pounded, my head swirled and my lady bits ached. I wanted him so bad I didn't think I could say no even if I wanted to.

Tom's hand snaked down my bare thigh, it was warm, soft and strong, leaving goosebumps in its wake, feeling so good I wanted him to wander over a little more. I so wanted him to. I wanted to feel him touch me. I wanted his touch to make everything okay, to make me forget the last two days, to make everything better. For just one night I wanted to forget.

His mouth moved down my neck and the sound of twinkling fairies echoed throughout the room from my handbag on the bedside table. I ignored it, begging for it to go away, knowing it was only mum and her blasted impeccable timing. I closed my eyes and waited for it to stop, but it twinkled and it twinkled and Tom's hand went back to my waist, his hot breath whispering in my ear, 'I promised.'

'Promises, promises,' I mumbled as the music finally stopped.

'Not like this. Not today.' Trailing his hand down my thigh, he whispered, 'when I make love to you Alex, it won't be to forget, it'll be because it's right and I'm going to need every part of you to participate. I want you utterly coherent because when that happens, it's going to be amazing,' he said, sending a shiver through my body

I shivered as he nibbled my earlobe and my whole body caught alight, then he stopped, 'Today is not a day for amazing,' he said, laying his head on the pillow and pulling me so close I could feel his heart pounding.

His heartbeat slowed with the rise and fall of his chest. My breathing settled and moved in time with his as though we fit, as though we were meant to be like some stupid story book romance. But I took it because I needed it.

Chapter 9

I woke wrapped snug and safe in Tom's arms, his body warm against mine, his breath soft and moist on my ear. If Tom weren't being hunted by crazy, gun-wielding Frenchman, if we weren't hiding in Henri's ridiculously fabulous chateau, everything would have been perfect.

'Good morning,' Tom murmured sleepily.

'Morning,' I replied, snuggling further into his warmth.

Tom softly kissed my neck, squeezing me tight, my body igniting with electrified goosebumps. Perhaps today was the day for amazing? Then he got out of bed. I rolled over to see what he was doing completely forgetting he'd slept in the buff. I blushed as I saw him standing perfectly naked beside the bed, or was it the impure thoughts of what I could do to that naked body running through my head that had the fire racing all over my body? I wasn't sure which. Probably both.

Tom caught me grinning to myself and smiled. 'Not now, Babe, I've got a mate to rescue.'

I sat up quick, the warm tingles in my lady land dissipating, 'What do you mean?' I asked, reality crashing down on me.

'Well Moe's not going to rescue himself, is he?'

'But you can't.'

'Why not?'

'It's too dangerous, Tom, they have guns.'

He climbed across the bed, kissing me so hard he forced me back onto the pillows, stealing my breath from my lungs. Pulling back just as my head began to spin, he said, 'I'm a big boy, Alex, trust me.'

I pulled his mouth back to mine.

'Nice try,' he said, winking. Climbing off the bed and pulling on a pair of board shorts from his backpack, he left the room.

I fell back onto the bed, exasperated. He couldn't seriously be going after the crazy Frenchman. Surely he wasn't that foolish?

Laughter drifted up from somewhere below the window. Washing and dressing in record speed I went in search of the laughter, hoping to find Tom and to stop him doing something stupid.

Everyone sat on pool lounge chairs in a circle under a shaded verandah beside a sprawling swimming pool glistening in the morning sunshine and surrounded by vines.

'Ah, there she is!' joked Lydia.

I smiled trying not to blush, even though I'd done nothing to blush about other than sleeping beside a beautiful, naked man.

A big granite table was pushed to the side and weighted down with fruit, yoghurt, croissants and a shiny silver coffee pot. Selecting a ham and cheese croissant and pouring a much needed cup of coffee, I sat in a lounge chair in the circle facing the others. I broke off a piece of croissant, shoving it hungrily into my mouth.

Tom had disappeared but Michael hadn't and Lydia had said I needed Michael and I wasn't waiting a minute longer to find out what was going on. Enough was enough. I'd gotten through the night. My mental stability was still in tact. Despite still being shaken and traumatised, I wasn't in a corner crying like a baby so it was time to demand some answers. I had to know, I had a right to know.

'So, is anyone going to tell me what's going on? Why Lydia and Tom are being hunted by crazy fat Frenchman on motorbikes? Why a gun was held to my head? Why Moe was kidnapped and why Tom is going to rescue him?'

I stared at my croissant, breaking off another piece, waiting, holding my breath, afraid of what the answer to my question might be. The possibilities were endless and I wasn't sure how I'd feel if I didn't like the answer.

Silence wasn't what I'd expected. I looked at Lydia to see why she was suddenly a mute. She was looking over my shoulder. Turning around I saw Tom, his face far from impressed.

I looked from one to the other, 'Well?' I demanded.

Tom pushed me forward on the lounge chair, sitting behind me, having one of his silent conversations with Michael.

'She has a right to know, I suppose,' Michael grumbled.

'Damn right I do,' I told him.

He smiled before adding, 'You're probably better off not knowing, though. I warn you, it could change everything.'

'Change what?'

'How you think about me for one,' Tom added.

'And me,' Lydia said.

'How could anything change that?' I asked. 'You said you were the good guys.'

'We are. But we're not who you think we are, not exactly,' Tom whispered, regretfully.

'What do you mean? Who are you? How much of it has been a lie?' I asked, suddenly afraid.

'Not a lie, not exactly,' Lydia said. 'We just haven't mentioned some things, that's all.'

'What things, what sort of things?' I asked moving away from Tom, thinking the worst. Were they criminals? Were they dangerous? Lydia had said they were on the run but she'd said from their families. Was that really all there was too it?

'See, you've already moved away.'

'Shut up and tell me what's going on or I'll do more than move to the end of the chair.'

'Ooh, she does have a feisty side,' Lydia laughed.

'Lydia!'

'Sorry, Alex,' but she was smiling too much to be sorry. I wondered how bad it could really be if Lydia was making fun? Then I remembered the shotgun that'd been aimed at my head and thought bad, really, really bad.

'Have you heard of the Harrington family?' Tom asked.

'Of course I have. The Harrington's own half of Australia, resorts up north, hotels all along the east coast, that new one they're building in Alice is supposed to be really nice.'

'Yes, that's them. That's us.'

'What?' I asked looking from Tom to Lydia. 'You know them? You're related to them. What exactly?'

'We are them,' Lydia added apologetically.

'I don't understand.'

'Which bit?' Tom asked impatiently.

'The life you live, the family, I don't understand how it all fits together and why crazy Frenchman are chasing you with shotguns.'

'Because Dad's an ass,' Lydia blurted.

'Lids,' Tom chided.

'Well he is.'

'Yes, he is,' Tom conceded. 'Our father, the great Richard Harrington himself, is nothing but an arse kissing fool. Anyway, we had some trouble on a site. There was an accident, a kid, a first year tradie, just turned 18, died and dad left me hanging.'

'That was the one on the Gold Coast, right? I remember that.'

'Yeah, that's the one.'

'The media went to town on you.'

'They did.'

'Tell her why,' Lydia interjected.

'It doesn't really matter why,' Tom added. 'I should have done more.'

'Still, Tom?'

Tom huffed. 'The building company in charge was owned by Lincoln Cummins,' he started.

'THE Lincoln Cummins?'

'Yes. He had no business being there or being on any site for that matter. Everyone knew he was a party boy, we knew first hand how much but George Cummins and Richard Harrington were BFFs so dad was always happy to do whatever George Cummins asked and when George asked for Linc's new bullshit building company to get the gig of building the Goldie resort, dad just gives it to him. I caught the little asswipe laundering money, swapping out materials for cheaper materials and pocketing the cash to party with because Old George was keeping him on a short leash through his trust fund. I caught him one night fucked up to his eyeballs in a dress going at it with the young tradie, Axl Barker up against the lobby wall. I knew about his extra curricular activities, he partied with our sister so I knew and didn't think it was a big deal, thought everyone knew so I just carried on with my business but then there's the accident and Axl's dead and right when I'm about to give my statement to the police I get a photo of mum and Jaz having brunch with Sue Cummins. I got the message, how easy it would be for George to do whatever he wanted to so I left out the bits about Linc stealing and getting wasted and fucking young tradies in a dress. A week later, Linc announces his engagement to that supermodel heiress from the states and moves an ocean away and I have George quietly in my ear reminding me how dangerous it is for their family's future that I exist. Linc knew I knew everything and threw me under the bus before skipping town.

'Of course, the great Richard Harrington didn't believe a word of it, couldn't believe that George would do that. Which was ridiculous considering the people he'd bought off to keep quiet about Jaz and the destruction she left in her wake. But George and his connections were far more important to Dad than I was. So anyway, George set his media conglomerate on me, they went to town with no restraint. I was guilty in the publics mind and left hung out to dry which was just great when it turned out young Axl Barker is the illegitimate but much loved son of an underworld boss who'd been so proud of his son doing the right thing and living life on the straight and narrow. I'd already been planning to skip town before the accident to get away from Dad. I was just waiting for this project to be done then I was leaving. After the accident, I took out my savings, added a little from my trust fund just in case and then as soon as the police gave me the all clear I left. Lydia wasn't meant to come but well... you've met Lydia,' he grinned.

'Wouldn't be anywhere else, bro,' she laughed.

'So who exactly has hired the Frenchmen? George?'

'We had a lot of threats from Axl's dad and his people before we left so I'm guessing it's them. George's media blitz was done on purpose to stir up trouble in the hope of getting Axl's dad to do his dirty work for him so he could keep his hands clean.'

I considered it all for a moment. The enormity of it. It had been so well publicised but I remembered thinking at the time that something was off. Tom was right, Linc was a well known party boy, had been scooped out of the gutter more than once. I wondered how much of it didn't actually make the television when George owned so much of it, how much worse it really was. I remembered being surprised to find out he even had his own building company, I'd thought he was just a trust fund bludger. 'So how do Michael and Moe fit into all of this?'

'They're our bodyguards.'

'You're what? Are you serious?'

'Deadly. It's the only thing we take from Dad. I'm not a

masochist. I don't want to die and there's Lids to think about. It keeps Mum happy. Not that we had a choice. They followed us here. I tried to get rid of them, called mum, pleading but she begged and it was mum and she promised to do what she could to make things easier if I kept them. They get an annual allowance to follow us around and protect us.'

'Right,' I said, letting it sink in as if that kind of information could possibly sink in.

'So you hate us now?' asked Lydia.

'Why would I hate you?'

'Cos we're not really backpacking bums?'

'Yes you are. You still work crap jobs to pay your way don't you?'

'Yeah, mostly,' they answered in unison.

'Then you're exactly the same people.' I moved back against Tom and he wrapped his arms around me. I looked at Lydia and smiled.

'I knew none of it sounded right at the time.'

He shrugged. 'The kid, he was young, doing the right thing, trying hard, in the end, it was just easier to blame the rich kid.'

'But why you and not Linc?'

'It was my project. Dad had made me the figurehead of the project, the face of it. Linc was all over Cummins media as the party boy come good, working hard, making an honest living. No one wanted to believe he hadn't changed.'

'But you were ex army, surely people had faith in that?'

'Yes, but he doesn't talk about it,' Lydia added. 'No one even knows what the hell he did in the army, he could have been a cook or a dish washer for all anyone knows,' she smirked.

Johnno laughed.

Tom huffed.

He clearly wasn't a dish washer. I'd seen him fighting off two burly meatheads so I was sure he was a lot more than anything menial. I'd thought he was just being modest when he'd avoided the subject but I wondered if there was more to it, if maybe he did something super secret or maybe it was just so awful he didn't want to talk about it? I tried probing a little, wanting to know as much as I could now the gates were opened.

'All you need to know is I learnt enough to keep you safe. The rest, no one needs to know those details, even if I were allowed to share them,' he said sadly.

My heart swelled of its own accord. Something about the way he spoke, the stories he told made me want to take care of him, to love him, to make everything better. He had demons, he had too may hurts bottled up inside. The running no longer seemed free and romantic and my heart broke a little for him. Is this what true love really was? Is that what was happening to me? I wanted to protect and save him, I wanted to love him enough to make the rest go away. It made anything I'd ever felt for Billy seem so insignificant. In comparison, I wondered if I'd ever had any romantic feelings for Billy at all. I'd fancied him in the beginning. I'd enjoyed kissing him and our time in the bedroom well enough but I'd never felt this intense need to hold him, to make the world a better place for him, to love away the pain, make him soup, I don't even know what exactly it was I wanted to do for Tom, it was a swirl of emotion that was I was feeling and strange but so incredibly intense.

'Hmmm...' Pulling his arms around me tighter I bent down

and kissed his hand. I knew this man would never intentionally hurt anyone, not now, not when he was 21, not ever. He was too good and beautiful and kind.

'So how are we going to get Moe back?'

'We?' Tom near leapt of the chair, 'You're not going anywhere near this, do you hear me?'

'Why? Because I'm a girl? What? Surely there's something I can do to help?' I shouted back before storming off feeling as useless and pathetic as that girl who stood in the dunes crying with a gun to her head. I didn't want to be that girl ever again. I couldn't be. I'd come too far.

I was partway up the stairs when he grabbed my arm. 'Alex, I'm serious,' his eyes pleaded. 'I can't have you in danger. Nowhere near it. I couldn't concentrate.' He took another step, levelling his face with mine, our eyes locking, my heart stopping for just a moment.

Touching his face I wondered what happened to his stubble. 'Tom, I couldn't cope if anything happened to you. I couldn't. I was a mess when you left before. I can't go through that again. I don't think I'd survive it again. Please,' I begged, 'there has to be another way. Can't Michael take care of it?'

Tom dragged me up the stairs, closing the door behind him. 'No, not after everything Moe's done for us. I owe him this. Johnno, Michael and I, we know what we're doing. We're trained for this stuff.'

'You're not army anymore.'

'Once Army, always army. We'll be fine. As long as I know you're safe and you'll be here when I get back, that's all I need.'

'I'll be here. Just make sure you come back.'

'Does that mean you've forgiven me?' he asked with that twinkle in his eye that sent my heart fluttering.

I shrugged but couldn't help smiling.

'I needed to hear that,' he grinned, taking a step closer. 'Now don't get mad, but I need you to look out for Lydia while we're gone, keep her out of trouble and get her home to Australia if anything happens.'

'What do you mean if anything happens?'

He closed the few steps between us, holding my face, kissing me hard, stealing the breath out of my lungs. Breathless, he answered, 'I swear, nothing will happen out there. I'm not dying without sleeping with you.' He gently stroked the side of my face as we stood there a moment, our breaths caught in all the possibilities before returning to normal.

Winking, he took a toiletry bag and some clothes from his backpack and left the room.

I flopped on the edge of our bed. I didn't think I could survive him dying without sleeping with me either. I waited for my heart rate to return, took some painkillers and then I wondered how Tom was getting by with his busted shoulder. He seemed fine, but he shouldn't be, should he? He'd just had a dislocated shoulder put back into place. That had to hurt, didn't it?

I found Michael heading inside and bailed him up against the stone wall. 'Tom's shoulder is still busted Michael, you can't let him go.'

'His shoulder's fine. He tougher than you give him credit for. He can take care of himself. You have to trust us.'

'Please, call for help, something, anything,' I begged desperately.

'Sorry, Alex, but I need Tom. Trust us,' He implored, holding my shoulders for affect. 'I'll bring him back in one piece, I promise.'

Old houses echoed, their staircases echoed, I looked up and Tom stood, furious, his hair wet, wearing black cargo pants, his black t-shirt in his hand.

'You good, Buddy?' Michael asked.

'Yeah, just give me a sec.' Michael nodded and continued on his way.

Tom wedged me against the hard, cold wall, his bare chest glistening with beads of water where the sun's rays snuck in through the doorway. 'You weren't trying to be sneaky, were you?'

'Me? Nope,' I mumbled, shaking my head.

'Babe, I need to know you aren't going to do anything stupid. Just sit tight, keep an eye on Lydia. Promise me. Promise,' he ordered, looming over me so I couldn't think straight.

'Fine. I promise.' I said, hanging my head in defeat.

Tilting my face up with his finger, he declared, 'I love you, Alex. I'm coming back.' His eyes never faltered, his face didn't as much as twitch. He pushed himself against me, his hot mouth melting onto mine, his tongue reaching inside; the soft gentleness of his movement confirming its new declaration. Butterflies desperately tried to escape my stomach, a groan escaping instead, saying everything I couldn't.

'Ahem.'

He stopped kissing me but didn't move away, our foreheads touching.

'We got a lead,' Michael said.

Tom kissed my forehead. 'Stay! Watch my sister. I'll be back by bedtime.'

Nodding pointlessly, unable to breathe, I watched them walk down the long hallway, their shadowed silhouettes moving in unison and out the front door where Henri and Johnno waited.

Andrea linked her arm through mine, 'Come. He'll be fine,' she insisted.

I let her lead me outside. I sat on a lounge chair beside Lydia and looked across the pool and the green vineyards beyond. We didn't need any words. There was nothing to be said. All we could do now was wait.

Chapter 10

I left the others sitting under the verandah drinking something cold and icy to walk through the vines. I couldn't sit still. My mind was jumpy, my heart was jumpier. I tried focussing on Tom's parting words, I love you and I'll be back by bedtime. I was holding him to the second because I was right there with him on the first. I couldn't say how I could love him after such a short amount of time but I did. Perhaps enduring so much adversity in such a short time accelerates things? Perhaps the life he led put things into perspective.

We don't have an infinite amount of time on earth, things could change in an instant, I'd learnt that in the last forty eight hours. If that bulldog of a Frenchman had pulled the trigger it would have been all over for me, they would have been shipping my body back to my horrified mother. Things like that change you. You don't sit around waiting for an appropriate amount of time to pass before voicing such declarations.

Perhaps Tom had learnt that doing whatever secret things he

did in the army? Perhaps he'd learnt it when he'd had to turn his life upside down to protect his family from George Cummins? All I knew was he'd left without me telling him how I felt. He left before I could tell him how the sun shone brighter when he was in the room. Before I could tell him that no matter what happened I'd forever be grateful for knowing him, for knowing what it feels like to be blown away by someone, not because they bought a fancy dinner or gave a fancy gift but because of their spirit, the way they love the ocean and come alive when it kisses their skin, the way they look at you as though the world turns with you as its axis. The way they look for you in a room before anyone else and their face comes alive when they find you. If I had to go home tomorrow, if I only ever got to feel like this for these few days, I'd never regret a single moment of it, even the bad stuff that would haunt me for the rest of my life, it all disappeared when I saw Tom's smile when I closed my eyes.

I knew that this trip had already changed me, I'd never be the same person. I would go home and I'd change my life. I wasn't quite sure how yet, perhaps that little bookshop I'd imagined, perhaps something else but I wasn't going back to my cubicle, I wasn't going back to laughing at Stan's bad jokes or being treated like someone's maid. Lydia had been right, this trip was just what I needed. But I couldn't leave until I knew Tom was okay. I wasn't sure how I would actually leave but I knew I couldn't stay. I'd be a burden to his survival. I had no visa and a life to fix and only I could do that.

I looked up at the sun, it was sitting high in the sky. Some time had passed since they'd left. The butler was laying out things for lunch and Bex's merry men were corralling everyone to eat.

'Alex,' Harry called.

I joined the others for lunch. Simple fare, fresh baguettes I suspected Marguerite had baked herself with ham and full bodied cheese. The butler put out some wine and we gratefully accepted but sipped with trepidation. It seemed everyone was keeping their wits clear of impairment. It didn't fill me with confidence.

Bex's Merry Men tried telling funny stories in an effort to lighten the mood but there wasn't much that could do that so eventually we sat in silence staring out into the vines until the sun began to sink.

I couldn't sit still. I kept moving, I left a voicemail for mum, called the airline to change my flight, I let Marguerite do a load of washing for me then repacked everything into my suitcase, making sure everything was neat and organised and ready to go with just my jammies, an outfit change for the morning and toiletries. I tried to read but gave up when I realised I'd read the same page three times and still had no idea what it said. When Bex hollered from the hallway I was grateful for the interruption and joined the others for dinner.

It was an even more sombre affair than the night before, more forced merriment until we all just gave up and ate in silence. It concerned me that the others must have been as nervous as I was and that couldn't be good.

Afterwards I found Lydia sitting by the fire, staring absently into the embers. She quickly wiped her eyes when I walked in and I felt bad for interrupting her private moment. 'What's wrong? Have you heard something?' I asked.

She shook her head, no.

'Then what?'

'He should have been back by now. He made it sound like they were just popping down the street to pick Moe up and they'd be back in no time. And they're not back,' she said quietly.

'Tom said by bedtime, he still has time.'

She shrugged. 'Dinnertime, bedtime, there's not much difference. What's taking them so long?'

It was my turn to shrug. I wish I knew. I wish I had words of wisdom, of comfort but this wasn't my world, I didn't know how these things worked.

'I don't know what I'll do Alex, if anything happens to him.'

'Nothing is happening to Tom,' I told her with as much bravado as I could muster. 'Michael will make sure of it. And he has Johnno, right?'

She nodded.

I heard anxious but hushed talking coming from the hallway. Lydia needed a minute so I went to see what was going on to find Bex's Merry Men, Chris and Harry, in a hushed but heated debate.

'What's going on?' I asked, clearly surprising them.

They clamped their mouths shut.

'Tell me,' I demanded, in no mood for playing polite.

'You need to tell her,' Harry said.

'Tell me what?'

'Yeah, tell her what?' Lydia demanded having composed herself.

'I got a message,' Chris said apprehensively. 'From Johnno. We have to go get Moe.'

'Moe? What about Tom?' I asked, my stomach sinking.

Chris shrugged. 'Message just says, not going to plan, need you to pick up Moe and he gives the address. That's all I know, I swear.'

'They've got Tom,' Lydia stumbled.

'What?' I asked, needing the wall to hold me up.

'They'll kill him,' Lydia whispered.

Harry held Lydia up as she paled to ghostly white. 'He'll be okay, Lids. This is Tom, he's invincible.'

She shook her head. 'No. They've been wanting this too long.'

'We'll know more once we pick up Moe,' Chris insisted. 'Alex, can you sit with Lydia until we get back?'

'What? No, I'm coming with you,' I said, pushing past them into the hallway.

'Then I'm coming too,' Lydia said, finding her legs and following me.

'What good is it going to do? Just sit here and we'll be back in a little bit,' Harry insisted.

'No Harry, I don't want to wait that long and what if there's a clue we need to help Tom? I'm not waiting until you get back to figure it out,' I told them.

'Fine,' he conceded, clearly wishing there was more he could do to convince us otherwise.

We all strode out with clear instructions from the butler on how to get to the address Johnno had sent and a promise from the butler to look out for Andrea and Bex while we were gone.

We climbed into the faded, sad blue van and off we went, down winding roads and narrow through fares until eventually we came to the address Johnno had sent through.

We stopped in front of the dark, dirty building with a non-descript flaking black door with not even a number on it. One of the windows on the second floor was haphazardly boarded up, forgotten and unwanted. We climbed out and stood in a row facing the building.

Across the street there was a sad looking jewellery store, its entrance closed and well secured for the night. A dull light shone from the back of the bakery beside it. Then there was a shop signposted as a butcher but it didn't appear to have seen any life in some time. Leaves and debris gathered at its front door, thick dust on the windows. But nothing on the street looked as sad and broken as the unnamed building in front of us. I got the eerie sense that bad things had happened here and there was no way I was waiting a second longer to find out what.

I was out of the van before Harry had turned it off, despite Chris' pleas ringing in the background to wait. I probably should have waited for them, to make sure it was safe but Johnno wouldn't have sent us here if it wasn't safe. He would have warned Chris and Harry, told them to bring backup, something. He wouldn't have sent them into danger blind.

The front door was unlocked so I walked in as though I had the right to, as though I'd somewhere along the way found the confidence to do so. I was on a mission. I had to know if Tom was okay because I had the sickening feeling deep in my stomach that Lydia was right and that Tom was far from okay.

I searched the rooms as I went, empty and held together with cobwebs, it had been a long time since they'd been used for much. There was no sign of anyone until I got to the final room at the end of the hallway. The door opened onto a kitchen that had seen better days. A chair sat in the middle of the room with ropes hanging from the bottom of the chair legs. That sickening feeling grew worse when I saw blood splatter on the chair and on the floor. But other than some dirty coffee mugs on the sink, there was no other sign of life. No Moe.

I opened the back door and stepped out into the cool night. It was quiet. No sounds of life from the neighbours, no children laughing or music playing or even the echo of a television or barking dog.

'Anything?' Lydia asked coming up behind me.

I shook my head at a loss for words.

'Harry's checking upstairs, Chris is checking the ally down the side.'

Amongst the overgrown garden a pink flower was blooming beautifully under the bright moonlight. I went over to look at it, desperate for something lovely in the madness. As I got closer I heard a pained groan from the shadows. I moved closer, slowly, not quite sure what I was hearing. It almost sounded like a wounded animal and they could be dangerous when startled but as I got closer I could see the outline of a man.

'Over here,' I called to the others, pulling out my phone to use the light to see what I was looking at. 'Moe?' I whispered, falling to me knees. 'Moe, are you okay?' I asked, trying to look him over with the little light I had.

Chris rushed up beside me, shone a torch onto Moe who

blinked up at us, relief flooding his face despite his apparent pain.

Harry joined us and checked him over for major injuries while Lydia and I watched on. Once they declared him mostly okay, just dehydrated and no doubt concussed, they carefully sat him up while Lydia went to rinse a mug and get him some water.

He bounced back remarkably well, well enough anyway to relay what happened.

'They kept me tied to the chair, didn't do much to me really other than taunt me with their bad jokes. It was all just to lure out Tom. Tom should have known that. But they all came anyway. They almost succeeded too, we were on our way out then they got Johnno. Tom being Tom did exactly as they knew he would and saved Johnno but now they have Tom,' he told us.

'Where are the others then?'

'Michael, Johnno and Henri have gone after them. I got thrown into the bloody garden and one of the bastards gave me a friendly kick to the head on his way out,' he said, rubbing the point of impact.

'Well, let's get you back to the villa and have Bex look you over,' Harry suggested.

'We should look around first,' Lydia suggested. 'See if we can find anything that can help the guys find Tom.'

I agreed, it was a good idea and I had to do something because the adrenaline pumping through my body was almost unbearable. All I could think was what they'd be doing to Tom now they finally had their chance. I watched too much crime TV because the images were plenty and disturbing. I suspected Lydia was thinking the same thing as she tore through the house burning off her frustration as she pulled out drawers and opened cupboards. There was nothing to find though. The house was empty of anything useful, it was empty of pretty much anything. They'd not taken notes or kept bills or anything else that could help us find where they'd taken Tom. There was nothing but the used mugs and some milk spoiling in the fridge and an almost empty jar of coffee on the counter. There were no leftover food containers or pizza boxes, no personal items or bedding, not even a pillow. This place had been used for one thing and one thing only, to set a trap for Tom. We had no choice to leave empty handed.

One of the boys had messaged Bex ahead so her mad and fear was well hidden when we returned and she was ready with first aid supplies to tend to Moe. The butler's wife was clearly well versed in the art of personal care, too but spoke no English so quietly assisted with the dabbing of creams on the few cuts Moe had while Bex made sure he wasn't lying about his lack of injuries. Everyone was charged with keeping an eye on Moe so he didn't fall asleep before his concussion was in hand. After my turn of feeding and watering him and trying to keep him good humoured while he tried insisting Tom would be fine when he was clearly feeling defeated, I went to sit on the loveseat on the front verandah where it was quiet.

Lydia was already there watching the curving drive as though by watching it could make them appear faster.

'He has to be okay,' I insisted as I held her while she sobbed.

'I'm just hoping he took his tracker,' she mumbled.

'His tracker?'

Michael gave us both trackers, they're little pins we can put on our clothes or the bottom of our shoes. We don't use them often though, especially as we've had no trouble for so long. I'm just hoping he thought to put it on before he left,' she said.

I hoped so too. Something like that could save his life right now and I really needed his life to be saved.

'Are you wearing yours?' I asked curiously.

She nodded. 'I am now,' she said, showing me the pin in her bra.

Eventually, as the pink of dawn kissed the sky, I woke with a start. My neck was kinked from sleeping twisted like a pretzel but I forgot about my aches as I saw four shadowed figures walking up the driveway, the stones crunching under their feet as they went.

'Lydia, Lydia,' I nudged.

She woke, jumping as she did. 'What?' she asked before also spotting them. 'Tom?' she whispered hopefully.

The others joined us, from where I don't know. Had they also been sleeping on the verandah or inside the door?

Finally, one by one the shadowed figures walked into the light. Henri and Johnno limped ahead. Then, Michael holding Tom up as they walked. I fell against the balustrade, holding on tight to stop from falling, sobbing. He'd come back. They'd found him. I'd begun to believe I'd never see him again, that it was over. He could barely walk, his legs looked like they were dragging through the dirt more than walking. He didn't even appear to be awake but he was there. Everything would be okay now.

Lydia ran to Tom. I couldn't move. The Merry Men placed their hands on my shoulders in comfort as I shook so hard my knees knocked against the wood of the balustrade. I had to get myself together. I had to breathe. Tom needed me. I tried to stand without holding on, the Merry Men steadying me.

Lydia returned to Andrea's side, crying as Andrea held her tight. The verandah light illuminated Tom as they got closer and I saw how his head hung, how it flopped unnaturally and my heart sank.

'What's wrong with him?' I asked softly, almost too afraid of the answer.

Tom lifted his head slowly, revealing his swollen, bruised eyes, almost not eyes anymore at all. Scabs had formed on his fat and split mouth, his cheeks glowed purple and blue, his wild, surf caked hair tamed with dried red blood.

'Alex?' he mumbled.

I cried before I could stop myself, thankful the Merry Men were close enough to hold me up. How could they do this to him? How could anyone do this to another human being?

I stepped closer. 'Careful,' instructed Michael. 'He's pretty beat up.'

Lydia and I followed as Michael near carried Tom up the stairs.

'Careful,' I fussed as they lay him on the bed. 'Does he need a doctor or something?' I asked.

'Not here,' said Michael. 'We won't make that mistake again.'

'What do you mean?'

'We think that's how they found us. When the doctor keyed Tom's information into his database, it must have triggered something somewhere and led them here.'

Marguerite and Bex came into the room with bandages, solutions and bowls of warm water. The butler hurried the others out of the room and handed me a pair of scissors, nodding towards Tom, so I began cutting off what was left of his blood stained clothes.

Rainbows of purple, red and blue swirls covered the beautiful bare skin of his body. Open cuts wept. His body hair was caked thick with dry blood. I sobbed cutting away the remaining fabric. Tom shuddered as each of my tears fell onto his bare, bruised skin. I sat in the chair by his bed stroking his sticky hair, soothing him through my own tears while Bex checked his bones as best she could and Marguerite tended to the cuts.

'You're going to be fine,' I insisted, not knowing if it was true, and, 'sshhhh,' as he flinched in pain. Tears spilled from the corners of his bruised eyes as Marguerite cleaned and mended his wounds.

Eventually they had him cleaned, stitched, taped and bandaged.

'He have good bones,' Marguerite smiled kindly before taking her supplies from the room.

I looked to Bex for more information. 'We can't be sure without medical equipment and we'll know more once the swelling goes down but it looks like his bones have remained mostly in tact. I'd suspect his cheekbone is fractured and at least a finger or two but there's not much more a doctor could do so I've patched him up and we'll just have to wait and see. Marguerite gave him some kick arse painkillers I don't even want to know how they got a hold of but he'll be comfortable for now,' she said before also leaving.

I couldn't even hold his crushed hand, it looked like he'd

fought back and that was something. I could hardly see into his swollen eyes or kiss his ballooned, torn mouth. I found an undamaged spot on his neck to kiss before Michael pushed me out of the room so he could rest.

Lydia waited on the floor in the hallway by the door, her knees drawn to her chest, tears running down her face. I slid down to the floor beside her, her head falling onto my shoulder. 'How bad is he, Alex?'

'Bad.'

She sobbed. Andrea sat on her other side, a comforting hand on hers. The others soon gave up trying to move us and left us be. Showers turned on and people fussed about throughout the house but I wasn't moving for anything or anyone. I had to be here if he needed me. I'd left the door open just a crack so I could hear him call. I couldn't move from his side ever again.

'How's everyone else?' I asked Lydia.

'Barely a scratch,' she smiled, shaking her head at the absurdity of it.

I must have fallen asleep. I don't remember doing it but Marguerite was nudging me out of a deep sleep. Opening my eyes, I blinked a couple of times until recollection set in. Marguerite stood above me, a kind, warm smile beaming down. Her husband stood beside her holding a tray with bowls. She took one of the bowls off the tray and offered it to me. I wasn't hungry but I took it anyway. Lydia and Andrea woke, accepting their soup before the butler disappeared like a ghost and Marguerite went in to check on Tom.

She returned a few seconds later and declared, 'Sleeping.' Then she was gone and we sipped our soup in silence.

Andrea eventually coaxed Lydia into a shower and I waited alone. I was drifting off again when I heard his voice. My eyes flicked wide. I sat still and listened until he mumbled again. Jumping to my feet I raced into the bedroom.

I sat in the chair beside his bed, leaning forward so my face was level with his.

'Ax,' he mumbled.

'Hey,' I smiled, carefully stroking his hair. 'You okay?'

'Mmmm...' he mumbled, clearly anything but okay.

'You want me to get someone?'

'No,' he stammered. 'Stay.'

He slowly half rolled to face the other side of the bed so I got on it and lay with him. I looked into his swollen eyes and smiled. He tried holding my hand but couldn't move his fingers, still too swollen despite the ice packs, so he just laid his hand on top of mine.

We lay face to face, so close we were almost touching, our eyes locked. It took everything to keep the tears at bay, tears for this beautiful man and the inhumanity that had broken him.

Softly I said, 'I don't know why you even fancy me, boring, ordinary me, when you're you, so perfect and wise and strong and funny and handsome, so beautiful and lovely and I can't understand at all why you love me, but life without you is now unimaginable. I don't know how in less than a week you've become more important to me than the air I breathe, I don't know. But you have. I don't want to live without you. It's as simple as that. So, I'm right here. Whether you like it or not. I'm staying right here,' I sobbed.

A tear rolled from the corner of his eye, I softly caught it before it crossed the broken skin of his colourful cheekbone. His eyes sparkled with more, I shushed him and whispered, 'sleep,' as I snuggled up beside him.

Marguerite was bathing and redressing Tom's wounds when I woke. Someone had covered me with a blanket while I'd slept and I was grateful for it as a slight morning chill settled on my nose.

Tom flinched with every movement Marguerite made, every dab of the cotton wool, the undoing and redoing of bandages. His eyes welled and I couldn't watch a second longer without my heart breaking into billions of pieces.

I left them to it and went to shower. Tom was sleeping when I returned. I took the coffee Marguerite had left me to sit on the window seat, my feet curled underneath me and watched our friends eating by the pool.

They laughed a little less freely than before but at least they were laughing, all present and accounted for. It meant they would be okay. Lydia sensing me watching, looked up and waved. I put my hand on the cool glass in a return wave before she rejoined the conversation around her.

I couldn't leave the chateau anytime soon, that much I knew. I couldn't leave Tom as he was, so broken with trouble still lingering who knew where. It wouldn't be over, not yet, not that easy, they'd come again. Or more would be sent. I watched Tom sleep. He wasn't leaving that bed any time soon. His face was unrecognisable. His eyes almost too swollen to open, his lip still fat and purple, and they were just the bits I could see from where I sat.

Taking my phone out of my bag and ignoring the missed call count from my mother, I called work.

Voicemail, thank heavens for voicemail. 'Stan, it's, Al...Lexi,' geez, I'd already forgotten my real name. 'I've been, um, delayed, here in Paris...'

'Hello? Lexi?' Crap! Diligent bugger was still in the office after everyone else had left, probably snooping through everyone's in-trays.

'Stan, hi, how's things?'

'Good. Great. Fine. What's this about you not coming in on Monday?'

'Well, um, something's come up.'

'Are you dying? In hospital?'

'No, no, nothing quite like that.'

'Then get your arse back to your desk on Monday or don't come back at all.'

'Oh, okay then,' I stammered. 'I guess I won't be coming back,' I told him, even though I knew that legally he couldn't fire me that easily.

I hung up, feeling an enormous amount of relief. I hated that job. I hated that miserable cubicle. Most of all, I hated that short, fat, opinionated fool. I'd just find another job when I got home. Something would sort itself out. I had my bits and bobs money and I didn't have to contribute to Billy's rent or utilities any more, so that freed up a bit more of what was left in the bank, so I wouldn't go hungry too soon and I could work like the others if it came to that. I'd need to figure out the visa regulations. I looked over at Tom. Life was way too short to live like I had been. Somehow I'd figure it out.

Chapter 11

Fat drops of rain fell beyond the window, shaking awake the vines that had been resting in the sunshine. I'd been watching life below the window for days. How many days, I wasn't sure. I'd lost track. The days had all begun blurring together. And now it rained, cleansing and fresh, forcing everyone away from their poolside joviality to somewhere else.

'I don't know why I'm still alive,' Tom said.

I was just glad he was. Johnno had walked around with the weighty guilt of the world on his shoulders for a couple of days but no one had said much about what had happened.

'Shh... we'll talk about it later. It doesn't matter. You're here and you're okay.'

He nodded as best he could. 'I don't know if they're done,' he said. 'They didn't kill me so probably not,' he mumbled.

I wanted to ask why they didn't. What was their end game, then? But I was afraid of the answer.

'They know there's more to the story. They know it doesn't

start and end with me. But George Cummins is still too involved. I couldn't tell if they were asking because George wanted to know what I was willing to give up or if Axl's family just wanted the truth. I just kept thinking of that picture George sent of mum and Jaz and I kept my mouth shut. Then the boys burst in. By that point I couldn't have said much if I wanted to. But it means one way or another, they're probably not done,' he said sadly. 'But now they have a taste, they'll want more, they'll want to finish it,' he added.

'Shhh... let Michael and Moe worry about it for now,' I insisted.

Almost a week had passed and slowly, Tom was coming back to life. Tom's bruising had faded and his cuts were healing. His face was less puffy, definition again returning to his handsome face and I could see his eyes and I smiled, blushing, when he caught me looking at him.

'Sorry, but you'll have to wait a bit longer to have a piece of this, Alex,' he smirked before grimacing.

I laughed. I'd wait forever if I had to. Already I couldn't imagine ever wanting to sleep with another man.

The butler came in with some soup and handed me my phone. 'It keep ringing,' he said before spooning soup to Tom.

I had no idea I'd even left it lying about. I must have left it downstairs when I'd gone down for lunch. 'It's just Mum,' I said, turning it off.

'Alex, she's been ringing for days,' Tom grumbled.

'I don't care. I'm not interested in a lecture today.'

'Shouldn't you at least let her know you're okay?'

'Well look at you suddenly so full of words,' I smiled.

He frowned at me as best he could.

'Fine, I'll call her in a bit.' I looked at the clock, calculating the time difference in my head. I waited until it was the middle of the night at home when chances were she'd have it on silent while she slept, if it was on at all.

Turning the phone back on, I scrolled through for her number and pressed the call button, crossing my fingers for voicemail. It didn't even ring, just as I'd hoped, before I heard her cheery, static voicemail.

'Hi Mum, it's me, Lexi. I'm fine, a little out of range but having a fabulous time. Will be back in touch soon. Love you. Miss you. Bye.' I hung up and threw the phone in the direction of my suitcase and lay on the bed beside Tom, reading my book.

Another week passed and Tom was ready to start moving. Michael and Moe had succumbed to letting Henri have a doctor friend take a closer look at Tom, just to be sure. The doctor asked no personal questions, took no notes and enjoyed a nice bottle of wine with Henri when he was done. He left giving Tom the all clear and some tips for recovery which included some work in the pool. He was still sore and too multi-coloured for my liking, but he insisted he was ready as Michael and Moe helped him down the stairs. I scurried behind them, admonishing them for going to fast. He should have still been in bed taking it easy but Michael and Moe dismissed my worry as that of the over-cautious, overprotective girlfriend. I wanted to say someone had to look out for him but knew it would come off snarly and they were looking after him, it was their job to make sure he was okay and Tom's mother would probably kick their butts if they didn't do their job to her motherly standards so I tried to let them work.

At the edge of the pool, they took off their shirts then Michael and Moe helped Tom into Henri's saltwater swimming pool. Henri had plenty of exercise equipment on hand to help with Tom's physiotherapy and rehabilitation, I suspected this wasn't the first time the pool had been used for such purpose.

They started with gentle walking and it all seemed harmless enough so I left them to do their work.

'How are you doing?' Lydia asked as I joined her and Marguerite in the kitchen.

I took the knife Lydia offered and began chopping vegetables. I shrugged, 'I think they're going too fast and Tom should be resting but they won't listen to me.'

She smiled. 'Those three never do. But don't worry, they do actually know what they're doing. I've given up asking Michael and Moe how they know what they know, they're more secretive than Tom, but they do know what they're doing and if Tom wasn't ready, he'd still be upstairs.' She gave my hand a reassuring pat then passed me some more carrots to chop.

Afterwards we ate lunch with the others and Tom's face almost glowed with happiness, despite some of the bruising that remained. Getting up and about had done him a lot of good.

By the end of the week Tom didn't need Michael or Moe's help, so I jumped into the pool with him and then after lunch we were taking walks through some of the nearby vines.

We were taking an afternoon walk, the sun high, enjoying the quiet. One of Henri's workers nodded as he passed, carrying some equipment from the shed to wherever Henri had banished his staff to during our stay. 'I have to leave,' Tom whispered.

My heart jumped to my throat and I felt instantly sick to my stomach. 'What do you mean?' I whispered, afraid of what it meant, of what he would say next.

'I can't stay here, the longer we stay here, the more chance they will find us. Too many people have seen us already,' he said, indicating the man disappearing over the hill. 'All it takes is for an innocent conversation at a restaurant to be overheard and I can't put Henri, Pierre and Marguerite in that kind of danger. Not to mention the others. They have to get back to their lives. I've held them up long enough. So, as soon as I can, in the next couple of days, I have to disappear for a while, lay low, stay out of sight, away from the others.'

There was no air left in my lungs, no air amongst the vines. I couldn't move, I couldn't speak, words disappeared from my panicked brain. I was busy trying to comprehend what he was saying, that he was leaving, again. I couldn't do it again. I couldn't go through that again.

He took my hand, made me turn to look at him, 'Alex, I want you to come with me. I know it's a lot to ask and I understand if you don't want to, if it's too much, but I'd really like you to come with me. I know everything will be okay if we're together.' He watched me, hopeful, afraid.

'Yes,' I said without even thinking about it. I didn't need to; there was no other choice to consider for me. Not anymore, I was too far in.

'That was quick. Don't you want to think about it or at least know where we'd be going and how it would work? How dull it is to lay low? How isolating it can be? You'd have to give up your whole life, your family, your friends, everything.'

'I don't care. As long as I'm with you, I don't care. I don't care about any of it. Knowing you're safe is what I need. I can figure everything else out if I know that every day when I wake up. And you're right; everything will be fine as long as we're together,' I smiled, my heart so full I thought it might burst.

'Good,' he smiled. 'I want you to stay. I want it like I've never wanted anything but I can't ask you to give up everything, your whole life, your family, your job, everything for me, for this stupid life,' he said.

'Even if I hadn't met you, I don't want any of my old life anymore. Well not my family, I love them but I don't want to be who I was then, who I was with them. I'm not ready to go back. I don't want to be that person anymore, that person so desperate for approval they give their life over to someone like Billy McRae. My family won't understand. They'll just try to squish me back into the box they built for me. With you, here, there are no boxes. I'm just me. I'm really liking me.'

'So am I,' he smiled, pulling my mouth to his and kissing me like he meant it.

He smiled, a little crookedly, but still his face managed to light the sky. Leaning over carefully, I kissed him. 'I'll go anywhere with you, wherever you need to go, Tom.'

'God I want to do very unsavoury things with you right now,' he laughed, groaned, then coughed, groaned again and leaned on my shoulder for support.

I wanted to soothe him, make it better, take away the pain,

but there was nothing I could do. 'All in good time,' I assured him, then we walked back to the villa so he could rest.

I lay down beside him, staring at the ceiling, trying to comprehend the choice I'd just made. There was no choice, I knew it, I would go anywhere with him, no question. But he was right, I was leaving a lot behind and not knowing when or if I'd see my family again was hard. They drove me mad. They pigeonholed me and there was no way Mum was going to understand any of it, especially me leaving her perfect Billy and running off with a man I hardly knew. I'd miss them. I'd miss Dad's quiet wisdom, my sister, Victoria's strength, my niece, Sophie's hugs and my mum's baking. But I'd be okay. With Tom, everything was right, the world was right, it made sense, my place in the world finally made sense and living without him would never be an option, not because I couldn't survive on my own, I knew I could, but because I loved him and I wanted to see his smile every day, I wanted him to be a part of whatever happened next and if I went home, nothing I did would mean anything if I couldn't share it with him.

Tom was speaking softly to Henri when I woke. I didn't even remember falling asleep but now felt as though I'd slept better than I had in days. It was because Tom was healing, because choices had been made, declarations given. Knowing Tom and I were going to be together, build a life together and have great adventures together had given me a sense of peace and great relief.

'Hey,' he said, sensing I'd woken.

'Hey,' I smiled back. 'What are you two up to?'

'Henri has somewhere for us to go. An apartment in Spain.

It's perfect, no one will be able to connect it to us and no one will even notice us in Barcelona.'

'What about the others?'

'Johnno, Bex, Harry and Chris are moving on in the morning. Lydia and Andrea are going back to Paris with Michael and Moe, so it'd just be us. Michael's not happy about it but an ordinary couple will blend in easier. He'll probably be lurking near by though or know someone who'll be keeping an eye on us and what's going on. Is that okay?'

'Of course. Are you sure you don't mind Henri? You've already done more than enough for us.'

'No, I do not mind at all. It just sits there going to waste since I've taken over here. Please. Use it. It is not much but it will be fine. I hid there many a time from someone or another,' he winked. 'So I know it is good for hiding.'

Leaving Tom and Henri to sort out the finer details, I went to farewell the others. The air was beautiful and warm. The sun was too bright for my unprotected eyes, but I didn't care. I headed poolside where my friends had made themselves quite at home, already way too merry.

The farewells were in full swing, regardless of the early hour. The others showed barely any signs of what had happened. Just sitting by the pool you'd think we were all just on a lovely holiday.

'A toast,' Lydia declared. 'To new friends, to old friends, to absent friends and to the ties that will hold us all together through the good and the bad, wherever we are.'

Raising our glasses we smiled with a resounding, 'Cheers!'

I'd miss these people. We'd been through so much together

in such a short time. They were like family. This new group of friends weren't like any I'd ever had before. Most of my friends at home came as part of the Billy package. Billy and I had been together so long, my friends, mostly from school, had all dropped away, moved on. I had nothing to go home to. I was more me with them, even amid the chaos, than I'd ever been in my whole life. I felt whole here, with them, with Tom. Even though they were all moving on, going back to their lives and not coming to Spain with Tom and me, I knew our paths would cross again, that we'd be forever entwined. They'd never be far.

Henri helped Tom down the stairs when it was time to wave the others and their smoking blue van off as they began their long journey back to Paris under the cover of the setting sun.

We had one more night to go. We'd be leaving before the sun was up in the morning and suddenly the house was too quiet without the others.

'Come, Marguerite has made us dinner, you'll need all your strength for tomorrow's drive,' Henri said.

As we followed him into the grand dining room, Tom asked, 'Pierre and Marguerite will join us won't they?'

'Certainly,' Henri nodded as he asked Pierre to set two more places. 'I believe Maggie has made her specialty of Coq Au Vin for you. You're in for a treat,' he smiled as Pierre brought in the pots of *Coq Au Vin* and potatoes, broccoli, wine and profiteroles for dessert.

'I don't know how we can ever thank you,' Tom said to our hosts.

'Ah!' Henri scoffed. 'There is no need. I do wish you would just stay here, though.'

'I can't do that. I can't put you all in any more danger than you've already been. The longer I'm here, the more chance there is they'll trace me here somehow. They always find a way and you've already done enough. Besides, you have a lady with a young son to woo,' Tom smiled. 'We will be fine in Barcelona, we'll lay low, stay out of sight and we'll be fine.'

Henri nodded and didn't push it any further. Perhaps because he knew Tom was right. But we enjoyed our last night with our hosts sharing stories.

Chapter 12

The sun was just kissing the horizon when the butler and his wife drove us down Henri's long gravelled drive. Despite my free will to go anywhere Tom wanted, I'd still been apprehensive about the actual going. It was a big step, walking away from my family, my job, the ruins of my life, even my new friends. But at the same time it felt good and right to be in control of my own life for the first time ever and nothing else mattered because Tom needed me. I needed Tom.

'You okay?' Tom asked, pulling me against his chest.

I nodded, stretching my arms around him, knowing I'd made the right choice.

Beside me, Tom's chest rose and fell with each breath. The echo of his heartbeat thumping throughout his beautiful body, sung me to sleep.

The sun was forcing its way through the heavily tinted windows when I woke. Tom was staring out the window, pain etched in his face. 'You should have moved me if you were hurting.'

'Not a chance,' he said, kissing the top of my head before turning back to the window. I marvelled at the miracle of his existence, that he was still there, in one piece and had suffered no more damage than bruises and cuts.

I sat up to watch the green fields whizzing by, their beauty mesmerising, hypnotic and soon I again saw nothing but the inside of my eyelids.

I woke when the car stopped. I could feel drool creeping down my chin and wiped it quickly before following Tom, Pierre and Marguerite out of the car and into the Barcelona dusk.

People moved around us, busy with their own business, coming and going about their own lives, too busy to notice us standing on the footpath. The butler placed our bags on the ground, handed Tom a set of keys and was back in his car before I could even blink. I mouthed a thank you to Marguerite who nodded almost imperceptibly before they drove away. It didn't seem enough for all they'd done for us, but under the circumstances, it had to do.

Then it was just us. Tom was still far too broken for any heavy lifting, so I threw his ridiculously heavy backpack across my shoulders, while I dragged my ridiculously oversized suitcase up the stairs. My case crashed against the steps as I slowly climbed behind Tom who limped and hobbled the whole way up, gripping the handrail as he climbed, doing his best to ignore the pain of so much activity until we eventually reached our second floor apartment.

Tom opened the door and one step inside I let the bags fall, crashing in a heap.

Tom enveloped me in his big arms, holding me close to his chest. 'Pierre could have helped us up the stairs,' he commented.

'They were outta here pretty quick.'

'They were, weren't they? Henri did say the less visible we were and the less attention we attracted, the better. So I guess it was a good thing.'

Tom let go and we walked into the apartment, our new home for who knew how long. The kitchenette was as we walked in and overlooked the small living room with a sliding door leading to a small balcony. To the right was a short hallway that led to the one bedroom on one side and the small bathroom on the other.

I dragged our luggage into the bedroom. The furnishings were much more modest than at the vineyard, but it was enough. There was a simple double bed, a chest of drawers, and a wardrobe. It was all we needed.

I put my toiletries bag into the small bathroom. There was a shower hanging over the bath, which could prove difficult for Tom. There was a small cupboard and a toilet behind the door. It wasn't fancy or glossy but it was enough.

I found Tom sitting on the balcony when I finished unpacking. There was a small metal table and two chairs overlooking the bustling street below. Tom pointed out Las Ramblas at the end of the street. 'It'll be full of tourists and easy to blend in which will be perfect. We can get everything we need to get by down there and we'll be hardly noticed,' he told me.

'So what now?' I asked after sitting a moment and enjoying the new sounds and feeling the sun on my face.

'Nothing, Babe. It's just you and me chillin' now.'

'Hmmm... I'll drink to that,' I said clinking our water glasses.

Henri had been pretty awesome offering us his apartment, but there was no food. Tom didn't want me wandering too far too soon so sent me downstairs to the pub next door for takeaway. The pub was dark as Tom had hoped. It was too early on Spain time for dinner but there were enough patrons drinking, some tourists in the back eating, just enough people for me to not be remembered.

'*Inglés?*' I asked the beautiful girl behind the counter.

'Of course,' she smiled. She had long, warm brown hair that waved just right. She had big brown eyes that smiled when she did, perfectly manicured eyebrows and a figure to die for. She could have graced a catwalk or the pages of a magazine but I got the impression she was completely unaware of just how beautiful she was.

I ordered a selection of things, some paella and tapas, assuring her I wasn't going too far and the food would remain hot and delicious.

I sat in the bar with a coke while I waited and watched a game of soccer on the television hoping the few backpackers also watching were oblivious to my existence. I sent a message to my mother while I waited, hoping it would placate her for a while and eventually left with my bag of food. As I left, the intrepid travellers were swearing good-humouredly at the television as though they were the only people in existence and I was glad for their ignorance.

We couldn't avoid the inevitable in the morning, when there was no milk for coffee or even coffee at that or a slice of bread to toast. I had to go in search of supplies. We needed to fill the kitchen so we didn't have to leave for a while and Tom needed all the sustenance he could get.

'I don't like it,' said Tom shaking his head as I got ready. 'I don't want you going out there alone.'

'We don't have a choice, Tom.' I cupped his face with my hands. 'We have to eat. I'll be fine. No one's looking for me.'

'Yeah, well, don't be so sure about that. You had a gun held to your head. You shot that bloke in the hand. They know who you are,' he said, extricating himself from my grip and going into the bedroom. Rummaging through his bag with his one semi good hand, he pulled out a purple cap. 'This was Bex's. She thought you might need it.' He twirled my hair into a rope and turned it inside the cap. He slid on my sunglasses which half hid my face and as easy as that, I was barely recognisable.

'Be quick,' he instructed. 'Only the necessities, yeah?'

I nodded.

'There's a fresh market part way down Las Ramblas. Turn right at the end of our street and just walk. It's on the left, you can't miss it. Bare necessities, Alex, promise.'

I nodded again and he handed me a wad of Euros.

Apprehensively, I headed outside into the throng of people moving towards Las Ramblas. I resisted looking back up to the balcony where I knew Tom would be watching. I didn't want him to see the fear on my face. The streets were full of people and everything was unfamiliar. It would take me a minute to adjust, his little speech hadn't helped much either. But I had to toughen up, this was my life now, I'd be no use to Tom or myself if I couldn't adapt. Taking a deep breath, I joined the sea of tourists and locals going about their business and made my way to Las Ramblas.

Souvenir stalls and silver painted men on boxes lined the sidewalk. People stopped to watch the frozen silver men in the middle of the walkway. I dodged them and the people crowding the souvenir stalls. I dodged the tables and chairs of restaurants awaiting patrons and keeping the panic in my stomach squashed down, I eventually spotted the market up ahead.

The noise of people bounced off the walls, the smell of fresh fruit and vegetables wafting in the air with the faint smells of fresh fish and meat from further in, all reminiscent of market places throughout the world, making me feel safe and at home. Everyone shouted in Spanish and Catalan. I could manage a *hola*, a *como esta*, or even a *muy bien*, thanks to high school Spanish. But the rest, the fast Spanish directed at me or shouted around me, I couldn't even pick out a word.

I'd have thought I'd feel invisible in a city where I couldn't speak the language, but I didn't. I felt alive as though I were a part of the delicate, rich, bustling, multi-cultural society that enveloped me with its warmth and happiness. Everywhere I looked people laughed and chatted with all the time in the world to spare. No hustle and bustle, just happiness.

Filling a basket with fruit and vegetables, I handed it over with my Euros and took the filled plastic bag from the smiling Spaniard with the best *gracias* I could manage. I was pretty sure he laughed at my poor pronunciation, but I didn't care, I felt connected and a part of something that filled my soul.

Moving on to the meats, I ordered some chicken and fish. I couldn't cook much in that small kitchenette but chicken, fish, rice and vegetables would be easy enough. Some fresh sliced ham and bread completed my essentials, although I could have shopped for hours.

I took my heaving bags back out on to Las Ramblas, where the silver buskers frozen on their perches now commanded my attention. The rich smells of Paella cooking wafted on the air. I bought some flowers from a stall and stopped into a small convenience store, buying milk, juice, coffee, tea and yoghurt, cheese, crackers, rice and Sangria, instinctively throwing a couple of boxes of hair colour into my basket just before I piled everything onto the counter.

I was pretty impressed with myself when I came back out onto Las Ramblas and began dodging and squeezing past the flood of tourists with ease. The Alexandra Deen that flew to Paris a couple of weeks ago was now unrecognisable and not just because of the hat and sunglasses, but the meek, mild girl who was duped by her cheating bastard boyfriend no longer existed. The sun beat down on my bare arms and I smiled. I was happy, happier than I could ever remember being. I liked this new person.

Our building was nothing but a white, paint chipped doorway between a three star hotel and the bar. Everyone was far too busy going about their business to even notice me entering this door they barely even saw. I imagined Henri buying it for that reason.

Tom opened the apartment door as soon as I reached the top of the stairs with a beaming smile as though I were returning from weeks away. 'That looks like more than the bare necessities,' he commented, raising his eyebrows.

'Nope. Just think our idea of what constitutes bare necessities might be different,' I said, returning his cheeky grin with one of my own and dumping the heavy bags on the bench top.

'Hmmm...' he groaned unconvinced as I found homes for our supplies. 'No troubles finding what you needed then?' he asked, reaching for a box of hair colour and raising his eyebrows in question again.

'This place is amazing,' I said regaling him with my story of Las Ramblas, the sounds, the smells, the painted silver men, while he laughed and nodded with a knowing smile. He'd seen it all before, fallen in love with it all before. But I liked the way he looked at me as I shared with him my tales as though whatever I had to say was interesting, as though he enjoyed seeing me happy.

'So who's this for?' he asked dropping a box of hair colour he'd been reading back on the bench top.

I shrugged and placed the other beside it. 'Thought they might come in handy, you were a very adamant about disguising me before.'

'With good reason. Don't underestimate the situation we're in.'

I left the groceries, moving over to where Tom stood. Sliding my arms around his waist, looking up into his green eyes that never failed to send my knees to jelly, I said, 'We'll be fine, as long as we're together.'

Leaning down, Tom lightly kissed me, 'You betchya.' He winced as my hold became too tight. Apologising, I returned to the groceries.

With the groceries away, I made us a sandwich and then we took the hair colour into the bathroom. I took a moment to appreciate how the sun had bleached my boring hair to sun kissed before Tom apprehensively attacked our heads with some blunt scissors and the hair colour. We waited our twenty minutes by sitting on the balcony and watching the people on the street below, guessing where they'd been, where they were going and if they were locals or tourists. I carefully rinsed his hair then rinsed mine then blow-dried us both before standing back to assess the results.

'You did a pretty good job,' I said, swishing my new black bob. 'A man of many talents, hey?'

He laughed. 'This isn't the first time I've needed to do a hair change and one of the many hobby jobs Lydia undertook to piss off Dad was hairdressing. He was mortified, *"that bloody over-priced education should buy me more than hairdressing,"'* Tom bellowed, mocking his father with another laugh. 'She only bothered long enough to learn some basics, but cutting was one of them and I paid attention when I needed to and now you're the lucky recipient of our misspent lives.'

'Well, lucky me,' I smiled, planting a quick kiss on his perfect mouth, running my hand through his new black neat haircut, already missing his blonde shaggy locks.

'So did Lydia ever settle on something more fitting her *'over-priced education?'* I asked as we tidied up.

'She'd finally enrolled in fashion design and was doing work experience with one of Australia's leading designers when everything fell apart. I should never have let her give it up to come with me,' he whispered, the last almost to himself, shaking his head.

'If I know Lydia, I don't think you had a choice.'

He smiled, 'Already you know us better than we know ourselves.' He kissed me, his mouth familiar and warm but he pulled away too quick, threw the empty packets in the bin and reached for his pain pills.

Patting his arm, I went to make some tea.

Chapter 13

The days passed. Tom slept a lot, exercised as much as he could and we watched a lot of movies. I caught up on a lot of reading and for the first time in a while, enjoyed cooking and baking. It was nice to cook good, tasty food without the fear of falling short of someone's expectations or having to cook for masses of people that were invited without my consultation. Tom just enjoyed everything I cooked, the fancy and the not so fancy and I enjoyed cooking it.

As the days and the weeks passed, Tom was getting a little antsy, a little claustrophobic. I'd been able to walk to the market a couple of times to ease my cabin fever, speak to the men at the market and breathe in the fresh air. Tom only had the two room apartment and the small balcony.

'I can't stand it anymore,' Tom groaned, pacing the small apartment like a caged animal. 'I have to get out before I go mad,' he said. 'Why don't we go down to the pub for dinner?'

'Will we be safe?' I asked, concerned.

'We've been quiet, we'll wait until it's busy and no one will notice us,' he insisted.

I agreed for the sake of his mental health. His spirit was seeming flat so I knew he needed it.

Tom sat with his back to the rear of the restaurant, facing the front. I watched as his eyes quickly assessed everyone in the dining area, the few tourists watching the mounted televisions in the bar, he watched, assessed and finally, exhaled.

'You alright?'

He smiled tightly. 'Sorry, habit.'

'Tom Harrington survival habit or army habit?'

'I don't think their exclusive. I'm army trained. Assessing people in social environments was one of my things. It's come in handy.'

'And what were your other things?'

'Most of it was classified. I did a lot of assess, react, plan, act, all in a moment, it's what kept me and my team alive. It didn't stop things from getting hairy but it kept us alive,' he said, a darkness clouding his beautiful eyes and his handsome face.

I nodded, feeling sad for him that he'd seen and experienced so much, that he carried so much on his shoulders. He needed to rest, to breathe, to feel safe. I reached for his hand, squeezed it and changed the subject.

Even though we were just two amongst the many in back end of the noisy pub, we huddled over the table as we spoke. We were deep in conversation about nothing in particular when the young, tanned bar tender flipped around a chair and flopped into it. 'Oi, oi, oi' he declared exhaustedly, as though we were all long lost friends.

Staring at him rudely, lost for words. I felt Tom's legs tense under the table. I could feel his apprehension and defensive instincts kicking in as he was trying to figure out, friend or foe.

'Sorry. Aussies, right?'

I nodded. Tom was busy assessing the situation.

'Thank Christ,' he declared. 'You guys don't mind hiding me for a minute, do ya? My boss is working me like a friggin dog and if I have to clean one more friggin, shining glass, I'm gonna throw it at his friggin head.' He smiled as he spoke, not really hating his boss but desperately looking for a rest break.

Tom's body softened as he relaxed and he smiled.

'Rick,' the bar tender extended his hand. Tom waved his bandaged hand to show he couldn't shake.

Rick held his hand in front of me instead, 'Alex,' I introduced myself reluctantly. Surprising myself really, it was the first time I'd ever introduced myself as Alex. It was strange but liberating. I barely knew who Lexi even was anymore.

'Bit beat up, eh?' Rick asked, nodding towards Tom.

'Car accident,' Tom lied.

'Hard luck, man,' Rick nodded as the waitress brought our Paella. It was the same beautiful woman from the first night I'd come in for takeaway.

'Rick...' she scolded with a smile.

He grinned back at her.

'Oh, it is you,' she said as she topped up my glass of sangria. 'You changed your hair, it looks beautiful,' she smiled before walking away.

'I didn't think she'd remember me,' I told Tom quietly, forgetting Rick was even there.

'Sarita is good at remembering faces,' Rick said. 'You also live across from us, we've seen you on the balcony,' he added. 'Well, I've got glasses to clean, see ya round, dudes,' he nodded and went back behind the bar leaving us to devour our food like animals.

'Should we be worried?' I asked Tom.

He shrugged, watching Rick and the waitress obliviously going about their evening. 'I don't think so. So far we're just the new residents across from them. The apartment's probably been vacant a while but they won't have noticed anything beyond that, I don't think.

'Not so bad, is it?' Tom asked when we climbed into bed that night and he draped his arm around me and pulled me close. 'Definitely my kind of hiding out,' he laughed.

'No complaints here. I could get used to Spain,' I said.

We kept to ourselves for the next few days. I did another grocery run to fill the cupboards but otherwise we stayed inside. We even avoided going out onto the balcony. We'd analysed Rick and the waitress some more and again come to the conclusion that there was nothing to worry about but Tom still thought it best we helped them to forget about us.

But despite the board games and the movies, Tom's constant exercising to get himself well, it wasn't long before he was going stir crazy.

'Perhaps just a walk?' he suggested. 'Come on, I'm going mad in here,' he pleaded.

'If you think it's safe, then we'll walk,' I told him.

'Its busy enough out there that we should go unnoticed,' he said.

We had only just stepped out of the building when we ran into Rick.

'Hey,' he called, sipping a cup of coffee. 'Where you guys been.

Tom shrugged.

'We're having a thing for the game inside. Please, come and save me from the soccer lovers,' Rick begged

Tom smiled. 'Drink then walk?' he asked.

I shrugged, I preferred him to sit but didn't want my over worrying to risk our safety.

Rick led us to a table in the back away from the soccer loving spectators.

'Rick, you're not serving?' Sarita said as Rick brought us a jug of sangria.

'I can't understand a word any of them are saying, Babe,' he complained.

She frowned at him.

'I just need a minute, they're all watching the game anyway,' he told her.

She smiled. '*Cinco*,' she said, then walked away.

'I need ten *cincos*,' Rick smiled. 'Please, talk to me about something that makes sense. How's the footy going?' he asked.

Tom frowned. He was probably as out of touch with Australian rules wins and losses as Rick. Lucky I wasn't.

'Carlton are having a big season,' I told him. 'So are Adelaide and Gold Coast.'

'Ah,' he moaned. 'It's good to hear the accent, hear things

from home. I don't usually mind but feeling a little homesick lately. Visa is nearly up and its making me think of home.'

Tom nodded, smiling and I suspected he knew a little something about feeling isolated by language barriers and being homesick.

I went to the ladies room and left Rick and Tom talking, returning to find them the best of friends, having bonded over the isolation in foreign countries, discussing the merits of Aussie rules over soccer and bull fighting as though they were just two regular blokes.

Rick waved his hand in the air whenever my glass was nearly empty and a new one appeared, filled with fresh Sangria. Rick ate paella with us, ignoring his duties to talk rubbish and loving every second of it until Guillermo, the tyrant bar owner eventually shooed him back to work as the bar filled.

'Papa,' scolded our beautiful waitress.

'Sarita, we pay him to work.'

'Oh Papa, stop,' she insisted before weaving her slender arms around Rick's waist.

Tom smiled as Rick raised a thumb in triumph; he won his fight with the attentions of the boss' daughter.

As the bar filled making Tom uncomfortable, we left with our bellies bursting, sangria flowing through our bodies and climbed the stairs back to our little flat to end the night with a cup of tea on the balcony like two old people.

'Are we in danger from going down there?' I asked.

'Nah, I think we're okay. We'll blend better, be less memorable if we're a regular couple. He'd have wondered more if he we were holed up and not seen at all for weeks but we'll have to be careful.'

I nodded, it made sense.

'Backpacking trip gone wrong you think?' I asked, referring to Rick and the crazy life he had going down in the bar with Sarita and Guillermo.

'Or right? Depends on how you look at it,' Tom smiled.

'Very true,' I nodded, laughing. 'Has that ever happened to you?' I asked him, fishing for information on his romantic past.

He grinned. 'Just the once,' he said.

'Right,' I nodded. 'What happened, how did it end?' I asked.

'It hasn't yet,' he smirked.

It took a second before I realised he was referring to us, to what we had going on. 'You idiot,' I laughed. 'There weren't any others? Surely there was? A good looking guy like you must pull women in with no trouble at all.'

He actually blushed. 'There's been women, yes. But there's never been anything serious. I've never stayed anywhere for any- one. We're always on the move but still, I've never met anyone I wanted to stop for. Until you,' he winked.

Now I blushed.

'Would you really have married that bloke you went to Paris with?' he asked.

I nodded. 'Sadly, I would have said yes. I had no idea about anything.'

'He sounds like an asshole though, all the womanising aside.'

'He was. But everyone told me how great he was, how lucky I was. I didn't know any different. I didn't know this,' I said, indi- cating the two of us. 'Who knew you even existed?' I smiled.

'Who knew,' he smiled.

I could definitely get used to living with Tom. Just Tom and me, laughing and joking.

It was nice to smile and laugh with Tom. Billy and I had never shared secrets. There'd never been lots of laughs when it was just the two of us, just comfortable companionship, none of the electricity that sparked between Tom and me. We sparked so much when we were close, it almost set Henri's little flat on fire.

Living with Tom was almost perfect. But barely being able to touch Tom's beautiful body was fast becoming torture. He was doing a lot better, the bruising was way less offensive, but he still hurt, inside and out. He moved slow and needed help with so many things, rolling around in bed was not an option. But all that intimacy, lying in bed with him, helping him shower and dress, it was killing me not being able to do with him as I pleased and pretend it was fine.

After locking up, I went into the bedroom where Tom was struggling with his t-shirt. I gladly removed his shirt, restraining my instinctive libido. 'Not easy, is it?' Tom asked.

'What?' I asked, trying to be innocent.

He laughed. 'You know what,' he said, raising his eyebrows.

'Stop it. I need to help you with your pants,' I scolded.

'Oooh, nice!'

'I'm serious, Tom,' I reprimanded.

He slid an arm around me. 'C'mon, that can wait, can't it?' he asked, leaning down to kiss me, the wet warmth of his mouth intoxicating every cell of my body.

'Um,' I stumbled, 'um, no, it can't.' Regaining my composure, I stood up straight, trying to pretend his naked chest wasn't the most delectable thing I'd ever seen, that his man bits weren't standing tall, begging for my attention. 'Can you lie down please?' I whispered, taking a deep breath.

He smiled, his eyes sparkling with all things naughty and very inappropriate. On the outside, he'd mostly healed, a few of the darker bruises still remained and some almost healed cuts, but mostly it was his insides. He still struggled with bending and stretching so I went about undressing him, focussing on just helping him get ready for bed, not what was responding to my touch.

I tucked him in and left, splashed my face with cold water and put on my nightie, which was pointless as it was just a flimsy slip of silk but it was all I had. Climbing in beside Tom I faced the other direction, laying as far from him as possible, not trusting myself, the temptation more than I feared I could control.

Rolling over, Tom kissed my bare shoulder, his hot breath lingering and tingling. He whispered mischievously, 'It won't be long, Babe and I'll give you some amazing. You'll be screaming down all of Barcelona.'

I smiled, my lady land aching at the thought. I couldn't wait.

As the days clicked over, we were finding our way. We'd made friends we ate lunch with or nodded to as we walked by. We were living, here in this beautiful faraway land, we were loving and we were living and we were smiling. We'd passed on a movie night with Sarita and Rick, still edging on the side of caution, but we toasted them across the balcony some nights and invited them over for a roast dinner because I could tell Rick was feeling homesick when he spoke of home. I'd never known so much happiness could even exist. I'd never felt so much like myself, my true self, the girl that had always lied buried so far down I'd forgotten she was even there.

Waking suddenly in the middle of the night, I nearly jumped out of my skin as someone banged on the front door. Tom was still sleeping so tentatively, with my heart pounding, I went to the door and checked the peephole. Rick stood on the other side, jittery, looking from side to side. Crazed nervous, sweat beading on his forehead.

I turned as I sensed Tom. He stood behind me in nothing but boxers looking at me questioningly. 'Rick,' I mouthed.

Tom nodded, so I opened the door and Rick burst into our flat, life and energy exploding into the air. He took in Tom's bruised body, 'Hell, man, you look like shit!'

Tom shrugged. Rick shrugged. 'Can youse hide me for a bit?' he asked.

'What's up, man?' Tom asked.

'It's Sarita. She's mad I'm going home. Papa G's looking for me blood for breaking her heart.'

I tried not to laugh. Tom and Rick went to the balcony while I emptied a box of crackers onto a platter, sliced up some cheese and put on the kettle. Cheese and crackers weren't too manly but they'd have to do.

I took a pot of tea and cups to the balcony where Rick was regaling Tom with the tale of him and Sarita. 'I was travelling with mates, just passing through, you know and there was Sarita serving us drinks in the pub and man, she's just so beautiful and when she smiled at me it was like the whole world stopped. How could I leave that? So the boys moved on and I stayed. Sarita got me a job at the pub and I moved in with her and Papa G in their flat upstairs and well, here I am. But now my visa's due to expire and to be honest, I wouldn't mind going home, seeing the fam, seeing the boys but she's gone nuts. I didn't want to hurt her, but what can I do if I have no visa? Papa G's going to kill me. You should have seen his face. I thought it was going to explode, he was so mad.'

'You don't love Sarita?' I asked confused. They'd looked very much in love when we'd seen them together in the bar.

'Sure, I guess. But she's a part of this world. I belong in another world, a world where we barbeque at night, play beach cricket and football in the park. I miss my family. I miss my mates. My visa's up. I don't have a choice, it's time for me to go home.'

Tom looked my way questioningly. Why I wasn't sure. But he said nothing and we finished the pot of tea and left Rick to sleep on the couch rather than ramble into the place he shared with Sarita and Guillermo above the pub in the very wee hours.

I climbed into bed beside Tom. 'You okay?' he asked.

'Sure, why?' I asked surprised he'd wonder anything else.

'We're not so different you know.'

'Than what?'

'Rick and Sarita.'

'Sure we are.'

'But don't you miss home?'

'No. Surprisingly.'

'But you'll miss it and everyone eventually.'

'Tom, I'd miss you more. I don't want to exist without you.

I'm not going anywhere,' I declared as Rick's snores echoed throughout the flat.

Tom held me close as we slept, regardless of the pain it caused as though it was all that would keep me there even though there was no way I was ever leaving.

Chapter 14

Rick remained splayed across the small sofa when I got up. I left him be, helped Tom into the shower and showered myself.

They were drinking coffee on the balcony when I'd finished my shower.

'Coffee on the bench for you, Babe,' Tom called.

They were laughing, a husky, worse for wear laugh that comes from a late night. It was nice to see Tom relaxed, not worrying about gun-wielding Frenchmen, his broken body or being hunted like an animal. They were just two blokes sipping coffee talking women and football.

I left them to their man business and kept myself busy in the kitchen.

'Alex,' Tom called.

I took them some more coffee out to the balcony with me.

'What's your opinion?' Rick asked. 'What should I do?'

'About what?' I asked absently, sipping my coffee.

'Sarita.'

'I can't help you, Rick. Answer me this though, what if she could go home with you?'

'That would be amazing!' he answered without hesitation.

'Perhaps there's something in that then?'

'Perhaps. But Papa G would never let her go, so there's no point considering it.'

'So you find a way to stay or you go?' I asked.

'You have anything stronger than coffee?' he asked.

Tom and I laughed. I was standing on the balcony near where Tom sat and he reached out, his arm gliding around my waist.

'We can't all be as lucky as you two,' Rick complained.

Tom and I shared a knowing look. If only Rick knew. I wondered what he would think if he knew we'd only met a few weeks ago when I split from my other boyfriend. That we were only living together because we were on the run.

'Can I just hold onto my freedom for a little bit longer? Do you guys mind?'

'Course not,' I smiled, shaking my head and leaving them to talk while I went on a supplies run while Tom was too distracted to fuss.

I moved slowly through the people on Las Ramblas to the market and took my time picking through the produce and thinking about what I might cook in the days to come. It was nice to be planning menus again, but planning them for what I wanted to cook and to eat, not to cater to someone else's dictation. It felt like we were making a home here, building a life together.

'Alex! Alex!' someone called.

I looked around panicked. No one knew me here, who would be calling to me. I went into survival mode, edging into the shadows, my brain quickly trying to assess the situation. Tom would never be able to find me if something happened. I edged further against a fruit stall hoping the more witnesses, the safer I'd be.

Then I saw Sarita, exasperated, squeezing her way through the crowd of market shoppers, her beautiful face tear stained, but smiling as her slender arms pushed people aside. 'Alex, it is you'

I nodded, smiling, unsure why she would be so surprised to see me at the market.

'Are you not coming for dinner tonight?' she asked, looking at my already bulging shopping bags.

'I have to cook sometimes or we'll be poor,' I laughed.

She nodded, her eyes welling with tears.

'Sarita, it's okay. I think the pub will survive without our patronage for a night or two.'

She smiled through her tears. 'No, sorry, I know. I don't mean to be sad.'

'What's wrong?' I asked, fairly sure I knew what was wrong.

I led her out of the throng of people to a bench and sat down.

'It is Rick,' she began. 'He is leaving me and I don't know what to do?'

Nodding as though it was the first time I'd heard such a thing, I asked, 'Can't you go with him?'

'He hasn't asked.'

'Would you go if he did?'

'Papa would be cross, but yes, I love him. I would go if he asked.'

'Have you told him?'

'No,' she shook her head with a giggle. 'I could not be that forward. He needs to want me to come, not agree out of pity.'

'Well that's fair,' I agreed. 'When is he leaving? Do you still have time?'

'Soon. Weeks. I don't know.'

I put my arm around her and let her cry on my shoulder a moment, ignoring the quizzical looks from passersby.

'Sarita, you just need to talk to him. I'm sure it'd all work out if you sat down and talked.'

'But I don't even know where he is. He didn't come home. He didn't come to work. I think he's already gone.'

'Come with me. I think I know where to find him,' I smiled.

Sarita helped carry my bags through the sea of tourists on Las Ramblas. She linked her arm through mine and started talking about her favourite parts of Barcelona. None of which I'd seen yet so I did a lot of nodding, but all of a sudden, I had a friend.

I opened the door to the flat hoping Rick wouldn't be upset I'd brought Sarita home. The boys were still on the balcony drinking coffee. I needn't have worried about Rick's reaction, his face lit up when he saw Sarita in the doorway and that told me everything.

Tom locked the two of them out on the balcony with a couple of beers. 'How did you do this?' he asked unpacking a shopping bag.

'It just happened. I ran into Sarita in the market. She wants to go with him to Australia. She was afraid to tell him.'

On the balcony, they hugged, they kissed, and they smiled. They finished their beers and came into the flat holding hands, grinning from ear to ear.

'She's comin' with me!' Rick declared.

'Now we just have to tell Papa,' Sarita groaned. 'Will you come to lunch with us first? Let me thank you for helping?'

Over a table filled with tapas, Tom and I laughed with our friends. We were adding bricks to the life we were building. We were forgetting all about crazy Frenchman. I liked it. I liked this life we were putting together.

'You must help me,' Sarita whispered over lunch the next day. She'd appeared at my door with her big pleading brown eyes insisting I come to lunch, she had something to discuss.

Tom was in the flat resting. Rick was behind the bar. It was just Sarita and I, two girls having lunch. We sat by the window at the front, Tom would have hated me being so open to passersby but it was such a gorgeous day with the sun streaming in and landing on our bare legs. My back was to the window so no one would know it was me with my new short black bob.

Laughter and cheering rose up from a group of backpackers enjoying a game of something on the television. Sarita sat across from me, grinning wickedly like a schoolgirl doing something she well knew she shouldn't be doing, like accepting invitations from Australian boys that would take her far away and have her father bursting with fury.

It was a bit sad really, Papa G had no other family apart

from Sarita. Sarita's mother and sister died in a car accident when Sarita was a teenager. How she would leave him I didn't know. I wondered if she even could when it came down to it. She wanted to fly free like anyone else, but I think secretly she wanted her Papa to fly with her.

'Sarita, you have to do something,' Rick declared, sliding into a chair, a tea towel draped over his shoulder.

'About what?' she asked.

'Papa G. I spoke to him, about us, about moving. All he did was grunt and nod and began googling pubs for sale in Australia.'

'Don't worry about Papa,' Sarita reassured him.

Frustrated at receiving no help at all, Rick huffed and went to serve a customer at the bar.

'Silly boys,' Sarita smiled, shaking her head. 'Now, back to girl business,' she declared as she put a forkful of chicken into her mouth with the delicacy of a pea. 'We must go shopping. You will know best so you must help me.'

'What?' I asked completely taken by surprise. 'Me?'

'It is just shopping, Alex,' she laughed. 'Please? You will know best what I should buy to live there,' she begged.

'I think what you already wear will be perfectly fine,' I told her, sure her bohemian style would fit in with no problems.

'Pah,' she scoffed. 'I will need new things, come, come, please,'

'Fine, fine,' I conceded, sure she wasn't going to give up.

'Excellent,' she declared, clinking her wine glass to mine. 'Okay then, let's hurry and eat and get going.'

'What? Now?'

'Yes, now,' she laughed. 'Well, when we have finished our lunch.'

'I can't go now. Tom won't know where I am.'

'What is it with you two? He gets nervous whenever you leave the room. I never see you two go anywhere. Do you, go anywhere? Just call him or send a message, it will be fine,' she insisted.

'Tom's still recovering from the accident, he can't really go very far.'

'Phooey, he holds you captive like a prisoner. It is not good to be inside so much. Surely he won't mind a little shopping? He's not a tyrant is he?'

She was making some interesting points. He was starting to sound like one of those tyrannical men who keep their women captive in a cellar. Sarita's comments suggested she may have considered our behaviour before, perhaps discussed it with Rick. To not go shopping would draw far more unwanted attention than we needed. So I laughed. 'No, he is not a tyrant. Shopping will be great fun,' I said, ignoring the butterflies in my stomach.

I sent Tom a message. 'Going shopping with Sarita. Don't worry,' even though I knew he would worry. I half expected him to come bounding down the stairs in a panic, but he didn't. He hated his phone and had probably left it lying in the lounge room on silent knowing Tom.

'You know what you need? You need a job, some independence,' she said. 'You come work for Papa.'

'Sarita, that's so kind, but I don't think I have a visa to do that,' I told her, not even sure I was supposed to be in the country.

'Pah,' she said, waiving the thought away. 'Papa will work it out. Now though, we shop for Australia. Come, come,' she said, calling out a farewell to Rick and hooking her arm through mine and leading me down the street in the glorious sunshine.

To any passer-by, we were just too best girlfriends out shopping. We wandered boutiques most tourists probably didn't even know were there, exclusive boutiques hidden above shopfronts as well as the multitude of fabulous shops filled by the masses. My eyes darted constantly as we went in and out of shops. Every sudden movement had me freaking out. I barely noticed any of the clothes Sarita tried on. I was far too worried about Tom to concentrate and afraid of what we might find on the street each time we left a shop. I smiled and laughed as required, giving enough good ooh's and aah's to get through the day without letting on I was so distracted, grateful for shop assistants I could agree with.

Time slipped by like sand. The sun had moved and shadows crept across the walkways. Tom would be panicking. I knew it. I could feel it. That rubber band holding us together was stretching too far. My skin crawled with fear, my head ached and my stomach threatened to heave with each new shop we entered. I sent Tom messages throughout the day while Sarita was in fitting rooms but it was doing nothing to comfort me now.

We came out of yet another shop and I saw him. The bulldog was standing across the road under the cover of a shop's verandah flexing the hand I'd shot. He was almost concealed by shoppers, but not enough to hide his bulk and his ugly fat head.

My heart pounded. I tried desperately to breathe. He was looking side to side on the street, for what or who, I didn't know, maybe me. Maybe he had already seen me, knew I was here on this street shopping. But he didn't look at me and I kept Sarita between me and his line of vision.

'What about that first dress? Is it good for the Australian Beach?' Sarita asked. Before I could reply, she added, 'Yes, I think I like the first one best.'

I nodded, smiling, barely hearing what she was saying just glad to be about to hide in a new shop.

As we walked away, I looked back to where the bulldog of a man had stood and he was gone, leaving me wondering if he had been there at all. I exhaled as though I hadn't taken a single breath in all the minutes since I'd seen him and told Sarita the dress was beautiful.

'Really?' Sarita asked, thankfully not noticing my momentary insanity.

'Absolutely,' I smiled, feeling awful for not even remembering what it looked like, just desperate to get home and off the street.

Sarita became giddy with happiness and we hurried back to the first shop. She tried on the dress again. I tried harder to pay attention this time and thankfully the dress really was beautiful even though it wasn't much different from some of the clothes she already wore.

'This will fit in, yes?' she asked

There wasn't a lot Sarita could do to just fit in anywhere, she was far too beautiful but the dress would be perfect on any beach or in any bar I knew of. 'Of course,' I smiled.

She clapped her hands together, grinning from ear to ear.

'Si, si,' nodded the sales assistant who quickly went about sorting out the finer points of the sale before we walked out of the store again.

Then we were finished. I tentatively looked out the shop window as inconspicuously as possible before going outside. But it was late in the day and the streets were nearly empty and there were no burly Frenchman lurking in the shadows.

'Are you alright?' Sarita finally asked, concerned.

'Of course. It's just been a long day. I've been couped up for a while remember?' I said, forcing a smile.

'Yes, this is true,' she smiled, raising her eyebrows. 'Come, let's go home.'

Sarita chattered all the way back about the move, carrying her multitude of bags like someone accustomed to that much shopping, excitement bursting out of her. I was happy for her, for her and Rick. They were good people but I was glad it was over and just wanted to be upstairs in the safety of the apartment. We hugged on the street in front of my building and she went into the pub while I climbed the stairs to my fate.

'Where were you?' Tom demanded, opening the door before I'd even reached it.

'I'm sorry, Tom, I couldn't help it. Sarita insisted and then she started asking questions and it was easier to go than not.'

'What sort of questions?'

'I think she thought you might have been one of those sickos holding me captive for sex or something.'

'Really?'

'Maybe she didn't mean it, but it did sound that way.'

'You should have woken me. I got your messages but you were gone for hours. I went down to the pub looking for you and Rick said you weren't back yet. I was going to call, but he hijacked me, told me not worry and talked football all afternoon. I was worried sick. Don't ever do that to me again, yeah?' he said, pulling me to him tightly.

His green eyes were so sad I wanted to cry. 'I was terrified the whole time. I couldn't even concentrate on shopping. It's so exhausting. I thought I saw him, Tom.'

'Who?' he asked concerned.

'The one with a watermelon head. The one I shot.'

'Really?'

'I must have imagined it though. I turned back again and he was gone.'

'They can't have found us. Not yet. Come here,' he said, holding me tight. 'I hate that that happened to you. That I didn't stop it, that I couldn't stop any of it.'

'I'm just glad it all ended okay,' I smiled.

'You know, any time it's too much, you are free to leave,' he offered, his eyes not meaning a word of it.

'I know. But I'll always rather be with you, no matter how hard it gets.'

He wrapped his strong arms around me, pulling me close, holding me too tight. 'I'm just glad you're okay. I couldn't bear anything happening to you.'

He held me a long moment, squishing all the air out of me, but it felt good, it felt safe. Then, kissing the top of my head, he led me to the sofa and handed me a much needed cup of coffee.

Chapter 15

Waking wrapped so tight in Tom's arms made the previous day's shopping trip worth every second. I'm not sure I'll ever get used to waking beside Tom, seeing his handsome face, feeling him squeeze me as soon as he sensed I was awake but not wanting the closeness to end. I was happy to keep trying though. He was a piece of perfection I never knew existed. I pulled his arms tighter, snuggling into his warmth, so glad I found him.

He kissed my ear and his man bits jumped to attention. That was my cue to get out of bed. 'Baaaaabe!' he cried, pulling me back.

Tom crushed me against him, all of him. I felt him everywhere. My body went limp, unable to protest as he kissed my neck with a purpose he hadn't managed since we'd been at the villa on the beach. My body tingled all over with pleasure and bliss, gasping for air as my lady land danced a celebratory jig of its own.

My heart pounded, my head spun, blood flowed too fast, all

my senses exploding at once. I groaned as Tom's strong hands roamed all over my body. All sense of reason left my mind. All I could focus on was Tom, my legs wrapping around his, my arms snaking around his neck, feeling the perfection of his body beneath my hands, his muscles rippling with his every movement.

Banging on the front door blended with the banging in my chest, in my head, in my ears. I was far away in another place. A bomb could have exploded and I'd have not cared. All I could focus on was Tom. All I wanted was Tom. I needed Tom. My lady bits begged for him.

The banging continued in the other room, another place, another time, but must have been just loud enough to penetrate Tom's mind and he pulled away. Our eyes caught for a never-ending moment, the intensity, the knowing, rippling through my body. The banging continued and he kissed my forehead, swung his legs over the bed, threw on a crumpled t-shirt and boxers and he was gone.

I lay back on the pillows exacerbated. Short shallow breaths were all I could manage. Tom's laughter drifted in from the other room and slowly I returned from that beautiful place he'd taken me to, that perfect place of happiness and the promise of ecstasy, where nothing else existed but the two of us, where we floated on clouds, electrical currents of pleasure surging through every single cell. Voices and laughter in the other room dragged me kicking and screaming back to reality.

'They're trying to kidnap me,' Rick explained when I joined them after my shower.

Tom didn't panic at all; he just smiled wryly, so I asked, 'Who is?'

'Sarita's aunts. They said because her mother's gone they wanted to make sure I was suitable to be taking her all that way. Sarita told me to run, so I came here,' he said, perspiration beading through his hair and over his face.

I stifled a laugh as the door rattled with another visitor. I sat with Rick while Tom answered.

'Where is he? Big chicken!' Guillermo was having way too much fun with torturing Rick.

Guillermo pushed past a smirking Tom and out to the balcony. 'But Papa G...' Rick proclaimed.

'No Papa G. You must go. They are Sarita's aunties. Now come. Big baby.' Guillermo dragged Rick up by the arm and out the door.

'At least you don't have to worry about my family coming for you!' I laughed.

'For now, but I'm sure they'll be hunting me just the same!' Tom said.

'Ah, but they'll never find us.' I smiled, leaning into him against the balcony door, kissing him, desperate to pick up where we left off.

He pulled away, kissed the tip of my nose, 'Go pack your swimsuit, Babe, today is a day for amazing,' he said, raising his eyebrows.

'Really? Amazing?' I asked wondering if that meant the same thing I hoped it did.

'Sarita was right. It's not healthy to be inside so much and it's time you got to see some of Barcelona, among other amazing things,' he winked.

'But are you well enough?'

He pulled off his shirt, my blood boiling, my mouth near drooling, 'See, no bruises.'

He was right, the bruising had almost gone. His face showed nothing but a few faint scars that would fade in the sun.

'Will we be safe?'

'We've laid low for a few weeks. We've changed our hair and as long as we're careful, we should be fine.'

'Besides,' he added, 'the ocean will be good for the healing and you need some fresh air if you're seeing Watermelon Head when you're shopping.'

I didn't care what the excuse was, I wasn't going to waste time arguing and went to pack a day bag while he went to shower.

'Are you sure?' I asked again as we were leaving.

'I swear Alex, I'm fine. Let's go to the beach like normal people.'

'What's even normal?' I asked. 'I don't mind being housebound with you, you know.'

'You're not so bad yourself. Much better company than Moe, that's for sure!' He raised his conspiratorial eyebrows as he edged into my personal space, extracting out all the air, smelling like earth and salt and man. 'Let's get outta here,' he declared, exiting my airspace and leaving me gulping in air.

The full extent of amazing hit me as we walked down the stairs and he trailed a finger down my back. My palms began to sweat, my heart beating too fast, my breath catching in my throat.

'You okay?' he asked as I felt a flush creeping across my face.

'Ahuh, sure,' I smiled, unable to stop the redness I could feel creeping up my neck. I was thankful we were at the bottom of the stairs, the blinding sun streaming through and covering my face as he opened the door.

Tom flung an arm across my shoulders. 'You ready for amazing?' he asked, raising his eyebrows with a smirk, pushing his sunglasses on as we headed down the street and onto the bustling Las Ramblas like every other tourist.

We turned left and headed towards the water, stopping at the statue of Christopher Columbus before crossing the road to the pier, which we walked all the way to the end chatting and laughing, the sunshine warming our faces.

Tourists and street sellers with their illegal knock offs bustled around us, but anything outside of our beautiful bubble was inconsequential. All that existed was Tom and me. I soaked in the carnival atmosphere, Tom and I laughing as the sun drenched us with goodness. I wanted to commit every moment to memory. Days like this needed to be remembered.

We strolled along the esplanade arm in arm until we found a part of the beach least populated and a large space on the sand for ourselves. I dropped my bag into the sand and pulled out towels and bottles of water. Ripping off his shirt, Tom ran straight into the water like a deprived fish. I sat organising myself watching him dive into the water. It was like air to him and he'd been land bound for too long, not even his lonely surfboard had made the trip, he'd left it with Michael and Moe. That's how serious this was, how deep in hiding we were.

Tom came out of the water, his body glistening, his hair dripping. He raced up the sand, his face beaming. Leaning over he kissed me, the salt water dripping into my mouth with his tongue. The cold droplets falling onto my flushed face, his cool, ocean coated leg draping itself between mine. I groaned accidentally, and he stopped, smiling, 'Perhaps not here, hey?'

I smiled, embarrassed, thankful for the unpopulated piece of beach we had.

'Come cool off,' he suggested with a naughty smile, leading me to the water.

We spent the afternoon laughing, swimming, splashing each other, flirting outrageously as we enjoyed being outside and having fun. As the sun began its evening descent, we walked back up to the esplanade and through the gothic quarter until we found a restaurant filling with locals. It was a little restaurant, a hole in the wall, a stone wall it seemed. It was quaint and authentic and beautiful.

'Eat where the locals eat and you'll never go wrong,' Tom told me. 'The food will always be better and you'll never be ripped off by tourist prices,' he insisted as we waited to be seated.

He was right, the waiter was generous, the sangria perfect, the tapas and paella to die for, perfectly caramelised at the edges. 'Don't tell Papa G we cheated,' he laughed.

It was dark outside, the streets filled with people, when we finally left, our tummies ready to explode, our heads a little giddy from the sangria mixing with the night air. I chatted and giggled like a schoolgirl, blaming the sangria, but knowing it was nervous anticipation for the day's finale that was now not far away, the big crescendo of our day of amazing. The mere thought of it had my heart palpitating. I was suddenly nervous and strangely unsure, there were a lot of expectations after all this time but I wanted him so badly, there was nothing that would stop me.

We walked down our street, the bar next door was bursting at the seams. Rick was serving by the window and waved us in. There was a soccer game on the telly so we went in for a quick look. It was hard to refuse, we couldn't exactly say, no thanks, we're finally going to get down to some business, see you in the morning.

'Geez it's crazy man!' Rick cried as he hurried to the bar to pour our drinks.

All around were young travellers with varying accents, Australian, English, various European, a couple of Americans, cheering along with the game on the screen. This was Tom's world and these were his people and the smile spread across his face was one of my favourite things to see.

Some strangers stopped and spoke as they passed by about nothing in particular. It was nice to chat to random people like regular tourists, like normal people. As the game was ending two guys were yelling closer to the telly. I guessed the game hadn't gone as well as one of them had hoped. Then they were pushing and shoving, throwing punches. Some bystanders cheered them on, not even knowing what the fight was about. Some people quickly disappeared out the front door or down to the back of the bar. Papa G and Rick came pushing through the remaining crowd and before we could move, before Rick could push Papa G out of the way, bodies, tables, chairs and beer came hurtling towards us, knocking us both to the ground.

I hit my head but barely noticed. My only thought was for Tom. I jumped up searching for him. He was curled into a foetal position on the floor, people stepping over him, moving around him, not even noticing him, as though he didn't exist while he lay there, writhing in pain.

I fell to my knees beside him, looking for blood or something, anything. I found nothing. It could only be his insides. They weren't healed nearly enough for that kind of an impact. He wasn't as well as he'd led me to believe.

Chapter 16

Rick and Papa G appeared at my side. 'I call the ambulance,' Papa G said.

'No!' Tom and I shouted in unison.

'No, I'll be fine,' Tom added, regaining his composure. 'I just need to get upstairs.'

'Are you sure?' Rick asked. 'You look wrecked, man.'

'Yeah, cheers!' Tom laughed. 'Seriously though, I just need to lie down.'

'Well, alright then, if you're sure, man.'

Rick and Guillermo helped Tom up, I looked towards the front door and the Frenchman with the watermelon head was sticking his head in the doorway. We were concealed enough for now but there was no way out and he was just standing there.

'Shit, shit, shit,' I huffed, trying to think.

'What?' demanded Tom, trying to straighten up.

'It's him Tom, standing by the door, there's no way out.'

'Do you have a back room?' he asked Rick.

'Yeah, course. What's going on?'

'Nothing you want to know about, can you help me get back there?'

'Yeah, yeah, come on,' he said, as we pushed our way through drunken revellers coming from the back trying to force their way out the front.

We went through the hallway that led to the toilets, through the door marked private that Rick unlocked and up the stairs.

He helped Tom lay on the sofa. 'You alright?'

'Yeah, thanks, man.'

'No worries. Can I get you anything?'

'Nah, thanks. Can we just lay low in here for a bit?'

'Yeah of course. I gotta go help Papa G deal with all the mess, though, just call out if you need anything, help yourself to the fridge and stuff.'

'Thanks.'

I smiled my thanks as Rick closed the door and left.

'Where are you hurt?' I demanded as soon as Rick was gone.

'I don't know. Here,' he said indicating his side.

'Is it bad?' I asked.

'I don't think so. Think it just took the wind out of me.'

I looked at him disbelievingly.

'Okay, there might be bruising of some organs too,' he said, smiling tightly.

'What can I do?'

'Just stay here with me, where it's safe.'

'What are we going to do Tom?'

'Nothing. We're going to stay here. He didn't see us, did he?'

'No.'

'Then we're fine. He can't know exactly where we are, he's just working on a hunch.'

'What if it was him yesterday? What if he did see me and followed us? I didn't see anyone but I'm not used to this hiding business. I suck at it.'

'It's okay. You didn't do anything wrong. He didn't come up to the flat so he didn't follow you. Looking in a pub filled with tourists is a reasonable thing for a hunter like him to do.'

'But why would they have even come to Barcelona, with all the places in Europe to look, why here?'

'They'll be looking in all the favourite tourist spots first, all the good surf spots where we'll assume we can blend in. That's where they'll start and it'll take a while. We just need to stay out of sight until they move on. It's a good thing even because once they leave here empty handed, we'll be safe for a while.'

I handed him a glass of water and sat on the floor, leaning against the couch with a cup of tea.

'It won't always be like this,' he said. 'I have to get better eventually, right?' he looked at me with a cheeky grin that made me giggle. 'When I'm better and all this has blown over, we'll decide on somewhere fabulous to live. We'll get our own place, maybe by the beach. I'll rescue my board from Moe who's probably snapped the fin off it. We'll get jobs and make friends and surf,' he smiled dreamily into nowhere.

'That sounds perfect, but do I have to surf? Can I watch from the beach?' I asked, hoping a surf chick for company wasn't in this big dream. His idea was lovely, except for me attempting to surf again. Someone as unlucky as me doesn't get that lucky twice.

He laughed and kissed the top of my head. 'You can watch from anywhere you like, as long as you're there.'

'Always,' I whispered, kissing his cheek.

I fell asleep against the couch praying Tom was right, that everything would be okay, that Tom would be okay. I wanted us to live a life, eventually. We couldn't live like fugitives hiding out forever. I would if I had to as long as I was with Tom, but surely the Frenchmen, Axl's family and George Cummins would have give up eventually and we could live in a cute beach-side village somewhere, just minding our business and living our lives. Lydia and Andrea could visit and Bex and her Merry Men could come by for barbeques and surfing weekends. I liked it. I liked it a lot.

Drums and laughter rose up from the street as I made coffee in the morning. Tom slept like a drunk oblivious to the party occurring on the street below. I left him to rest. His body needed all the help it could get. Rick, Sarita and Guillermo had only returned for a couple of hours sleep and were already back to work, Sarita leaving a note to say there were leftovers in the fridge. Sitting on their balcony, I watched the spectacle of paper maché giants bobbing up and down as they paraded through the street below accompanied by percussion drums and cheered on by an array of jolly bystanders.

Down the street they went, giant medieval kings and queens dancing amid marching bands of trumpets and flutes, trombones and drums, belting out medieval festival tunes that had me tapping my feet and the people below clapping and bouncing in time. The giants looked ten feet tall, but gracefully danced their jigs with the greatest of ease. Medieval horses bounced around them amid the sea of red and yellow marching bands creating an amazing visual spectacle.

Masses of people filled the street below, spilling into Las Ramblas in the distance where a sea of colour awaited. Children sat atop parental shoulders for better viewing, everyone around them clapping with the drums, cheering and waving. The sounds rattled and shook, bouncing off the buildings, echoing all around, yet somehow Tom still slept. I checked he was still alive a few times and was relieved to find him still breathing each time.

The pub below was exploding, people spilling out of the large open windows. I considered going down to check on them. But I couldn't bear the thought of leaving Tom, not even for a minute. Not to mention, the protection the balcony provided was a little more than welcome after the night before.

Even as the last of the giants and their entourage spilled into Las Ramblas and beyond, the people still milled below on the street and in the bar. There was nothing more for me to see so I left them to their shenanigans, closing the balcony doors, muffling the sounds and making them sound far away.

I'd just put some more food in the microwave when Rick walked in. He planted a quick kiss to my cheek and made his way through to the kitchen. I made him tea.

'So,' he started. 'How's Tom?'

'He's okay. He's slept most of the day.'

'What, with all the noise of Le Merce?'

'Is that what all that was? I know, I had to check he was still breathing, I even pinched him to make sure he wasn't in a coma.'

Rick smiled. 'So, there was a guy in the bar before.'

'Right,' I said, not sure where he was headed. 'What guy?'

'A big, fat, hairy French one.'

I nodded.

'Alex?'

'What?'

'He wasn't a nice kind of guy. He was asking after Tom. What's going on?'

Tom shuffled into the kitchen. 'What did you tell him?' he asked Rick.

'Nothing. He and his meat head friend spoke with Papa G. They had a YouTube video of you on their phone from last night's fight. Papa G said you were celebrating your last night and should be long gone by now. I didn't hear anything else. He sent me up to let you know.'

'Thanks,' Tom nodded, pouring himself some tea.

'So what's going on, guys? Are you in trouble?'

Tom looked at me, clearly unsure how much he should divulge. I trusted Rick. I trusted Sarita and Guillermo. I nodded to Tom; I thought he should tell Rick everything. It wouldn't be fair to keep it from him. He was involved now. They all were. They'd hidden us and lied for us. They deserved to know what was going on.

Guillermo and Sarita came in.

'Who's watching the bar?' Rick asked.

Papa G waved his hand, 'People. We have staff you know. Are you okay?' he asked Tom.

'Yeah,' he said as I poured more tea. It was going to be a long night.

We sat on the sofa, dragging over a dining chair or two and Tom began with the whole sorry mess, who his family was, why he was living like a nomad, what had happened in France to bring us to Spain. All of it.

'Shit!' Rick responded.

Tom shrugged. He was used to it.

'Well I tell them you go to London to see the doctor,' Guillermo said.

'Thanks Papa G,' Tom said.

We sat quiet for a moment as the others took it all in. Tom and I realising how close they'd come to finding us. They'd only been metres away, at the bottom of the stairs. If I'd ventured into the bar for some dinner with Sarita, that could have been it. It could have been all over.

'I have to call Michael,' Tom said, pulling his phone from his pocket.

'Who's Michael?' asked Rick.

'Bodyguard,' Tom said as he put the phone to his ear, waiting for Michael answer his call. 'We have a problem,' he said. 'Yep, yep, 'k.' Then he hung up. 'He's going to see what he can find out.'

The tension in the room was thick. Papa G made more tea and put more food in the microwave. We were all trying to pretend everything was okay and shovelling food into our mouths when Tom's phone started singing.

'Yeah?' he answered, forgoing pleasantries. 'You sure? Shit. Yeah. Righto.' He hung up.

'They didn't believe Papa G and have checked into the hostel down the street.'

'They're sure it's them?'

'Yeah, Michael has a man in the hostel.'

'Shit.'

'Yeah, shit.'

'So what now?'

'We gotta get out of here. Michael's going to call with details. We'll leave tomorrow night, hopefully all the people around for La Merce will make it too hard to spot us. Until then, we can't leave the flat.'

'Where will you go?' asked Sarita softly.

'I don't know,' Tom said. 'I don't know.'

'I have a boat, big boat,' declared Guillermo. 'You take it. Harder to find you in the ocean, can't sneak up on you. I give your man the details when he calls. I give the dock the details. You go where you need.'

'Are you sure?' Tom asked. 'What if you need it? I don't know when we'll be able to get it back to you. We will, I just don't know when.'

He waved his hand dismissively, 'I don't need it. I go to Australia with Sarita and Rick.'

Rick rolled his eyes. A thrilled Sarita hugged Guillermo. 'There is nothing for me here without them,' Guillermo said. 'I buy them a restaurant already as wedding gift. I think I will retire though and sit on the beach like bum,' he declared with a big, satisfied grin.

Rick almost groaned at the word wedding but everyone knew it was inevitable.

Guillermo and Tom sorted out the details of the boat with

Michael, then in the early hours of the morning, Rick helped sneak us back up to our own flat without being seen.

'I'm sick of running, Alex,' Tom said as we were getting into bed. 'I just want to stop and be with you, make a life with you.'

'It doesn't matter where you are Tom. I'll be with you, so that's no different.'

'How can we have a life like that?'

'I don't know, but we'll find a way. We'll make it work.'

He took my hand in the dark, kissing it, declaring, 'I love you Alex.'

'I love you, too.'

Chapter 17

We lay in bed well after the sun had risen, snuggling as best we could with Tom's bruised insides. Silently we stared at the ceiling, our brains running overtime. I was wondering where we were headed. If I should call mum again and let her know I was okay. We had to pack up the apartment. I'm sure Tom's train of thought was a little more specific regarding the escaping death and the particulars of where best to hide.

I didn't want to move from the bed, I could have lain beside Tom forever. It was safe with Tom's arms around me hidden away in Henri's flat. Nothing could get us there. No one could find us locked in our own little corner of heaven. I was sure if we just stayed locked away we'd be safe. Sarita would be bring us food. We'd make do. But eventually we'd slip up and they'd be right there waiting. Now they knew we were somewhere to be found. Moe said moving was best so that's what we'd do while we had the cover of La Merce.

Someone knocked on the door, rescuing me from my restlessness. 'Check the peephole,' Tom instructed as I threw on a t-shirt and shorts.

I let Sarita in. She put the box she was carrying on the small dining table and hugged me. 'How are you?' she asked.

'I'm okay. I just worry about Tom. He doesn't need all the moving about.'

She nodded. Out of the box she pulled containers of food and helped herself to plates in the kitchen. 'Papa thought you might need some good food.'

'Your dad is a Godsend!'

I took a plate into a very grateful Tom and Sarita and I went onto the balcony to eat. It was easy to whittle away hours with Sarita, chatting over Guillermo's amazing paella that he knew was my favourite, then over tea and then when my disposition couldn't handle any more tea, far too much coffee. Some farewell Sangria was what I really fancied but I needed to keep my wits about me for the evening to come.

Sarita kindly avoided speaking too much about the coming events. She talked about her move instead, a safe, distracting topic.

'I'm going to miss your farewell,' I said sadly.

'I know. But it's okay. It is better you are alive,' she smiled. 'I'll send you photos when we get to Australia,' she said.

She passed me a piece of paper with a Gmail account and a password.

'I set up a special email for us to use, no one will know. It will be just for us and you can tell me you are okay and I can send you pictures.'

'That's brilliant,' I smiled. 'You would make a very good going into hiding person, you know.'

'Yes,' she said. 'I always fancied I could be a spy,' she said, the last dramatically but with a smile and we laughed. It was nice to laugh.

Then the day was coming to a close. Sarita rinsed up her containers and took them back to the pub in an old plastic shopping bag.

I showered. Tom showered. I packed our toiletries and picked all our clothes off the floor, clean and dirty merging into one big stinky mess in our bags. I made sure all the perishables were thrown out and the bins were emptied and the apartment was left as we'd found it.

The sounds below were changing with the day. As the last of the afternoons La Merce festivities moved on, so did the people, now they were slowly returning as they gathered for dinner and after dark revelry.

'Come, sit,' Tom asked. He'd swung his legs over the edge of the bed so I sat beside him. 'You can stop anytime you want off this train; I just want you to know that. You never need to feel obliged. This is a stupid way to live.'

'Would you stop it,' I scolded. 'We've had this conversation, Tom. I'll be happy as long as I'm with you. You've gone and ruined me now. I can't live without you. I don't want to go home, there's nothing there for me. Not anymore. Everything I need, everything I want is here, with you. Who we are, how I feel, who I am when I'm with you, I don't want to lose that, not for a minute. It's more than I ever dreamed could be possible. Who knew a person could be so happy?'

He pulled my mouth to his. 'I never knew I could love some-one, that it would feel like this, that I even had it in me,' he smiled, blushing ever so slightly. 'I just want us to stop, to breathe, to just live, with you. I'm exhausted.'

'We'll be fine. When we get to wherever we're going, we'll be fine. We'll rest well then, we'll lie on a beach and soak up the sun. They'll forget about you and we can just live. We'll be fine,' I said, smiling as best I could, not even sure I believed me, I kissed his stubble covered cheek.

'You're amazing, you know that?'

I smiled, kissed him softly. 'Besides,' I smirked, 'you have a promise to keep. You promised me a night of amazing and I'm not leaving until you come through.' I raised my eyebrows with more cheek than I think I'd ever mustered and went back to zip-ping our bags and giving the lovely little flat a quick once over.

'Babe...' Tom called.

'Is it time?'

'Yep,' he smiled tightly, putting his phone into his pocket before putting two more pain pills in his mouth and following them with a glass of water.

At the bottom of the stairs we swapped luggage so I could hobble along like a hunchback and he could roll my case along without any strain.

Clad in caps and sunglasses, even though the sun well on its way down, we blended into the sea of people, looking just like everyone who'd been amongst the festivities all day.

On Las Ramblas people moved like sheep in the opposite direction, heading towards the plaza. People hurried through the crowds carrying enormous sparklers sending off sprays of fire. A dragon and a devil raced past us on their way to one of the events.

We headed through the crowds, pushing and shoving our way towards Christopher Columbus. The boat was making an unprecedented pick up near the pier. Guillermo knew people it seemed and people liked Guillermo.

By the statue of Christopher Columbus, we casually milled amongst the many others coming or going from one side of the road to the other. Only we were waiting for our signal.

I apprehensively switched on and fiddled about with my phone while we waited. Sixteen voicemails from my mother now flashed on the screen. 'Crap,' I mumbled.

'You should probably call her,' Tom suggested. 'Who knows when you might get another chance?'

I contemplated it for a moment, but before I could even dial her number, it rang. I answered instinctively before the noise attracted any attention.

'Mum, hi!' I answered annoyed and surprised and worried, not needing a lecture as I was running from gun wielding Frenchman. 'What's up?' I asked as though I'd spoken to her that morning.

'What, that's it?' she asked, offended.

'Sorry mum, just, kinda in the middle of something here.'

'Well, I'm sorry to interrupt, Lexi, but we're kind of in the middle of something here, too.'

'Of course, sorry I haven't been in touch...' She cut me off as I was about to launch into a lengthy apology.

'Lexi, it's Nanna.'

'Nanna? What about Nanna?' I asked, suddenly panicked.

'She's dying.'

'What?' I cried too loudly, some passers-by turning to stare, Tom jumping to attention.

'Sorry, sweetheart, I didn't want to ruin your holiday, but you didn't come home with Billy and you haven't been answering your phone and I just had to get it out before you rushed off somewhere else.'

'What's wrong with Nanna, Mum?'

'Cancer, dear.'

'What cancer? Is she having treatment?'

'No, no treatment, it's too far gone for that.'

'How is it too far gone?'

'Well, you know how stubborn your grandmother is. She thinks she's invincible. I spoke to her doctors and well, she doesn't have long to go. She's pretty much stuck in that bed now and I thought you'd want to know before you missed getting to say goodbye.'

Tears flowed down my face as I hung up the phone. It couldn't be true. Not my Nanna. Not her. It couldn't be.

Tom pulled me to him, letting me cry into his shirt. His body was warm. I drank in his smell and listened to his heartbeat as mine slowed to beat in time with his.

'It's okay Alex,' he said. 'You have to go.'

'No. I can't leave you. No. I won't.'

'You have to. I'll be fine with Michael.'

'But where will you go?'

'I don't know, but I'll let you know when we're there. I'll use that address Sarita set up.'

I nodded. Confused, dazed. None of it was real. I couldn't contemplate leaving Tom, but I had to see my Nanna.

'Alex?'

'Yeah?'

'Run!'

'What?'

'Just run!' he shouted, grabbing my hand and near dragging me along the esplanade.

Out of the corner of my eye watermelon head and his meathead buddy who were far too big to run, ran, reaching inside their open shirts flapping against white singlets. Shit! They had guns. This wasn't good at all.

We dodged in and out of tourists, Tom's backpack bouncing up and down on my back. People shouted at us as we pushed through mumbling apologies as best we could. We crossed the road, cars honking. We ran towards the pier, Tom holding his phone to his ear.

Hidden by a horde of people, he wrestled his pack off my back, handing me my case as a taxi pulled up beside us. 'Get in the taxi and just go. Don't look back,' he demanded. 'Michael has a card, he'll make sure there's a plane ticket for you at the airport. Do you have taxi fare?'

'Um, I think,' I nodded, tears pouring down my face, goo sticking in my throat.

"K. Alex?'

'Yeah?'

'I love you,' he declared, kissing me hard on the mouth. Then he was gone, swallowed by a sea of tourists on the pier.

Chapter 18

I watched the fat Frenchmen through the rear window as they ignored me, running right past my taxi following Tom, pulling their guns from inside their shirts regardless of all the people on the pier. I watched as long as I could, tears pouring from my eyes, until the taxi was finally able to get past the crowds of happy people heading to festival celebrations and the gunmen blended into the masses on the pier and then the pier itself melted away in the distance.

I'd barely had time to choose between Tom and Nanna. I wasn't sure there was a choice. But all I knew now was it was too late. Tom was gone to somewhere unknown and I was on my way to the airport. There was no changing any of it now. It was done. I couldn't go back, I could only keep going.

In the distance a spray of water spat into the air as a speedboat raced towards a much larger boat bobbing in the water far off shore. My phone vibrated with a message from Tom saying, 'made it, love you. You okay?' I replied that I was then sat back relieved that at least he'd made it that far.

As promised, a ticket had been booked in my name. I checked in at the Emirates counter, surrendered my bag and numbly walked through security. I went to the gate with a cup of coffee, sat on the floor, stretching out my legs and waited.

All the way to Dubai, I worried about Tom. I called him but got his voicemail then I sat in the bathroom at the airport during the transfer and cried hoping he was okay, wondering when I'd see him again, if I'd see him again.

On the flight from Dubai to home, I worried about what I would find when I arrived. I worried about Nanna, Mum, and the mess created by stupid Billy bloody McRae.

I disembarked as though I were a prisoner walking to my death, desperate to see my Nanna but hardly able to move for the giant hole expanding in my stomach. Nanna was one of my favourite people in the whole world. If I'd had more time to make my decision, I don't know who I would have chosen, Tom or Nanna. It didn't matter now. There was no undoing any of it. Tom was on the other side of the world. I had no choice but to get into a taxi and go back to my real life as though the last weeks, Tom, everyone, all of it, had been a dream. I'm sure someone would have collected me if I'd given them my flight details, but a sixth sense had told me I'd need all the moments of freedom I could get.

The taxi turned down my parents' street, the street I'd grown up on, the street where Lexi had become Lexi and it was torturous, painfully horrible having to push Alex into a box and be boring, miserable Lexi again. I hated that most of all. Going back to being Lexi might be what would actually kill me.

My parents lived in an old double fronted stone cottage. The cottage had always been too small for a family, so it had always been overcrowded and cluttered with all our stuff. Quiet corners had been a thing of daydreams as was privacy. The cottage had one bathroom, three double- sized bedrooms, a small kitchen and dining room and a cosy living room. Mum loved the place, it was her dream home. It just wasn't built for a growing family. It was either a starter or a finisher, not much good for in between. But we'd made do and been happy enough. Happy enough seemed to be the motto of my life until I met Tom, until I met Lydia and seen how else you could live, that there could be so much more than happy enough. Despite their reasons for being where they were they did things every day that most people only ever dream about. They were free and happy and alive. I suspected they'd live that way no matter where they were.

Three cars lined the kerb in front of the house. The shiny black Subaru was my sister's, the well-worn four wheel drive, belonged to Aunt Veronica, a quirky, man loving, middle aged woman who didn't like fuss or trouble and the third car, a faded yellow beetle belonged to Aunt Veronica's only child, perky Felicity, who was a rare sight. She was usually off studying something ridiculously clever at a university far from home. Dad's car of course reigned supreme in the driveway. It was like a matching set of family, all ready and waiting to judge and condemn and I wasn't in the mood, I wanted a shower and something to eat and to see my Nanna. There were more important things than having to justify myself to them. I wasn't Lexi the lovely doormat anymore and I wasn't ready to be put back in that box and I was sure they weren't going to be thrilled to find that out. Lexi the lovely doormat was much easier for everyone else.

I quietly let myself in, standing a moment in the hallway, breathing in the familiar smells of home. Chatter and laughter drifted through from the kitchen at the back of the house and I relished my last moments of freedom.

'Aunt Lexi!' Sophie, my eight-year-old niece cried. She was the product of my sister's misspent youth, cute as a button, attention seeking, pretentious, spoilt rotten and always for-given. She clutched at my legs as though I'd been gone for years. 'I like your hair,' she said, grabbing my hand, dragging me through the house to my reckoning.

'Oh, look who it is!' mocked my dad as I entered the kitchen.

Reluctantly raising a hand I said, 'Hey.'

They were all sitting around Mum's old, round timber table staring at me like I was a foreigner.

'You look tired, Lexi, sit,' commanded my mum, placing a tea cup in front of me and slicing me an enormous piece of cake. 'What have you done to your hair? What are you wearing?' she asked looking at me suspiciously.

I shrugged. I'd forgotten the shorts and black and silver Ooh La La tank top I'd bought as a souvenir for my sister but had since worn to death. In my defence, I was supposed to be on a boat in the middle of the ocean not my mother's kitchen await-ing judgement.

My mother wasn't a teabag kind of person and in the centre of the table was a pot. I reached for it and poured. It was always excellent tea and she made the best cakes. Everyone continued staring silently as I went about making my tea.

'So?' My sister Victoria eventually asked, never one for suspense.

'So, what, V?' I asked like a petulant teenager.

Everyone watched me expectantly, as though my head might start spinning any moment. Aunt Veronica sat in the corner shaking her head, Felicity beside her smirking at the spectacle about to unfold. They all waited. I didn't like it. I didn't want to tell them about Tom, about what we'd shared, it didn't feel right. I wanted it to stay mine, to stay in my beautiful bubble of happiness, not be judged by their versions of mediocrity.

'Well if Lexi doesn't want to tell us where she's been or why we haven't been able to contact her, or why Victoria and Glenn had to go and get her stuff from poor Billy's place, then that's up to her.' Mum's face was deadpan as she delivered her little speech, pouring more tea into the array of cups around the table, not daring to look me in the eye. But I knew my mother well enough to know that that look, that tone, meant she was mad, really, really mad.

But her take on it all pissed me off just as much. How could she take his side over that of her own daughter? 'Poor Billy! My arse poor Billy!' I defended, deciding too bad if mum was pissed off. 'The dirty sod's been cheating on me for years mum, so don't go poor Billying me!'

'But he was heartbroken, Lexi. He popped in just the other day, his eyes were red from crying.'

'Yeah, right. If he'd been crying, it'd have been for his housekeeper and chef that put out whenever he wanted it, in between him sleeping with those skanky sluts. He asked me for a ménage a trois for crying out loud, in a restaurant full of people, in front of our friends. You can't win this one mum, so don't even try.'

I stood up too quickly, knocking the table, Aunt Veronica's freshly poured cup of tea swishing onto the tablecloth as I stormed out of the room to go in search of Nanna.

'She's sleeping, Lexi!' Mum shouted to me as I walked away.

'Not after that she's not!' I called.

I found Nanna in Victoria's old room. Lucky for her too, as the third bedroom was mine, the smallest, and as I poked my head in on the way past it had morphed into some sort of ironing room. Clearly mum wasn't expecting me home. That could be a problem.

Perhaps I could sleep in the storage unit my sister had apparently rented for me. I'd scanned an email from her when I'd checked my emails in Dubai. I could pay her back as soon as I sorted myself out, no hurry. So it'd said.

I shouldn't be too harsh on Victoria though, it was kind enough for her and Glenn to go and get my stuff. After all, all I sent was a very short, very random email explaining nothing. Their house isn't as small as mum and dad's, but it is immaculate and they're a growing family with stuff of their own, so there really wasn't anywhere for my stuff to go and I didn't exactly give V the chance to discuss the options. But I'd need to pay a visit to the storage unit soon. I was sick of seeing the clothes I'd taken with me, rinsed and rinsed and rinsed. I had begun dreaming of clean underwear like the others. I'd somehow become a backpacker.

Nanna was sitting up in her bed when I walked in, trashy

romance novel in hand and a billion fluffy pillows propping her up. She hadn't been sleeping at all.

'Don't tell your mother,' she smiled. 'Well, don't you look very French,' she said, looking me over. 'Sit,' she commanded, laying her lace bookmark into her place and putting the book beside her on the bed.

I sat in my Grandfather's worn brown leather recliner, wondering how Nanna had ever convinced mum to let her bring it and realising so much had already changed since I'd been gone.

'So what's his name?' Nanna asked directly.

'Who?'

'Don't play dumb with me, Alexandra.'

'Tom. His name is Tom,' I said, blushing and smiling all at once. 'He's handsome and funny and kind and strong and beautiful. He makes my heart stop when he looks at me and with him, Nan, I'm something, I'm someone. I'm so much more than I've ever been. I'm so damn happy it should be illegal.' I smiled as I told her the story, the whole story, start to finish from when I walked out on Billy, the finely coiffed lady who'd handed me fifty euro, the hostel, the trip to the beach, falling into the basement, Tom kissing me, Tom leaving, the crazy Frenchman holding a gun to my head, Moe's kidnapping, Henri's chateau, the rescue and our hiding out in Barcelona, Rick, Sarita and Guillermo, the bar fight, all of it up until now. I told her who Tom and Lydia were and how they couldn't come home without putting their mother and sister in danger and their father trying to control them and even more people hunting them. I told her how I'd surfed and drank sangria and eaten paella. And I told her how I'd left Tom running for his life down the Barcelona pier, jumping into a speed boat racing towards a bigger boat that would sail him to somewhere else, somewhere safe, somewhere far away from me.

She sat up high in her bed drinking cold tea, enraptured. 'Wow,' she said, when I'd finished. 'That's better than one of these books,' she declared, waving her book in the air.

'Only we never got down to that kind of business Nan,' I smiled, embarrassed.

'What? Never? Not any of those times? I thought you were just sparing me the details. Why ever not?'

'He was injured remember. He could barely move after he'd been beaten to a pulp in France.'

'Oh, that,' she nodded. 'Well, why are you here? Why aren't you off somewhere exotic hiding out with him?' she asked with a wishful naughty glint in her eye.

'Mum called, she said you were sick.'

'Poppycock.'

'You're not sick?'

'Well yes, but that's beside the point. I was always going to die someday. It didn't mean you had to leave the love of your life to come back to say goodbye. You could have just called.'

That was my Nanna. Never one for fanfare or fireworks or big to-do's. What was, was, that was it. There was no need to be fussing over any of it. She never held back whether she was right or wrong. She was the strongest, bravest, most fabulous woman I knew and in that moment I didn't mind a bit coming home to hear her rules on the world one more time.

'So what's going on?' I asked her.

'We found it too late, simple as that.'

I nodded, tears in my eyes.

'Now, now, Lex, don't be like that. I've lived a good life, you know. A darned good life. I'm okay with whatever is in store for me next. And you know who'll be there on the other side, don't you?'

I smiled. I knew.

'Yep, that man better be there waiting for me.'

'He wouldn't be anywhere else, I'm sure,' I said, patting her hand, knowing all too well the great love story she shared with my grandfather.

'I feel much better knowing you got rid of that ghastly Billy fellow though,' she said, smiling. 'You deserve more than he could ever give you.'

'You didn't like him? I thought everyone loved Billy?'

She laughed. 'No, everyone tolerated Billy. Only one who liked him was your mother. He charmed the pants of the poor thing and she never saw it coming.'

Mum fussed about in the hallway clearly wanting to interrupt. To save a war, I got up to leave. 'Do you need anything?' I asked.

'You couldn't sneak me some jelly beans, could you?' she asked like a naughty five-year-old.

'Sure I can. Why do I have to sneak them?'

'Your mother has me on some health kick. She says I need to be healthy to keep up my strength. I don't think she realises I'm going to die soon either way. I might as well be allowed some bloody jelly beans. Haven't I earnt jelly beans?' she asked.

'Then jelly beans you shall have!' I laughed. Typical Mum, trying to control the world.

'Oh, and another book?' she asked, holding up her spine wrinkled, page bent book, the lace bookmark hanging limp and bright between the yellowing pages.

I nodded, smiling and left. Mum rushed past me like a tornado. I shook my head, poor Nanna would be stuck listening to a lecture now.

Chapter 19

The sky outside looked like it wanted to open up and collapse. My back ached, reminding me I'd slept on the couch. The distinct swishing of the newspaper echoed from the other room and it was like reality smacked me in the face. In an instant of realisation, my stomach retched, my chest burned and my heart shattered into a billion pieces.

Tom was somewhere else. I didn't know where. I didn't know if I'd ever see him again. How could I? I didn't have the money to fly back to Europe. He couldn't come home. How could we ever be together again? There'd been no time to consider any of that before I'd left Barcelona, before Tom had near thrown me into a taxi as he ran from the gun-wielding Frenchmen.

The blackness crept along the walls, swallowing the tiny pin rosebuds on the wallpaper. I could feel it stretching for me, begging me to let it in. I couldn't, even though I wanted to, I desperately wanted it to engulf every part of me, swallow me whole and numb the pain and desperation that surged through my veins.

The very thought of Tom being with someone else, of me touching and loving someone else the way I did Tom had last night's dinner whirling in my stomach desperate to be out.

Mum pottered about in the kitchen, not so subtly clanking bowls and cutlery as she prepared breakfast. The noise echoed everywhere, the sounds penetrating my ears, my eardrums threatening to burst in protest, my calm ready to erupt with every step she took, every spoon she dropped, every page of the newspaper Dad turned. I had to get out. I had to be somewhere else, somewhere with air, somewhere without sound, or at least without their sound.

I threw on jeans and t-shirt that I'd left on the floor, grabbing my handbag I called out a 'See ya's,' barely hearing their grumbling protests as the front door flew closed behind me.

Hunching on the front step, I gasped for air, the green grass and footpath and road all swirling into a mixture of sun-drenched colours. I closed my eyes, waiting for it to stop. Then I began walking, walking to nowhere in particular, anywhere but the claustrophobia of a home with no Tom, a life with no Tom. It was a mess I couldn't run from. I couldn't hide from, but I had to try before I suffocated.

The streets had looked the same ever since I could remember. The Robinson's roses were a bit bigger, the gums lining the streets, taller, rounder, the petunias in the strange corner house, multiplied, but really, it was the same. There was comfort in the familiarity of things being the same, sadness in nothing changing when so much had changed in me. The world had turned just as it always had while I was on the other side of the world, engulfed in my whirly wind of magic.

There was an early morning quiet hanging on the sweet cool air. The sun promised warmth but it was still getting around to it as it slowly crept higher and higher into the clear sky. It was perfect spring weather, the pollens floating in the air, both beautiful and torturous, the gardens blooming with buds ready to burst, the scent of freshly mown grass hanging on the morning dew. All so familiar, all a reminder that I now existed somewhere Tom did not.

The local shopping centre was old, brownish, tired, the car park already bustling with people pushing filled trolleys and nine to fivers racing in and out for lunch supplies. I walked through the mall; nothing had changed there either since I'd been gone. I hadn't been gone long, after all. But it felt like a lifetime. I'd changed so much that seeing everything remain the same seemed wrong and out of place, strange, surreal, like I'd been in a time warp.

I bought a giant coffee and made my way into Kmart, taking comfort in the familiarity of knowing what was where, knowing I could have found my way around the shop with a blindfold, taking in the familiar smell of cheap cotton and the sounds of a shop revving up for the day.

I picked up a basket and turned to head towards the lolly aisle on the way to the book aisle and I smacked into a person moving way to fast for that time of day.

Shit, I thought as I looked up into a familiar set of eyes.

'Lexi,' Marley, mumbled, almost as surprised as me. 'I was going to call you this week, see if you were home yet, see if you were okay. Are you? Okay? Billy said you needed some time and went travelling. I don't blame you.'

I shrugged. 'I'm fine about Billy if that's what you're asking.'

'Oh,' she mumbled. 'Well, that's good. Did you want to get a coffee or something?' she asked, checking her watch. 'I have some time,' she said.

'Well, isn't that good of you?' I told her. 'Where was your time and concern in Paris when I was blindsided and left walking the streets alone in the middle of the night relying on strangers? Where were any of you then?'

'I'm sorry, Lexi. We were all sorry. We just didn't know what to do,' she said.

'What, that night or all the nights before? All the months or was it years, that Billy was cheating on me, making a fool out of me? What, was there not enough opportunity while you ate and drank my food and wine? Could you not have found just a moment, just one time, to say, hey, Lex, there's something you should know?'

'I'm sorry,' she stumbled, her eyes filling with tears. 'I'm really sorry. But there's no need to be so mean. I thought we were friends,' she pleaded.

'So did I. But clearly it was one sided. It doesn't matter anyway. I'm not that person anymore, the person you knew. I'm not going to be walked over anymore. I expect more from my friends and I wouldn't ever be able to get past what you all did, the way you all lied, how you all let me fall on my arse in a foreign country and left with nothing, while you all sat there and watched like it was entertainment. Perhaps that's why everyone was always so happy to come to our place for dinner? They got a free show with their meal?'

'Lex, no, no way,'

'Well, I'll never know for sure, will I? That's the point. It just is what it is. It's unfortunate for everyone, no matter which way you look at it, but it's done and I have to move on. Like I said, a lot's changed since that night. I've changed and I can't go back to being a walkover. I expect more. But I'm grateful and thankful to you for stopping and explaining yourself and apologising. It does mean a lot.'

'Well, you know where to find me if you change your mind,' she said, with a tight, sad smile.

I put Marley and the rest of them out of my mind. I was here for Nanna. Nanna needed me. I put a few bags of jelly beans in a plastic basket with some black and white boiled lollies I knew Nanna also loved and headed for the books still in disbelief Mum had denied my dying Nanna such simple luxuries. I guess there were all kinds of love that needed prolonging any way you knew how and Mum's way was to control the situation as best she could.

The good romance novels that got your heart beating lined half of the back wall in the book section. I happily killed time sipping my coffee, reading the backs and random pages, forgetting my troubles in the heaving bosoms and throbbing loins of randy housewives and their repairmen, the sheiks who sweep ordinary suburbanites off their feet and turned them into princesses. I eventually selected a few of the steamiest historical gems I could find for Nanna to enjoy, a swashbuckling pirate falling for the charms of a well bred heiress, a handsome cowboy up to no good, a lady and a duke in a forbidden affair. She'd love them. I might even borrow them.

I exited through the self-serve checkout, threw my empty

coffee cup in the bin and merged with the crowd that had thickened while I'd shopped. I popped into the supermarket for a few things and then headed back outside before I ran into anyone else I didn't want to see. I couldn't bear any more confrontations, the questions, the rumours, whatever Billy had been circulating while I wasn't here to defend myself or offer up the truth.

Reluctant to return to the confines of home any earlier than I had to, I sat in the park making my way through a bag of chocolate sultanas, watching the runners, the mums with prams, the pre-schoolers on the swings in the distance, the dog lovers in the dog park over the other side, all going about their day as though the world was fine, as though the world, my world, hadn't just imploded.

I lay my head back, closing my eyes, letting the sun drench my face in golden light while I listened to the cockie's squawking cacophony above, loving the deafening sound that blocked my thoughts for just a moment. They were always in control, always sounded like they were having a good time.

Eventually, I had to give in. I couldn't postpone going home any longer. I'd consumed the entire bag of chocolate sultanas and a can of lemonade, so while I was on an extreme sugar high, it seemed as good a time as any. Nanna would be wanting her jelly beans anyway, so I headed back to the confines of my new hell, a life without Tom and watching my Nanna die.

I sent him another message that went unanswered and gave up. I had other things to worry about. He was fine. He was in the middle of the ocean keeping safe. Our lives were now worlds apart. Perhaps this was always how it was meant to be?

I passed a few neighbours dishing out confused half smiles, obviously aware of my recent disappearance, equally surprised at my sudden reappearance. Then I looked up and saw what I didn't want to see, had never wanted to see again. I forced my legs to move, one foot in front of the other up the street and then step by step up the drive, past Billy bloody McCrae's iridescent green Hyundai Veloster that he treated like a Porsche or a prized Ferrari.

Mum was lavishing all the good chocolate cake she knew was my favourite on stupid Billy as he sat, grinning like a fool, as though he were the guest of honour at a fancy feast, the prodigal son-in-law returned. I wanted to hurl, right there on mum's kitchen floor, it was disgusting and infuriating. How could she do this to me? Pride clearly meant nothing to her. This was going to be one hell of a showdown.

Hiding my bags of goodies behind a cupboard in the living room, I leant in the doorway, silently. Billy looked up, smiling. He got up from his chair, sauntering over to where I stood, reaching out his arms to hug me as though he'd retained some right to do so, as though he hadn't confessed to being a disgusting human being. It made me sick, head spinning 360 degrees and exploding off my shoulders, mad.

'Oh fuck off Billy.' I said, pushing past him and into the backyard.

'Lexi!' my mother cried horrified from the kitchen.

Outside under the verandah, Dad's camp consisted of a high-grade outdoor recliner chair, a plastic coffee table that housed his ashtray, beside which he sat quietly smoking a cigar.

In his other hand, he held a beer as he watched the sun sink over his beloved garden.

'You give in to him Lexi and you'll regret it for the rest of your life,' Dad said, after I sat in the much less fancy foldout guest chair beside him.

'I'm not giving in, Dad, not this time.'

Dad was smiling under his bushy Tom Selleck moustache, 'Good girl,' he nodded and that was it. He went back to watching the trees with nothing more to say.

Billy eventually announced his entry into Dad's haven with the squeaking of the screen door. Took him long enough, he must have finished his cake before bothering with me, his priorities clearly as screwed up as usual.

'What?' I demanded without looking at him, continuing to watch the sun dancing between the trees with Dad.

'C'mon Lex, we've got to talk about this.'

'I thought I was pretty clear in Paris? I've nothing more to say.'

'C'mon, you were a little dramatic, don't you think? And what was with you getting into that van with those, those people? And what have you done to your lovely hair?'

'My hair is none of your business anymore and those people, Billy, are ten times the people you'll ever be. There's no way in hell you're weaselling your way back into my life. Besides, I've already moved on.'

'What? With who?'

'No one you know.' Dad was nodding and smiling beside me.

'Your mum seemed to think you hadn't meant any of it, that it was all a misunderstanding.'

'Well, Mum was wrong and if she'd listen to someone else once in a while, she'd have stayed out of it. We're finished, Billy, we're over. We're so over. You can leave whenever you're ready because I have nothing else to say.'

I pushed past Billy to go inside, I took the next piece of cake mum had sliced for him and went to sit with Nanna, waiting until the front door slammed shut and Billy huffed down the driveway into his equally stupid car and drove away.

Nanna patted my hand as I stood to leave. It was comforting.

The doorbell rang and I heard mum scuffling down the hallway in her slippers.

'Lexi, it's for you!'

Opening Nanna's bedroom door, I yelled back, 'Mum, not again, I'm not talking to Billy, we're finished! Get it through your blooming head!'

She stomped down the hallway, standing in Nanna's doorway scowling. 'Well, miss high and mighty, smarty pants, it's not Billy.'

'Then who is it?' I asked.

'I don't know, do I? Seems I know nothing about you anymore so why would I know who's at the door?'

My first thought was Tom. But I knew it wasn't possible.

'Just answer the door, Lexi, you can't leave people like that standing around all day,' she said, turning and storming back to the sanctuary of her kitchen.

People like what? Who even knew I was home? Who had Billy enlisted with his lies? I didn't care. I didn't want to see anyone. I certainly didn't want to speak to any of Billy's lying cahooting friends.

Standing on the other side of the screen door were two men with shaved heads, goatees, big, broad shoulders, tattoos dancing up their ridiculously thick arms that protruded from black t-shirts far too tight for their build. They were almost cartoon cliché's of mobsters. Could George have sent some locals after me already?

Their eyes narrowed as I approached, one asking, 'Alexandra Deen?'

His deep, gravelly, emotionless voice made me uncomfortable. I didn't want to answer. I wanted them to go away, step off my mother's floral doormat and go bother someone else. But eventually I stumbled, 'Ahuh.'

'You need to come with us,' the same man told me as though the other was a decorative mute.

'Um, nope, am pretty sure I don't.' I didn't mean to be smart, but I was unable to stop myself. I was nervous. They were making me sweat uncomfortably and the tone just kind of blurted out. I couldn't stop myself. I should have. These men could have been sent by George Cummins or Axl's mobster family. Who knew? All I knew was I had to stay inside the house. I'd be safe if I could just make them go away. Surely my family would protect me, wouldn't they? Call the police at the very least?

'Look little lady, some very important people need to see you. We don't want to be rough, but you do have to come with us one way or the other.'

'Nope, nope,' I said, shaking my head stupidly, 'am busy, my Nanna's sick.'

'What's this about?' Dad and Glenn demanded, trying to

be tough behind me, pushing their chests out like schoolboys about to engage in a brawl on the school oval.

'We need to speak to Alex about her boyfriend, that's all.'

Glenn laughed, 'For starters, dude, her name's Lexi, she'd never answer to Alex.' He laughed again as though the whole idea was hilarious, 'Never, and secondly, she just kicked her boyfriend's sorry arse to the kerb and he just drove off in his stupid green car. Seriously, you just missed him, he probably passed you. I'm surprised you didn't see him, that car practically glows.'

The scary men looked at each other confused, turned, then left without another word. I closed the door and stood quivering, frozen to the spot. I knew they didn't mean Billy. I knew they were looking for Tom. I probably should have called Billy to give him the heads up, but I was pretty sure they knew what Tom looked like and after scaring the pants off Billy, they'd do no more harm than that and Billy could do with some pants scaring.

'You okay, love?' Dad asked, draping a protective fatherly arm across my shoulders and leading me out to his backyard haven. He handed me a cigar he knew I'd never light but holding it felt purposeful and soothing. Besides, Dad's cigar let off enough stench there was no need for more.

Chapter 20

When I was a kid and I'd spend the night at Nanna's, we'd stay up late, snuggled in her bed with bags of lollies, mostly the hard boiled ones that clink against your teeth while you suck them until they were small enough to crunch to smithereens. We'd watch old black and white movies on the television she'd wheel in from the lounge room and gossip about everyone we knew. It probably wasn't the most appropriate thing to do but it helped me make sense of a world where I'd never fit in and it made Nanna and I closer than anyone. V hated boiled lollies, she only liked jelly babies and snakes and she didn't get black and white movies. She needed the colour and glitz and as for perky Felicity, she hated gossiping, so she said, and anything that didn't make her look like a genius, even when she was five she was like that. So it was just something Nanna and I shared.

Last night there'd been an Audrey Hepburn movie on Nanna's telly and multiple bags of lollies consumed until my teeth ached from the sugar and my head buzzed and my stomach swirled in circles listening to Nanna tell stories about all the old movie stars until mum started prowling the hallway and we'd mute the television, turn off the light and giggle like schoolgirls until eventually, when we'd emptied the lolly bags, and Audrey had taken her final bow of the night, we gave up and let mum have some peace. I'd snuck a piece of chocolate cake out of the fridge and crept back to my makeshift bed on the couch, climbing under the covers in the wee hours.

I woke with my head pounding from dehydration and too much sugar, all the detoxing and clean living of my adult life had cleansed my body of boiled lolly addictions and my head ached as my stomach frantically tried to digest all that sugar. The sun had decided to shine through the window, Dad was making a hell of a racket with his newspaper and mum was stomping about like a bear with a sore head. It couldn't hurt any more than mine though.

'I hope you didn't come home to camp out on our couch like a dole bludging bum?' my mother asked, her voice dripping with disdain as she huffed her way around the room with the vacuum cleaner.

I smiled and went in search of more cake to ease my sugar hangover. Sugar was like any other drug. Once you started consuming it in large quantities, you needed to keep adding more into your system, so I went into the kitchen until I heard the vacuum cleaner creeping its way down the hallway.

With my smartphone charging, I sat at mum's ancient computer wishing my laptop wasn't in storage. I'd have to make a trip there soon to get a few necessities, some fresh clothes and underwear, my cosmetics and laptop and some books to take my mind off things and keep me company. When mum returned all my other clothes that is because I certainly couldn't leave the house in my pyjamas. They weren't even my pyjamas, although they may have been once upon a time, they did look vaguely familiar but mum had found them buried in the back of a cupboard. They were all she'd left me while she washed the rest of my clothes and my teensy slips of nothing and unmentionables and hung them all outside on the line where poor dad was pretending not to see my underwear.

I logged into the Gmail account Sarita set up for us but there was just one email from Sarita, still nothing from Tom. I was getting worried that something was wrong. He should have at least let me know he was okay, that he was breathing.

There was a short message from Sarita with a picture of the house they were hoping to rent but that was it. Nothing else from anyone even though I'd sent them all a quick email from Dubai.

I should have emailed Sarita. I'd promised to let her know I was okay, but what would I say? I lost Tom, I'm sleeping on my parents couch, my life is a mess, my Nanna is dying and I can't stop or control any of it. No one needs that sob story. I'd find something nicer to tell her soon.

I took a deep breath, steadying my hands, holding the insides of my stomach down, focussing on breathing in and out, in and out. I tried telling myself not hearing from Tom meant nothing. He was probably just in transit, still in the middle of the ocean deciding where to go or in a small town where the internet hadn't yet reached or had sporadic connections. I had to give him time.

My phone had finished charging under the kitchen bench so I sliced another piece of cake and mentally crossing every limb and extremity I could as I checked for missed calls, messages, voicemails anything, but there was nothing. I put the phone in the pocket of my pyjamas, disappointed, tears welling in my eyes.

I sat slumped at the desk as though a message might magically come through while I waited, until mum stumbled through the back door with a basket full of washing. I took it from her and went to fold it in the lounge room. She smiled and minutes later joined me in the lounge room with a cup of tea. She bent to pick up a piece of washing, but I stopped her, 'It's no problem Mum, I've got it.'

'Oh, thanks, love,' she sighed.

'No worries. And thanks for the cuppa, mum. Love you,' I called as she walked out to tackle her next job with a smile tugging at her eyes. I did love her, even though she was neurotic and overbearing at times. I knew it was because she always wanted the best for me. It's just our ideas of success were a little different. But she did make me accountable, made me think. She was always the annoying little voice of reason nagging in my ear, keeping me honest.

Right now that voice was telling me to buck up and get on with my life. There was no way I could get back to Tom if I didn't have any money, to get money, I needed a job. I wasn't even sure I could focus through a job interview with everything that was going on but I had to, if I wanted to be with Tom at some point,

I had to get a job. I'd had a lot of time to think on the flight home and the time since and I wanted that life I had in my head. I wasn't going to be a passive servant to life anymore, I was going to make that vision in my head a reality. I had ideas on how I wanted to live, there had to be a near uninhabited beach somewhere no one would think to look where I could do something useful, where Tom and I could build a life. But for any of it to happen I had to get off my mothers couch. I had to find a way back to Tom which was going to take some time but I was going to make it happen. I had to make it happen.

I opened up the seek app on my phone and started scrolling for jobs with my skills. The idea of being another gofer with no future made me ill but I had a purpose this time, a goal, an end time. As soon as I had enough money, I'd be off. Providing Tom ever returned my calls and messages that is. But he would, I was sure he would when he was back in civilization. Being on the run in the middle of the ocean had to be a hindrance for technology.

So for my needs it didn't really make much difference what I applied for so I opened up the laptop in the kitchen and shot off a bunch of applications for everything from a receptionist at what sounded like an escort agency, an assistant for a private pilot and a bottom of the ladder admin job at a boutique city hotel.

I went back to the folding, pulled out the ironing board after going to get some cake and set myself up in front of the television with some afternoon retro comedies to keep me entertained. When I was finished ironing, I went to spend some time with Nanna.

I had only just sat down in Grandpa's squishy chair when

my phone rang with a local number I didn't recognise. My heart sank as I realised it wasn't Tom.

'Hello?' I answered.

I regretted my casual answering when a professional woman on the other end asked for Alexandra.

'It's Janelle from The Old Regent Hotel in Adelaide, I'm calling about the job application you just sent through,' she said.

I only just stopped myself from blurting, '*already!*' But my well trained manners took over and I went with it, not even remembering submitting that application. I remembered the fancy boutique hotel but the Old Regent Hotel, although beautiful, was old and tired but a job there was as good as a job anywhere else.

'We would love to interview you this afternoon,' she told me. 'I know it's short notice but we have all the decision makers in house today and it would be great if we could see you while they're here,' she said.

'Sure, no problem,' I replied without even thinking about the fact I had no clothes here other than my travel clothes and borrowed pyjamas but I went with it anyway, wrote down the address and the time before thanking her and hanging up.

Nanna was more jubilant that I was after I'd hung up. 'Why aren't you more excited?' she asked.

'Because it's already three in the afternoon, I'm still in my pyjamas and all my clothes are in V's storage unit.'

'You best get cracking, then,' she grinned from the bed, picking up her book.

I sighed heavily and left her to her book. As I showered, the realities sunk in, I had less than two hours to get into the city and to the hotel. I had no car at mums and no money to waste on car parking so it had to be the bus which meant I had to leave in forty minutes leaving no time to get to the storage unit my sister had stashed all my clothes in. I groaned in actual pain as I wrapped the towel around me because it meant I had to raid my mother's wardrobe.

She poked her head out of Nanna's room as I exited the shower and followed me into her room where she began pulling things out. There was a brown pencil skirt, red pants she wanted to pair with a billowing white blouse. When she pulled out the black dress she wore for funerals I snatched it out of her hands and made a run for it.

I at least had my own shoes and after a quick makeup job and blow dry before putting my hair up I was ready to go. Mum dropped me at the bus stop and the nerves set in. I wasn't ready. I wasn't supposed to be here but I had to focus on selling myself, I needed this job if I was going to make my way back to Tom and I had to make my way back to Tom, there was nothing here that made me as happy as I was when I was with him. But if I was going to change my life, with or without Tom, I needed to make some money.

Chapter 21

I would have liked to be wearing a jacket, something smart and professional but mum had nothing suitable so it was just the dress and my strappy heels.

Janelle was behind the desk in a smart blue and white spotted dress, her hair immaculately pulled back and still managing to look like she hadn't put in any effort at all. 'Hi, thanks for coming in,' she greeted, shaking my hand. 'Come on through,' she said, leading me through a door off the lobby into a meeting room.

I'd just sat down when there was a knock at the door. A man in an expensive suit stood in the doorway. He looked me up and down with a creepy look that sent a chill up my spine.

'Christian,' Janelle said with surprise in her tone.

'I thought I'd sit in on the interview,' he told her.

It took a moment before she covered her surprise. 'Of course,' she agreed.

Christian sat and the tension in the room amped up exponentially. I reminded myself it was money. Nothing else mattered but finding my way back to Tom.

Janelle struggled to get a word in. Every time she asked a question about my skills, Christian interrupted asking things like do you travel and hinting at what I do with my free time. I couldn't figure out what he actually wanted to know and going by the look on Janelle's face I doubted she knew where he was going either.

As I was trying to decipher a question about where I liked to eat, another knock interrupted me.

'Oh, Mr Harrington,' Janelle gasped, standing up and almost tripping over her chair.

I looked up with as much surprise but unable to move. The man taking up all the space in the doorway looked like an older, greyer, less charismatic version of Tom. My mouth went dry. So this is why I got an interview so quickly.

'Christian?' Mr Harrington boomed. 'Do you really need to be in here?' he asked.

'I thought it worthwhile one of us asked the questions that needed asking.

Mr Harrington sighed.

'Come on Dad, you really weren't going to leave it all up to Janelle to vet her? Who is she? We don't know a thing about her other than she was sleeping with Tom.'

'Hey,' I defended, not sure what I was reeling from the most, the insult or the fact that this Christian, this weedy, creepy man in his overpriced suit was Tom and Lydia's brother. 'If you have any job questions, then ask them. If you have any questions about Tom you can get lost. Actually,' I stumbled as my brain caught up. 'Don't ask any of them, because there's no way I'm working for you.'

I reached for my handbag feeling a little pleased with myself when I caught Janelle's stunned look. I doubted anyone told off Richard Harrington.

'Before you leave, Alexandra, a word?' Mr Harrington asked with a do not disagree with me voice.

I could tell Janelle didn't quite know what to make of the exchange and she just stood there mute.

'Fine,' I sighed and followed him out.

He led me through the hotel and into an old, rattly lift. The two big burly men who'd been at my house earlier joined us, quietly nodding at Mr Harrington and I recognised them as bodyguards. Not nearly as discreet as Michael and Moe but they'd probably never needed to be. I was just relieved they were Harrington hired.

The lift opened into what must be the penthouse and I followed him into the room, feeling the breath of one of his bodyguards on my neck. I turned and gave him a scowl but he barely noticed.

We walked down a short, bland hallway until Mr Harrington opened the door to a dark wooded study. 'Please, have a seat.'

I sat and waited for him to speak because I had nothing to say and was getting more annoyed by the minute that I'd gone to all this effort when I doubted there was even a job, it had probably already been filled but I was sure it was never going to be mine.

'We need to talk about Tom,' he told me.

'No, I don't think we do.'

He sighed, exasperated and rubbed his temples. I took a sick sense of satisfaction that I was causing him any amount of discomfort.

'Tom's in trouble, you have to know that?'

'Not as much trouble as he was in a few weeks ago, thanks to you,' I said, completely forgetting my ingrained manners.

He sighed again. 'I can't get hold of Michael or Moe which means they're all in trouble,' he told me as though I were a stupid child that didn't understand what he was saying.

'They're not in phone range at the moment, that's all.' I had no intention of telling him they were in the middle of the ocean, who knew what he would do with that information.

'Are you telling me you haven't heard from him at all?'

'Not since I left him in Barcelona running for his freaking life,' I told him.

He sighed again. 'It was never meant to be like this, to get like this. I need him to come home. His mother needs him and Lydia home where they're safe. It's getting harder to protect them. They need to stop. We need to sort it out.'

'I think the time for sorting it out has passed and while your wife and daughters are in danger there's no way Tom will come home and sort anything out.'

'He was overreacting. George Cummins is one of our oldest friends, there's no way he would hurt them.'

'Really? Are you really that stupid? What would you do if everything you were planning was on the line because someone knew something that could ruin everything?'

'If you're right, I can't protect them from bloody George Cummins when they're on the other side of the world,' He cried, clearly frustrated at the whole situation.

'If? There's no if. I saw what they did to him. He was black and freaking blue for weeks. He could barely walk or even sit up. They beat him to within an inch of his freaking life. So yeah, I'm right and it's your fault. You should have listened to him when he came to you. When he told you George Cummins had threatened your wife.'

'He didn't threaten her.'

'He did as much by sending Tom a photo of her and your daughter right before Tom spoke to the police. The meaning was pretty clear even to a regular person like me and I know you're not that stupid.'

He huffed at the insult.

'It doesn't matter anyway because like I said, I haven't spoken to Tom since I left him in Barcelona. So I can't help you. Now can I go seeing as this whole interview was clearly just a waste of my time,' I said, standing up.

'You don't need a job then? You did apply after all,' he told me.

I thought about it for a fleeting minute, 'if it means I have to work for you, then, no.'

'I don't actually work here, I just own it, you'd be working for Janelle,' he said.

'Then maybe you and that Christian should have let her finish the interview.'

'I'm sorry, my son can be a little over zealous.' He sighed. 'I'll walk you out but the job is yours if you want it.' After seeing the look on my face he added. 'Alexandra, I didn't pick you for a fool. You need a job. We have a job. It's simple mathematics.'

'I doubt anything is simple with you,' I told him as we walked through to the living room.

Someone called him from one of the other rooms. 'Would you mind waiting, you'll need my pass to get you back down the lift,' he said, leaving me before I'd responded.

I stood awkwardly in the living room waiting for him. It was not a particularly grand penthouse. I was surprised because everything I knew they owned was grand and fancy but this was nothing like any of their other properties.

'It's not particularly impressive, is it?' Christian asked as he walked into the kitchen. He opened the fridge and pulled out two bottles of water and offered me one. 'It will be when I'm finished with it,' he added proudly.

'You're going to fix it up?'

He nodded. 'Bring it back to its former glory, keep its old world charm but make it beautiful,' he said proudly.

'That would be kind of amazing,' I said, surprised and almost wishing I could be a part of that.

'So, is he coming back?' he asked.

'Tom?'

He nodded.

'Not that I know of.'

He nodded, seemingly satisfied.

'How are they?' asked a kind looking lady with a sweet soft face and shoulder length hair pulled back because it looked like it had a mind of its own. She could only be Lydia's mother.

'They're okay,' I assured her, not wanting to worry her with the truth.

'I miss them. I need them to be home. It's too quiet without them. I need to see that my babies are okay,' she insisted.

I nodded, understanding the hole they must have left in their family when they left, how loud their absence would be.

'I'll see what is keeping my husband,' she smiled, tightly.

'How is Lydia?' Christian asked after his mother had left.

'Okay. Headed back to Paris I believe.'

'I miss her.'

'You could visit her you know.'

'No I can't. Those two are like conjoined twins, wherever he is, she is.'

'Not right now.'

He shrugged. 'It won't be long and he'll be dragging her along behind him into whatever new mess he's found.'

'You don't like Tom?' I asked, taking a long drink of the cold water.

'What gave you that idea?' he smirked.

I watched Christian as he moved across the room. He was shorter than Tom, his face thinner, more angular and harsh, his slim body appeared toned under his expensive suit. He looked serious and strong but his eyes, not the dark green of the ocean like Toms, but a lighter, jade green, were sad and lonely. He didn't even look related to Tom. They couldn't possibly have come from the same gene pool.

'So you work with your dad?' I asked pointlessly.

'Of course. Some of us understand family responsibility.'

'Right,' I nodded, amused.

'Tom could have had anything he wanted, but he's an overindulged pretty boy who's used to getting things his way. I'd never have deserted in the face of crisis. In fact it was me who cleaned up his mess.'

'His mess?' I asked surprised and more than offended but seeing no point in challenging him. I smiled tightly and looked down the hallway to where Mr Harrington had disappeared. I wondered how much of Christian's dislike of Tom was for Tom himself or for having to live in the shadow of Tom all his life. Christian was serious and studious, he didn't carry the tanned, strong, athletic good looks of Tom and I wondered how that had played on a young boys mind, how often his father had openly compared the two.

Christian could have stood anywhere, sat at the table, on the couch but he chose where I was standing. He walked over, standing too close, looking at me with an expression I didn't recognise, almost something of distaste, distrust, the look of a predator I'd never seen before. Or I had, the anger and hate of it anyway, in the eyes of a Frenchman when he'd held a gun to my head. Suddenly I froze to the spot and couldn't move. I had to move but I just stared into his eyes that looked at me as though challenging me to defy any move he made.

Finally finding my legs out of sheer self-preservation, I went to move, to give him space. He grabbed my arm pulling me close, right up against his body. My stomach flipped, fear racing through my body. My eyes darted around the room but I couldn't see or hear anyone.

'You know, there's no mess of Tom's I can't fix,' he said, his groin pressing against my leg, his hot breath stinking of scotch on my neck.

'Are you kidding me?' I stammered jamming my knee into his groin.

'Christian!' his father scolded as Christian doubled over clutching his crown jewels.

Christian inched away from me, looking at me warily and once he'd caught his breath, snatched his bottle off the bench then he skulked away.

'Alexandra?' Mr Harrington called as he came into the room.

'I'm sorry,' he began, 'Where were we?'

I wasn't sure if he was apologising for having interrupted our earlier conversation or if it was a poor, exacerbated apology for his inadequate son? Either way I thought it would be best to forget what had just happened and focus on getting out and going home.

'Christian will be managing the project from our head office, so it really will just be you and Janelle working on the day to day management of the property. Let me show you out.'

He walked me all the way through the lobby. I couldn't see Janelle and wondered how annoyed she would be if I accepted the job without her even being able to interview me. It didn't matter, I wasn't accepting it anyway. I couldn't work for them, not after what they'd done to Tom. I'd have to find another way.

Chapter 22

'Where on earth have you been?' my mother screamed at me as I walked through the front door. Before I could even answer, she declared, 'You were gone for ages, you missed dinner. We've been worried sick. You've got to stop with the disappearing.' She must have been doing dishes when I'd walked in and she wiped her hands on a tea towel hanging over her shoulder and walked towards the kitchen.

I followed her, 'You're overreacting a little bit, Mum, you know where I was, it just went longer than I thought it would. That's a good thing, right?'

'It's a good thing if they offer you a job, Lexi.'

I stayed quiet, I couldn't tell her the job was mine if I wanted it and I couldn't tell her I'd turned it down but she saw it on my face anyway.

'They did, didn't they? They offered you the job?'

'Calm down, Mum. Yes, they offered me the job but I said no.'

'Lexi, you can't turn them down when you've already thrown away a perfectly good job. Jobs don't grow on trees you know.'

'You don't understand,' I tried reasoning.

'What exactly is it I don't understand? Because I don't seem to understand anything about you anymore,' she moaned.

'I'm still me, Mum, I'm just a better version. I'm tougher. And some creepy guy rubbed his man bits on my leg so no, I'm not working there.'

She rolled her eyes and turned on the kettle.

I hugged my mum, 'I'm home now so it's fine. I'm sorry you were worried. I should have messaged you while I was waiting for the bus,' I conceded, understanding how worried she must have been when I'd disappeared in France. I hadn't meant for her to worry or to make her such a nervous wreck that she worried when I was at a job interview too long.

She patted my shoulder. 'Well,' she huffed happily, 'I'll make some tea then, shall I?'

She went one way to make tea and I went down the hallway to see Nanna and update her on my crazy life. She lay asleep against the big fluffy pillows, her little white-tipped head so tiny and frail. She had her arms under the blankets, holding them tight to her chin. Her face had drained of colour, the pink cheeks from the morning gone. Her lips were pale with a slight bluish tinge and even though she was sleeping, dark rings arched upside down under her eyes.

Back in the kitchen with a hot cup of tea between my hands, I said to Mum, 'She looks worse.'

'She had a bad afternoon,' Mum said, keeping busy.

'She wasn't worried about me, was she?' I asked, my heart sinking and guilt already rising.

'No, she's been sleeping, she didn't notice you were missing.'

'I wasn't missing, Mum,' I sighed. 'She believed you though?'

'Whoever knows what goes through that woman's mind,' she smiled warmly. 'You know,' she started again, waving a teaspoon in the air at me, 'you and her are the same. You're like two peas in a pod with your mischief.'

'What mischief? I've never gotten into mischief.'

'This new boyfriend you speak of, he sounds like mischief. Disappearing in France with barely a phone call. That's mischief. Secret giggling sessions with your Nanna in the middle of the night, that's mischief, although that could have been her fault, she's hard to say no to. You, my dear,' she said waggling her spoon again, 'are as much mischief as your Grandmother; only she's been alive longer, she's sneakier, craftier.'

I liked the idea of being like Nanna; she was the most fun person I knew. She was strong and crazy and so much fun. 'What'll we do when she's gone?' I asked, suddenly realising that a world without Nanna was far too close.

'I don't know, Lexi,' she said pouring more tea into my cup and flopping in the chair beside me. 'I really don't know.'

Mum's eyes welled with tears, her face sagged, weary with strain and sadness. I don't ever remember Mum looking so worn or afraid. Mum mightn't have inherited Nanna's sense of adventure, but she did inherit her rock hard strength that anchored our whole family when Grandpa died. Whenever there was a crisis or times were tough and sometimes times were really tough, she was always the one that pulled us through, made everything okay. Seeing her without her armour, letting go of the rope that held us all together, was new. I didn't like it and I was pretty sure she wouldn't be enjoying the experience.

I couldn't imagine what she was going through. She was losing her mum. Even though we fought a lot with our differing opinions on the meaning of life. She was one of the most poised, strong, beautiful women I knew and I couldn't imagine for a second what it would be like to lose her. She was my compass, my barometer, my home. How do you keep going without that? She was soon going to have to learn to.

Draping my arm around her shoulders, I suggested, 'Let's go out.'

'No, no,' she said, shaking her head.

'Why not?' I asked, knowing her answer.

'I have to keep an eye on Nanna.'

'Where's Dad?'

'He's out the back.'

Opening the door I called to him. Dad was in the corner trimming a hedge. Putting down his clippers he came over, 'What's up?'

'Mum needs to get out for a bit. She's exhausted. She needs a break. You need to keep an eye on Nanna, okay?'

He stared at me. Mum never gave Dad instructions. He just went about his business, keeping out of her way and doing as he pleased. But he'd be fine, I was sure. Nanna was sleeping. He just had to stick his head in every fifteen minutes or so while we zipped out for a while.

Eventually Dad nodded. I smiled and kissed him on the cheek.

Mum was fussing about in her spotless kitchen. 'Come on, then,' I commanded. 'Dad's going to keep an eye on Nanna. You and I are going to go have some dessert.'

She opened her mouth, a defensive argument ready to spill into the air. I held up my hand, 'Don't even!' I said, reaching for her hand and dragging her to the front door.

'When did you get so bossy?' she asked, stumbling behind me. 'I'm not sure I like this new Lexi,' she declared breathlessly as she fell in step beside me. I just smiled, glad I hadn't lost Alex altogether since I'd come home.

I decided walking to the local shops where I'd gotten Nanna's supplies was the best idea. Mum could use some exercise and fresh air. It fixes everything, Lydia would say. Mum could use some naughty food, too. She'd become as thin as a rake. She was always slim. Good genes, I guess, but she'd become nothing but skin and bones since I'd been gone. There was a nice little café at the local shops; I'd order her a big slice of apple pie with ice cream or something. That'd give her back some strength.

The whole world around us continued about its business, neighbours waved as they watered their garden, Mum picked one of Mrs Bailey's famous roses at Mrs Bailey's insistence. Birds chirped about getting ready to settle in for the night, small children rode past on bikes making the most of the warm evening, their parents chasing behind. Normality was all around and the creases in Mum's face were smoothing, her lips curving into something of a smile. Yes, walking was a good idea.

I phoned V as we walked and she was waiting for us when we arrived. We were a little breathless and pink in the cheeks, laughing and much better for the exercise. We sat. We ordered. We ate sinful desserts, shared cake, and apple pie and lemon meringue pie. And we laughed some more.

I spoke of French beaches, the Eiffel tower, which really I'd only seen in the distance and the buskers on the streets of Barcelona. V told me all that had happened in my absence, the new couch she and Glenn had fought over until she'd gotten her own way, the dance class Sophie was taking, the trip to the Gold Coast they were planning for the school holidays. It was all lightness and good fun, and after some naughty frappuccino's, V left to go and put Sophie to bed and Mum and I walked home.

Nanna sat propped up in her bed reading one of the trashy novels I'd bought her. I handed her another I'd picked up as we'd left the shopping centre, much to Mum's protesting.

'Lexi, she doesn't need that kind of excitement,' Mum huffed.

I told her if ever there was a time a person needed some excitement, now was it. Nanna chuckled like she was watching a comedy show but she was thrilled with her new book.

'So, where were you this afternoon? How did the job interview go?' she asked in a whisper as though she knew she wasn't supposed to know.

Sitting in Grandpa's recliner, I told Nanna the story of the Harrington's and how the interview was a rouse and I was offered the job without even trying so they could keep an eye on me and find a way to Tom. I told her how Christian rubbed his bits on me and we had a giggle. Captivated by this new turn of events, nodding at each of the details, some of the colour slowly crept back into her cheeks, her smile widened and her eyes came alive.

Eventually the day ended, lights were switched off, the doors locked and the house breathed a sigh of relief as everything went quiet. Alone on the couch, in the dark and the silence, I held my breath and checked my messages. Still nothing from Tom, nothing from anyone that could ease my breaking heart and the sinking feeling I had in my stomach that I'd never see him again. Never hear his laugh. Never be able to ask for his advice or hear his stories or his movie commentary. Could he have so easily given up what we had? Could he have just walked away when our souls and hearts had moulded into one? No. Because if he could walk away so easily it meant I was delusional and none of it was real and it was real. All of it was real. He didn't lie, that much was true. I could believe in that.

Thoughts rumbled randomly around in my head, my stomach knotting and twisting, my insides getting caught up in each other ready to snap. Where was he? Why hadn't he called? Why hadn't he emailed? Something. Anything. I kept thinking about what Mr Harrington had said, hoping I was right to trust Michael and Moe, hoping neither of them had done the dirty on Tom and switched teams. It could happen if their own families had been threatened or they didn't want to give their own lives for Tom after all. Who knew what those bad guys were willing to do to get the job done? Round and round the thoughts went. What if Moe had made a deal when he'd been kidnapped? What could that mean for Tom? Could he protect himself against Moe? There was nothing I could do about any of it.

I wondered if his insides were healing? Was he resting? Was

Moe taking care of him? Feeding him properly? I pictured him, remembering the way his eyes lit up and the way his face relaxed in sleep with the moonlight glowing across his handsome face, the feel of his breath on my neck, the touch of his hands on my body. Would I ever see him again? Would I ever feel that alive again? Was he gone for good? Was he safe? Was he in more dan-ger than ever? Had he been hurt? Killed? My stomach flipped at the thought and I raced for the bathroom, expelling every crumb of cake mum had fed me.

Chapter 23

I woke on the cold, hard tiles, the whole side of my body aching, aching right through to my bones. Gripping the rim of the toilet bowl, I hauled myself up, my legs shaking like jelly, my stomach burning from heaving and my head pounding like I had my own private thunderstorm crashing inside it.

I opened the bathroom door, the house was lit up as though it was the middle of the day. Mum raced past with a jug of water rattling with ice cubes, water splashing over the rim. Mum took her jug into Nanna's room and suddenly my aches and pains were gone. I raced in after her. 'Mum, what's going on?'

'Nanna's just had a bit of a turn, go back to bed.'

I fell to my knees beside Nanna's bed, taking her bony, limp, cool hand in mine, holding it while mum fussed about. I watched her translucent peaceful face for signs, of what I wasn't sure. Her eyes fluttered open as she tried to smile. Mum shoved in an ice chip and Nanna happily sucked on it.

When the ice was gone and whatever mum had given her

finally kicked in, she looked at me, 'You look like shit, Lex,' she whispered.

Her bluntness meant she was okay. For now.

'You're not making yourself sick over that boy, are you?' she asked.

I shrugged.

'What did you tell her, Lexi?' my mother demanded.

'Doesn't matter, Mum.'

'Oh Caroline, hush, an old lady is allowed to hear an adventure story or two. It's not going to do any harm at this point. It's not like it's my heart that's killing me.'

'Mum, stop it.' My mother scolded before leaving the room.

'She's still not ready to face it, is she?' I asked Nanna.

'Don't you worry about her. You really do look like shit, Lex.'

'Thanks, Nan, like you can talk!'

'I'm serious. Don't you brush me off.'

'I'm not brushing you off. I hear you. But I'm fine, I promise. You just rest.'

'I'll be resting for eternity before long, so stop willing me to rest now. While I'm still alive, I'm still allowed to ask questions, aren't I? Don't go shutting me out like I'm dead already.'

'You know I don't mean that.'

'I know. I suppose it's just the pain.'

'Is it bad?'

'Eh, it's not pleasant, but what are you going to do, hey? And I doubt I could look any worse than you right now.'

She wriggled herself higher in her bed, sipping the water mum had left her. 'Now tell me what's going on.'

'I'm worried sick about him, that's all. I haven't heard from him. He's not answering his phone. I don't know where he is and not being with him hurts so bad. It's like someone's sliced open my insides and there's nothing left in there but a big black hole of nothing.'

'Oh I've been there,' she smiled warmly. 'First when your grandfather went to war and I didn't hear from him sometimes weeks at a time. People were coming home dead and injured every day, so every minute I didn't hear from him stretched to an eternity, my heart pulling and cracking. When he walked through that front door with a bunch of daisies from the neighbours yard...Lex, the relief I felt was indescribable. But mostly, I felt whole, like I could finally breathe.

'Then when he died... Goodness, I never thought I'd breathe again. He was the love of my life, Lex. He made every day worthwhile. Even when he was being a grouch,' she laughed, remembering. 'He laughed at my jokes like I was Lucille Ball. He smiled at me like I was Audrey Hepburn and in the bedroom, he'd drink me in like I was Marilyn Monroe. Oh, and when he smiled, Lexi, he lit my insides on fire. I felt I could conquer the world, save everyone with all the love I had in those moments. Then when he was gone, the world shifted, the air changed, a hole grew somewhere inside me that couldn't be filled with anything. It got better and goodness knows I love you girls more than life, but even now, I miss him every day. I miss his conversation. I miss him holding my hand when we walked. I miss him holding me close and telling me everything will be okay. He gave me strength and reason and more happiness than I ever imagined possible.'

Nodding, a tear in my eye, I knew, I knew what she meant. I'd felt what she'd felt, and now I saw the life and the love Tom and I might never get to have.

'Is that how you feel for this boy?'

'Yes,' I whispered.

She nodded. 'You're a lucky girl, Lex. Now you should go shower and clean up,' she said dismissing me.

Leaving her to her memories, I washed away the stench of vomit and fear seeping through my pores. Mum had washed some of my travelling clothes. I really needed to get to the storage unit housing the rest my clothes. Soon. I was sick of the sight of the same shorts and t-shirts and cotton pants and dresses it was too cold to wear. But right now, it all just seemed too much trouble

Lemon cupcakes lined the kitchen benches when I came in hunting for a sugar fix. They all appeared to be in various stages of cooling and decorating. There was a row of cupcakes on a wire rack smothered in thick white frosting that I knew from experience would explode in a lemony fizzing frenzy on my tongue.

Baking was mum's stress release. What she baked told us the severity of the crisis. Lemon cupcakes came with lemon curd and all sorts of fancy inclusions. Lemon cupcakes were the big guns. Mum was stressing. There was no consoling her when she was baking these babies. I noticed she wasn't even waiting for them to finish cooling before icing them which meant she was in a bad place. Icing drips were all over the benches; waterfalls of icing stalactites hung off the edges of the cupcakes and wire cooling racks, but somehow only made them even more enticing. I took as many as I could carry, and went back to my bed in front of the telly.

Putting the reserve cupcakes on the arm of the couch, I shoved them one by one into my mouth, savouring the icing tingling on my tongue, the sugar surging through my veins. I unravelled my folded blankets, flipped on the television and began on the last cupcake.

I woke to some afternoon cooking show when Victoria and Sophie came stomping through the house. V had never known how to be quiet. Thankfully, they walked right by me. I wasn't feeling particularly social.

I checked my phone again, my email, my Facebook, everywhere I could think of, but there was nothing. I put my phone on the lamp table, ate a forgotten cupcake I'd left there and pulled the blankets up high, wishing the whole world would go away, that I could go back to before, back to Barcelona, when everything was perfect, when it was just Tom and I building a life and being happy.

It had only been a matter of days since I'd last seen Tom and it felt like a lifetime. Already, I felt like an empty forgotten shell of nothing. How would the next sixty years be without him? I could feel myself, moment by moment, slipping away without him. I felt weak and stupid because of it, but he was my person, he made everything better, he made me better and somehow I had to find a way to live in this colourless, empty void without him.

I had to find a way to go back to a job, to care about what was going on around me. I'd have to find somewhere to live, perhaps get a cat. But I couldn't figure out how to get off the couch. Without Tom there was no purpose, no reason, no light, no air.

'Aunt Lexi?'

I opened my eyes to find Sophie standing inches from my face, twisting her head sideways, trying to look into my eyes.

'Yeah, Sophe?' I tried smiling, squeezing her tight instead so she wouldn't see the tears in my eyes.

When I felt brave, I let her go. She said, 'Nanna wants to see you.'

"K,' I said, smiling better this time, ruffling her hair and handing over the remote. Cartoons were squealing out of the television before I'd left the room.

Taking some deep breaths as I approached Nanna's room. I regained my composure and knocked.

Every day Nanna was paler than the day before. The light was slowly leaving her body. We were watching her die. She smiled despite the pain her face told me she was in. 'Sit, sit,' she insisted.

Sitting in Grandpa's chair, I held her tiny, frail hand.

'Oh Lexi, don't be so melodramatic. We all knew there wasn't that long to go. That's why you came home and left your man behind, isn't it?'

'Yes. But I don't mind at all, Nan, really.'

'Well I do,' she said, startlingly.

I smiled. She was going to be a tough right to the end. I guess at some point you earn that right and I loved her strength, I loved her spirit, she could boss me about as long as she liked.

'I'm serious, Lexi. Here,' she said, handing me an envelope.

I opened it, money spilling out. 'What's this?'

'It's for you to go find your man.'

'Nan, don't be silly,' I said, shaking my head.

'It's not open for discussion, Lexi,' she said, her pale face serious. 'I phoned the travel agent and they've booked you on a flight. You leave for Paris this afternoon. Paris is okay isn't it? That's where his sister is, right? She'll know where to start, won't she?'

'Nan! No!' I cried, shocked that she could even suggest such a thing. 'I can't leave you. Not now.'

'Why? Because I'm dying? Don't be ridiculous. I'm going to die with or without you watching and I'd much rather die knowing you were on your way to take back that great love. We all deserve our great love but few of us get to find it. You're one of the lucky ones, Lex, you found your great love, now you have to go get him. You have to. You have to make a life with him, you have to find a way, find a corner of the world no one will find you and make a life, do something great.'

'Nan, I can't. There's other things. There's mum for a start.'

'Poppycock Alexandra, your mother will be fine and you know it. And what other things? My funeral? You think I want you to miss out on your life, your one chance, so you can watch my coffin lowered into the dirt? I don't want any of you to have to watch me die, to bury me. It's not necessary. Besides, I know you'll be here in spirit and I'll be with you, wherever you go, whatever trouble finds you, I'll be right there with you.'

Tears rolled down my face, I wiped my dripping nose on my sleeve. I bent to kiss Nanna's hand.

'You better hurry or you'll miss your flight.'

'No. I can't.' I shook my head. My voice was stuck. My chest ached. My eyes burned.

'Yes,' she insisted, leaning over and taking my head in her hands. 'I love you Lexi, there's so much of me in you, you've no idea how happy that makes me, how proud I am. I'd never be at peace if I didn't see you go to get your man so this, this is my dying wish. You can't deny an old lady her last dying wish can you?' she asked smugly.

I looked at her incredulous. I couldn't believe she'd pull something as low as the dying wish card. I shook my head, sobbing like a baby. I couldn't go. What sort of a selfish cow would I be to leave Nanna, leave my family now. But she lay there begging, insisting, how could I deny her? I kissed her cool cheek, hugging her too tight. 'I love you, Nan. I love you so much.'

I left the room, closing the door, sinking to the floor, crying, my whole body shaking.

Chapter 24

Nanna had already spoken to everyone else before she'd spoken to me. Mum gave me a container filled with cupcakes and a tear filled goodbye. Dad was much less emotional but he squeezed too tight during his goodbye hug. Victoria was ready and waiting to take me to the airport. Emptying Sophie's schoolbag that'd she'd dropped by the front door, I shoved in the pile of clothes mum had just folded and left on the end of the couch. Sophie handed me my handbag and I left before I changed my mind or fell to pieces.

V and I didn't speak all the way to the airport. There was nothing to say perhaps. Or perhaps with a single word we both knew we'd never go through with it. V pulled the Subaru up to the drop off zone, but I couldn't get out. My legs wouldn't move. I was stuck.

'She insisted, Lex. It's her dying wish. You have to go get your man.'

Tears blurred my vision, distorting my sister's lovely face.

Watching her tears streak through her carefully applied makeup, I saw all the moments she'd been there for me, the firsts only a sister can guide you through and let you know you're not alone. I wish she was coming with me. It'd be easier if she was. But she couldn't and all I could say was, 'Take care of Mum. She's not handling this as well as you think.'

'I know, Lex,' she nodded.

Wrapping my arms around my sister's neck, not knowing when or if I'd ever see her again, I declared, 'I love you, V.'

I raced out of the car, grabbing my bag and hurrying across the courtyard, too afraid to look back, for even a last glance. I didn't know how long I'd be gone or if I would ever return once I'd found Tom. That's if I found Tom at all. But I was afraid if I looked back, I wouldn't be able to take another step forward. I heard the tyres of V's car screech and knew she was gone.

The flight was long, the food was ordinary, a man snored behind me and a ten-year-old boy fidgeted beside me. Then I had three hours to pace the terminal in Dubai before I had the pleasure of doing it all again with a chatty solo traveller talking about her cats with her stale coffee breath for another seven hours before I finally, gratefully landed at Charles De Gaulle airport.

I waited in the taxi queue, swarms of butterflies filling my stomach with dread and anticipation, my body aching, sagging from exhaustion. But I pushed myself to keep going as I finally climbed into a taxi.

'Hostel de Paris, merci,' I asked.

'Where?' the driver asked in his heavy French accent.

I repeated my request but he had no idea where it was and

I had no idea how to direct him. I'd barely found it the first time. But I did remember the hotel Billy and I had stayed in so I asked for that instead. I'd find my way to the hostel from there. I knew once I got to the hostel, everything would be okay. Andrea would be back to work and she'd know where Lydia was and then I could relax, I could breathe. Lydia would know what to do.

Parting with more of Nanna's money than I wanted to, I got out of the taxi and stood on the footpath with my small backpack, waving off the kind porter from the hotel. I wondered if he'd remember me? Unlikely, I'd been quite a sight that night with tears and make up distorting my face, now I just looked tired.

Turning away from the hotel, I walked down the street, retracing my steps of that dark, rainy night that now felt a whole lifetime ago. I was thankful this time the sun was high, the sky was clear blue and the streets were filled with people. I was far too tired to defend myself. I still couldn't believe I'd walked the streets of Paris that night, alone, in the rain, so late at night. Anything could have happened. I hoped the universe would take as good a care of me today as it had that night.

Two girls were walking a distance behind me, carrying a map, having a lovely time no doubt exploring Paris. A very coiffed lady with a small white dog walked ahead of me. People jogged around me in the sunshine. It was a beautiful day.

I'd walked for a while, not nearly as panicked as the last time. I recognised some of my surroundings so I knew that at some point, the hostel would appear out of nowhere nestled behind the trees, proving the whole experience wasn't just a figment of my imagination, which I'd wondered when the taxi driver had no idea where the hostel was. But I wasn't insane. Not yet, anyway and I was rewarded for my patience as the sun was sinking in the sky, the coach lamps shone through the trees up ahead. I'd found it. I'd made it. Everything was going to be okay.

I pushed open that surprisingly light wooden door and then my heart sank. Seated behind the reception desk was a nice looking girl with long brown pigtails and black glasses. She looked up and smiled. I tried returning her smile, but I was heartbroken. Where was Andrea?

'Can I help you?' the girl asked.

'Is Andrea working today?'

'Andrea? No, she is still on her holidays.'

I nodded, tears welling in my eyes.

'Can I get you a room?' she asked, sympathetically.

'Sure.' I said. I had to sleep somewhere while I figured out what to do.

She handed me my key and linen. I told her I knew the way and started up the stairs. Checking the room number on the brick attached to my key, I couldn't believe it. I stopped on the stairs in disbelief. It was the same room, the same bed.

'Is everything okay?' the receptionist called.

'Yes...yes,' I nodded, going up the rest of the stairs quickly.

Everything was the same. Only the room was empty, no debris anywhere signalling I was sharing with anyone. I showered and put my things away, climbing into the familiar, lumpy, heavenly bed, pulling the little curtain closed even though it was still the middle of the afternoon. I just couldn't face another moment of disappointment, not with the jetlag kicking in.

Rustling from the other side of the room woke me in the middle of the night with a start. Could it be? It had to be. Opening the little curtain, my heart pounded with anticipation, but there was no Lydia. No Andrea. A short brunette offered her apologies with a soft Irish accent. I tried smiling, then too disappointed for anything more, I closed my curtain and went back to sleep.

Morning came and I was dazed. *What should I do? Where should I start?* I had no idea. Coming here was stupid. If the bad guys and Mr Harrington's people couldn't find Tom, how was I supposed to find him? Just little old me with nowhere to start, not even a clue for where to begin. As if it was ever going to be this easy. Nanna and her romantic notions. 'Go get your man,' she says as though all stories end like those in one of her books.

People stirred in the beds that had filled during the night. I'd heard nothing after the Irish girl's rustling, but there they were, unfamiliar heads on pillows. I showered, dressed and left as quickly as I could. The hostel had become a dull, drab, sad place. Without Lydia, Tom, Bex and her Merry Men, it was grey and lifeless. The chipped paint on the walls no longer looked quaint and quirky. It looked sad and forgotten and miserable, as did the worn staircase, the dull lighting, it was all too visible without their brightness to overshadow it all.

Opening the front door, sunshine smacked me in the face and I dove for my sunglasses, hid my eyes and walked. I didn't know where I was going. I just walked. Anywhere would be better than the emptiness of the hostel. Doing something, however pointless, would be better than doing nothing.

I passed patisseries with window displays that made your

mouth water. Buildings older than Australia. Ladies dressed in Dior and Chanel and then, weary, I sat in the shadow of the Louvre. I stared numbly with no concept of time at all, watching the tourists fill the square, going in and out of the Louvre, passing through to somewhere else, going about their business. When people started to look at me strangely as they passed time and again, in and out of the Louvre, I headed for the Eiffel Tower I'd seen in the distance earlier.

A rich green lawn stretched up to the tower as though a humble servant of its beauty. I found a space on the lawn and basked in the enormity of the tower. I'd stopped for some wine, then at a bakery and filled a bag with croissants and scrolls and custard filled pastries and now worked my way through the supply. Everyone drank wine on the lawns, couples made out and groups of friends were scattered everywhere having their lovely picnics of crusty breads and fancy cheese spreads and bottles of French wine, so I drank too, straight from the bottle. That's just how bad my life was, no little plastic cups for me, no friends to care anyway and I wondered again what I was even doing here, in Paris, alone, without as much as a starting point.

How stupid could I have been to think it'd be that easy, that I'd even find him at all? He'd completely vanished from everyone, including his dad and his highly paid super spies. There was no way I was going to find him, not now, not ever. Leaving Nanna, my family, it had all been for nothing. This was what life would be now; this is how it would be forever, nothing but emptiness, a dark giant void of lost possibilities eating away at my insides until the day I died a miserable, lonely old crone.

Raising the bottle to my lips, I took a long gulp. It was fruity and sweet and in seconds was filling my veins with a false sense of something less miserable than how I really felt, so I drank some more. The couples and groups of friends enjoying their picnics didn't see me. A tour group gathered around, their lavish spread across the lawn, their laughter carrying on the gentle breeze, saw no one but themselves. None of them saw me falling into my black hole.

The sun had begun its slow descent as I finished the last of my wine and a chill settled on the air. All that was left of my picnic were the pastry crumbs sprinkled over my pants. Brushing them off, I wobbled to my feet. It reminded me of that first day at the beach when I'd surfed, gliding across the water, wobbly and unsure, happy with Tom laughing beside me, the sun glistening like diamonds as water beaded on his beautiful body. When everyone had been together. When Tom and I fell in love. When everything had been perfect.

I concentrated with every step not to stumble down the street. The wine had made a beeline for my head and now buzzed about at will. The last thing I needed was the French police to throw me in gaol for disorderly conduct so I tried to keep walking in a straight line.

Crossing one of the many bridges slowly, dreamily, I found the road leading back to the hostel. A car passed, a pop song I faintly recognised the tune of drifting out of the open windows. The beat was familiar if the words weren't and it bounced around in my head. Couples strolling by hand in hand to dinner looked at me strangely. *'What are they looking at?'* I wondered.

Then, a few steps on and a few more wry looks, I realised I'd been humming the tune of the song I'd heard out loud. I clamped my mouth shut with my hand, checking no one else was around then breathed a sigh of relief and continued on my way.

A Police car passed, stopping at the corner, turned and headed my way. Clenching my lips together I kept moving, pretending I didn't see them until they stopped beside me.

'Mademoiselle?' They called from inside their car. They asked me a question in French that I didn't understand, so I stared at them blankly.

'Sorry,' I eventually stumbled. 'I don't speak French.'

The passenger got out of the car and asked, 'Are you okay?' in English.

'Ahuh,' I nodded, tears rolling quietly down my cheeks.

'Where are you headed?'

I told them the name of the hostel, waving my arms randomly in its vague direction.

'Get in.'

I didn't even care anymore if they were taking me to gaol. Suddenly everything around me spun, lights blurring together outside the windows. It was over, all of it and on top of everything I'd now have to sleep in a foreign gaol, branded a drunk and become someone's prison bitch.

It was like a miracle when the hostel glowed before me. Praying it wasn't just my inebriated imagination, I just stared at it as we approached until the police car came to complete stop. One of the officers smiled kindly as he opened the door, letting me out.

'Thank you,' I said sheepishly.

The officer nodded with a smirk buried under his little moustache and left.

Pushing open the hostel door as the police car drove away, I took the room key from the bemused receptionist and stumbled slowly up the stairs to my room, collapsing onto my bed fully clothed, pulling the little curtain shut, the blanket up and rolling over to face the wall, pretending the whole day had never existed, and that was the end of that.

Chapter 25

It was a dream. It had to be a dream. There was banging, the bed shaking from the force. Then more banging. It couldn't be. I'd already fallen for that wish once and had found an Irish girl unpacking her underwear. Ignoring the stupid dream that had woken me, I rolled over, but there was more banging. Rolling back to face the curtain, I opened my eyes and waited, listening but all was quiet.

Breathing a sigh of relief, it really was just a warped drunken dream after all. I was about to close my eyes and slip back into beautiful sleep when the whole bed shook again, the poor timber surround near exploding, the sound echoing throughout the room. Shit! I thought, it's really not a dream.

I slowly opened the curtain, not daring to hope, but there, beaming down at me like the cat that got the cream was Lydia. Standing beside her was Andrea holding a tray of coffee, smiling.

Bouncing out of the bed, banging my head but not caring at

all, I hugged Lydia so hard I almost snapped the poor thing in two. Tears exploded from my eyes with the relief of familiarity, the relief of Lydia, my saviour, again.

'Hey, hey, hey,' she laughed.

'Watch the coffee,' Andrea grinned, holding it up in defence when I looked her way.

'Come on, before we disturb everyone,' Lydia said.

In my crumpled, stale clothes, I put on a jacket and followed them downstairs to a breakfast room at the back of the building.

'Here,' Andrea said, handing me one of the coffees.

'Thank you. Do you reception people have some sort of secret code?' I asked her.

'Something like that,' she smiled.

'What are you even doing here?' Lydia asked, excited.

'Looking for Tom.'

'He's not with you?' she asked, confused.

'No. I left him in Barcelona. My Nanna's dying so I went home and the last I saw, he was running from the crazy Frenchmen with guns and jumping into a boat with Michael. I haven't heard a thing since. He was supposed to call me, or email or something. He wasn't answering any of my calls. They went straight to voicemail. I hoped you guys had heard from him.'

'Not a word since the boys left to rescue you guys. We've been out to visit Drey's family. I thought you two would be holed up on some remote beach getting up to all sorts of mischief,' she said winking.

I blushed. 'Sadly, no,' I smiled, wishing her version was right. 'Did Moe go too?' I asked, even though Mr Harrington had referred to Tom and his team, so I'd assumed he had.

'He's with Michael. I'm usually safe enough on my own despite Tom thinking otherwise. It's Tom they're after. He didn't say where they were going, just said they'd sort it out and let me know.'

'Huh,' I mumbled.

'Is he in trouble Alex?'

'Yeah, well, he was when we left Barcelona. But he promised to let me know he was okay when they landed somewhere.'

'And nothing?'

'Nope, not a peep. Then your dad lured me into a meeting at some hotel, then he gave me a grilling. He's lost contact too.'

'Dad's heard nothing either?'

'Nothing.'

'That's not good at all,' she said, shaking her head in thought.

Lydia pulled her phone from her pocket, scrolled through the numbers and pressed the call button and waited. 'Bloody voicemail,' she groaned. 'Tom, where are you? Call me,' she demanded before dialling again. 'Michael, it's Lydia, call me ASAP,' she said. She repeated the process for Moe.

'What now?' I asked.

'I dunno, keep trying I suppose,' she said, shrugging her shoulders in defeat.

'I don't think I've ever not been able to get at least one of them, even at four am,' Lydia said softly. 'What time is it in Australia?' she asked.

I calculated the approximate time difference, ten, eleven hours or so, give or take. 'It's around lunchtime. Why?'

She made another call on her phone. 'I can't find him. Where is he?' she asked the person on the other end. Then added, 'Well what's the good of all your bloody spying if you bloody lose him anyway?' she shouted before hanging up.

'What's the good of him?' she asked, frustrated.

'Your dad I'm guessing?'

'Yeah, pointless bastard.'

Her phone rang, 'Hello,' she said hopefully. 'Oh,' she said, not liking who was on the other end. 'Fine,' she groaned and hung up. 'He says use the card for anything we need. You've had some minders on you the whole way so we should be safe,' she smirked.

'What are you talking about?' I asked. Surely I'd have known if I was followed?

'They'll show themselves soon enough.'

'In the meantime, you two should go shower, come back down for breakfast and start again with fresh heads. You can't call anyone else this early anyway,' Andrea said.

'She's right,' Lydia agreed

'I've got to get ready for work. Let me know how you get on,' Andrea said.

'Come on,' Lydia said, dragging me up by the elbow. 'We'll find him Alex. We always do.' She laughed, even though always only equated to one time and technically we'd lost him and Michael and Moe had done the finding. But the point was, he'd been found I suppose, so he could be found again.

'It's Tom we're talking about; he's made of steel, right?' Andrea said nudging me.

'He knows how to survive,' Lydia promised. 'Michael and Moe will look after him.'

'If you were so sure Lydia, we wouldn't be sitting here in the early hours discussing it,' I smirked.

'Hmmm...good point,' she smiled. 'He'll still be fine. When we find him. He's probably on some remote beach without his phone charger, completely oblivious to time and if so, then he really will be in trouble, because I'll beat the crap out of him!'

I had the quickest shower in history then dressed for anything in the crumpled jeans and t-shirt I'd brought with me.

Lydia was waiting for me at the table we'd recently vacated with a pot of coffee and a plate of croissants.

'Anything?' I asked.

She shook her head. 'Eat,' she said indicating the croissants. 'We might need our strength.'

I took a warm croissant.

'Straight out of the oven,' Lydia told me. 'Drey always does them best.'

I nodded and broke off bite-sized pieces and forced them into my mouth. I didn't want to eat. I had no appetite, no saliva, I just wanted to get on with it and find Tom. But I ate anyway because Lydia was right we needed to be fuelled and ready and they were amazing.

'So, your mum was asking about you,' I told Lydia just to make conversation.

Instantly her eyes welled, but her voice remained the same, 'Is she okay?'

'Sure. She's worried about you two, misses you a lot.'

'Which hotel did you go to?'

'The Old Regent.'

'Ah, a new one?'

'Christian says it's going to be beautiful when he's finished with it.'

'I'm sure it will be. He has an eye when it comes to hotels,' she smiled.

'How was the old man?'

'He seemed worn. I don't really know what he was like before, but he was definitely worn, and gruff.'

'Always gruff,' smiled Lydia. 'But he's never been worn.'

'Perhaps it was just Tom missing.'

'And how was Christian?'

I shrugged.

'What does that mean?' she asked with a smirk.

'He's, um, not like you guys.'

She laughed heartily, 'That's the understatement of the year! He's a good guy though, when you get to know him, if he lets you get to know him. Did he use his manners?'

'No, not really,' I said, avoiding her eyes, not wanting to share what had gone on.

'What did he do, Alex?'

'Nothing. Well, not really. Your Dad kind of saved me.'

'From what?'

'Christian's slimy advances.'

'He hit on you?'

'Well, more like tried forcing himself. Told me he could fix any of Tom's messes. But I kneed him in the groin and your dad came in before it got out of hand.'

'Tom will kill him.'

'I think your dad might have already taken care of that.'

'Oh, won't Christian love that Dad's still sticking up for Tom after everything that's happened,' she sniggered, almost to herself. 'You really kneed Christian in the groin?' she laughed.

I nodded, smirking.

'That's priceless,' she said shaking her head. 'That'll teach him. Poor thing won't know what happened, no one challenges Christian Harrington,' she chuckled as two nice looking, girl next door types, approached our table. 'Ah,' Lydia said, extending her hand and introducing herself. 'This is Alex but I'm guessing you already know that.'

They smiled sheepishly, nodding. 'Celine, Alana,' Celine introduced.

As the breakfast room began filling with other patrons we went out to the foyer so Lydia could make some more calls.

'I don't know what else to do, who else to phone,' Lydia moaned.

'Well, where would he go, does he have a favourite place he likes to hide?' I asked.

'Well, there's a few,' she said, thinking. She moved Andrea out from behind her office computer and started tapping away and calling hotels and hostels looking for a Tom Blake, 'Famous surfer,' she whispered while she waited for the first to check their records. She hung up, searched and called another and another.

I'd left my bag and everything upstairs so I asked Andrea to find me the number for Papa G's bar in Barcelona and she handed me the office phone to use.

'Papa G?' I queried when he answered the phone.

'Alex, is that you?' he asked.

'Yes, Papa G.'

'What is wrong, why you calling?' he asked.

'I'm looking for Tom, have you heard from him?'

'Tom? No, how did you lose him?' he asked as I heard Rick asking questions in the background. Papa G shushed him. 'Are you okay Bella?' he asked.

'No, Papa G. No one can find him and I don't think I'll be okay until I do.' Andrea handed me a post-it note with Lydia's mobile number on it and I gave the details to Papa G. 'Will you call one of us if you hear from him? We just need to know he's okay.'

'Of course, of course,' he said.

'Found him!' Lydia called from across the room. 'He's in Tangier,' she said.

'Papa G, it's okay, we found him, he's in Tangier. I'll get a flight and we'll be fine.'

'Tangier is not safe, Bella. I send someone to meet you. Good man, he'll look after you. He have a sign. Do not leave the airport without him.'

I hung up from Papa G and Lydia wrote down the details, handing the piece of paper to Celine and booked our flights with her shiny, hardly used family funded credit card.

When she was finished, she sighed with relief, collapsing in the club chair by the window. 'Bastard scared the shit out of me,' she said. 'I am so going to punch him when we get there,' she laughed.

Suddenly I froze, suddenly I wondered, what if he didn't want to see me. He was fine. He was in Tangier. He hadn't contacted me. He hadn't picked up Lydia's calls. What if he was shacked up with someone else sorting out all that pent up sexual energy I'd left him with? What if he was living the life of dreams and perfectly happy doing it?

'What?' Lydia demanded while I sat contemplating the inner workings of Tom Harrington.

'What if he wants it this way? What if not contacting me or you or whatever, is just fine with him? He's moved on, happy as Larry with whatever he's doing.'

'Come on, you know Tom better than that. He came back for you at the beach. He whisked you off for supposed eternity to Barcelona. Trust in him. There'll be a good reason.'

'Yeah I know. I guess, it's just, there's still so much I don't know. You guys had the whole amazing, fabulous, gypsy life before I came along. What if he liked that better?'

'Don't be ridiculous. Tom is in love with you. The way he looks at you, the way he protects you, the way his face lights up when you walk into the room, I've never seen him like that. Besides, I can't imagine our lives now without you. It's like you were always there. You fit in so perfectly. I forget you weren't there with us on all those adventures.'

'Really?' I asked, unsure, never having truly fitted in anywhere in my life.

'Yes, you fool!' she laughed. 'I couldn't imagine our lives now without you in it. You're one of us whether you like it or not!' she smiled. 'Now would you go get your stuff before we miss our flight.

Running upstairs, I chucked all my stuff in my bag, ran back down, my legs burning. 'Okay, let's go,' I said hugging Andrea goodbye.

'There's a car waiting outside, come on. Let's go find that stupid brother of mine,' Lydia said.

'It's going to be okay, Alex,' Lydia said, holding my hand. 'It has to be, he has to be. I can't live without him either. He's my rock. I don't think I can go forever without him. A couple of weeks, yeah, but that's it. That's the most I could survive. He's a part of me.'

I squeezed her hand in comfort. I had no words to offer. I just wanted him standing in front of us, smiling, anything. I didn't even care anymore if he's sunburnt from spending too much time at the beach, or wobbling from too many Pina Coladas. I don't think they drink Pina Coladas in Morocco. In fact, I don't think they drink at all, but that's not the point.

'You know, he knew I was gay, even before I did,' Lydia smiled. 'He told me, Lids, be whoever you are inside. It makes no difference to me who you love. I'll love you anyway, just as long as you're happy. Not everyone was as supportive as Tom. In fact, I don't think my parents would even remember the conversation. They were much happier to nod and assume it was just an attention grabbing antic and mostly ignored the whole palaver. But not Tom. He was so cool, about the whole thing and it made it easier. I knew I would be okay at a time when nothing made sense. I don't think I could do this life thing without him. Besides, if anything bad had happened, I'd know right? It's a twin thing, he gets sick, I get some sickness? Isn't that how it works?'

'Is that what usually happens? Were you in pain in France?'

'Well, no. But if he were dying, I'd know. That's different. It'd be a part of me dying too. We share too much DNA for it to go unnoticed.'

'I sure hope you're right.'

'I am, I know it,' she declared, laying her head on my shoulder, staring out the window.

'You ready ladies?' asked Alana as we landed and people starting gathering their things.

People surged forward as though we were prey as soon as we came out of customs. Alana and Celine flanked Lydia and I and slowly, hesitantly, we moved forward. Papa G's man was going to be holding a sign so we scanned the onlookers for one but saw nothing. A few men in Fez hats and robes covering their jeans and cargo pants closed in on us, their eyes greedy. Then from behind the crowd came a commotion. Alana and Celine became instantly protective pushing us behind them, which was no good. These people were like hungry piranhas circling us from all sides.

A young man, flustered, red and sweaty from hurrying, pushed through the crowd of people now offering us tours, warning us of the dangers of Tangier, trying to sell us all manner of things. A sign dangled by the young man's side as he pushed through the crowd, the sign, jiggling about as he ran towards us.

'Ladies,' he bowed breathlessly. 'Uncle G has sent me to be your chauffeur.'

Alana and Celine looked him up and down as the men he'd just pushed through got restless and angry at him stealing their sales but they soon moved onto other tourists looking much more confused than us. How this man had known we were his guests I was trying to figure out when he smiled and held up his mobile phone and the photo Papa G had sent him.

'You are younger than we expected,' said Celine, untrusting.

'Ah, Uncle G phoned my father, he is busy, so he sent me.'

'You speak very good English,' Alana stated.

'Yes. I've been living and studying in London. I am home to marry. Father thought this would keep me out of trouble.'

'Uhuh,' nodded Celine, deciding if she should believe him. She must have decided in the affirmative, sticking out her hand she introduced herself.

'Ilyas,' the fresh-faced young man replied. 'You can call me Illy.'

Alana and Celine nodded. 'Let's go then, shall we?'

We followed Illy to his car. He was tall and lean in a slightly awkward way and ambled rather than walked. He had thick black hair under his fez and tanned skin showing from under his *djellaba*. His phone rang and without breaking stride, he picked it up. Near forgetting we were following, he endured a heated conversation, his hand slapping his forehead numerous times, his tone exasperated before he finally remembered us, said something quietly, disconnected and looked back to us with a strained smile. 'Fiancée,' he said holding his phone up as way of explanation and apology.

Illy's car was too much of a luxury sedan to be his and he was too pleased to be driving it. I guessed his father had offered it as a compromise so he could be busy with doing nothing as Uncle G had told us he did with passion.

Everything outside my window was unfamiliar as we drove. I had no points of reference, so sat back and enjoyed what I saw, cataloguing it all for another time when it would eventually make sense. How we would ever find Tom in that labyrinth was beyond me. I just hoped he was in the hotel, laying low and safe.

I closed my eyes as we drove, imagining a place more familiar, imagining Tom's arms around me and smiled. I would see him soon. In minutes we'd be together and if there was a dirty skank in his lap aka Billy bloody McCrae, I was never dating again.

The sun was setting when Illy pulled up in front of a hotel.

'We are here,' Illy said turning off the car.

All the streets around us looked the same, tall cement buildings, long cement footpaths stretching in all directions. Nothing green, nothing distinctive

We got out. 'This way,' said Illy. 'Stay close,' he insisted and I almost grabbed a hold of his *djellaba* as people filled the footpath.

The hotel was three star, maybe. It was derelict and sad but I daresay a great place to hide. Illy spoke to the receptionist and I waited for him to translate. After what seemed a tense, frustrated conversation, Illy said, 'He is not here. He is gone.'

'What? He can't be gone. This is where he was.'

'I am sorry. He is not now,' he said apologetically.

'Well where is he?' I asked looking around the small foyer as though he might materialise.

Illy asked the receptionist but before she could answer, her phone rang. She answered and we waited.

Alana's phone rang and she went outside to take the call. When she returned she told us, 'That was your Dad. Tom's used his credit card in Casablanca.'

'What?' demanded Lydia. 'No. It's Dad's credit card, Dad's

money and it's traceable. Something's wrong. He'd never ever use that card. Never'

'What does that mean?' I asked.

'I don't know but we have to get to Casablanca and find him.'

'I will drive you,' insisted Illy.

'What? No, we can't ask you to do that, we'll get a flight or something,' Lydia said.

'No, really, I insist. Uncle G would never forgive me if I didn't take proper care of you,' he said.

'Alright, thank you,' Lydia said.

'We will make some calls along the way and see what we can find out,' said Alana.

'Great, let's go then,' said Lydia.

Illy thanked the receptionist for us. She smiled shyly in return then was looking past us to her next customer.

We turned to leave and I stopped dead, looking into the face of a man that looked like a bulldog. The man who'd held a shotgun to my head. If I'd moved faster he mightn't have recognised me but I'd frozen and given his puny brain too much time to process what he was seeing. Even with the new hairdo I still looked like me.

'Shit, hurry,' I said as I could see recognition slowly dawning. I grabbed Illy's arm and we pushed past him. 'Run,' I said as soon as we were outside and we ran all the way up the hill to the car. Thankfully the bulldog was too heavy to keep up. We couldn't go straight back to the car though, he could see it, he would know what we were driving and he'd be able to find us, so we ran past it, further up the hill and around the corner onto a busy street.

The street was full of people going about their regular business. We worked our way around them as they went bustling by, snaking in and around us. I focussed on the bobbing of Alana's head as we surged through with the crowd but the crowd became thicker and the noise louder and soon there were so many people I could hardly see any more of Alana than the occasional bobbing of her ponytailed head amongst the crowd until I couldn't see it anymore. I couldn't see anyone.

Her head fully disappeared into the crowd and I took sharp shallow breaths to control the panic surging through my body. It had only been seconds and already she was gone, swallowed whole, no sign she'd been there at all. I twisted and turned like a lost child. I had no idea where to go, how to weave my way back to the car, if it was even safe to do so.

How had it happened? How was I lost in a foreign country? I was supposed to be with Tom. He was supposed to have been at the hotel. I hadn't expected to return without him. How could we have missed him? He'd just been there a few hours ago and now he was gone and I couldn't see anyone and there were all these people around, pushing by with their funny hats and *hajibs* and robes. My eyes welled with tears as I looked around in panic. I stopped. I stood still. Maybe they'd find me? I'd arrived at a junction in the street and I had no idea which way to turn, left or right? I wanted to cry.

'What, no friends to protect you, you make it all too easy,' a man whispered in my ear, his hand on my elbow, bringing me back to the present.

I turned, startled, bile swimming in my stomach but I couldn't see anyone. Was I losing my mind? Masses of people were crossing the junction, had he been swept away by them? I didn't know. I didn't know anything anymore. Only that I was lost. I'd failed at finding Tom and now he was in even more trouble and there was nothing I could do about any of it.

Someone pulled my arm, dragging me into a doorway. I stumbled, tripping up the small step, my ankle rolling the wrong way. I fell to the floor, pain shooting up my leg, too afraid to look up at my captor. But when I did it was Celine. She held a finger to her mouth to shush me so I squished further back into the corner awaiting instructions.

She bent down and whispered, 'Are you okay?'

I nodded, wincing, my eyes filled with tears threatening to erupt.

Celine stood, flattening herself against the whitewashed wall and peeked around the corner and flipped back into position, her breathing concentrated and focussed. Waiting a few minutes she tried again, this time taking long enough for a proper look. She returned to me, 'Can you walk on it?'

'I don't know,' I whispered, trying to stand.

It hurt. I winced in pain.

'Lean on me,' she offered, holding out her arm.

'No, I'm okay, let's just hurry,' I insisted, ignoring the pain shooting up my leg.

Carefully we stepped out onto the street, which had quietened with the surge of people having reached their destinations. Only a few people now walked casually in conversation with no hurry at all.

We were only a few steps down the street when a car horn beeped scaring the bejeezus out of us both. My heart couldn't take much more of this. Illy's car stopped beside us and we quickly climbed in and Illy began the drive to Casablanca.

'You should sleep,' he suggested. 'It is a long drive.'

Sleep was the furthest thing from my mind after running from the bulldog and nearly being kidnapped off the street but I closed my eyes and again tried blocking out the sounds of people and horns that seemed to bounce off all the buildings.

I must have slept despite my protesting because we were out of the city when I opened my eyes.

'Here,' said Illy handing me a bottle of water.

I sipped the water and then slept some more, sleeping like the dead, catching up on missed sleep and letting my poor exhausted body recoup some energy until eventually the car came to a stop.

'Are you okay?' Illy asked.

'I think so,' I said. 'I don't really know. I'll be better when I find Tom,' I told him.

'Do not panic just yet,' soothed Celine. 'We will be there soon enough, right Illy?'

'Sure, soon,' he said wearily.

'How is your ankle?' asked Celine.

'It's okay. A bit sore,' I said trying to get comfortable again so I could rest some more. I wanted to be rested and ready for anything when we got to Casablanca, when I found Tom. I just hoped Lydia was wrong and him using that credit card wasn't a sign something untoward was happening to him. I had visions of him bound and gagged while someone else used his card and it was all a trick and we'd never find him.

Time had almost stood still while we drove the last few kilometres before Illy finally pulled the car to a stop and everyone began piling out. I hobbled along with Illy's help, my ankle was a little swollen and stiff, I was sure it would be fine in a minute or two. We walked into a nearby café, Lydia was desperate for the bathroom. We were finally in Casablanca, a city I'd love to have seen, the smells and the sounds exotic, but I was too preoccupied to even notice them.

As soon as we walked into the café a woman screamed Illy's name and he near pushed me out of the way as she raced into his arms.

Celine caught me and we all stood staring at him. This girl was beautiful. She was movie star beautiful. He held her close and turned to us beaming, 'This is Aya, my girlfriend.'

We tried smiling and saying hello but really we were too confused to be fully coherent. Was this really the girl he was going to marry? The girl going bridezilla on him in Tangier?

He smiled at us, amused, 'It is okay,' he said. 'She knows I am to marry Merryem.'

'Right,' I said without thinking. So at least that explained his keenness to get out of Tangier and drive the ridiculously long journey to Casablanca.

'Aya and I met at University,' he said, as way of explanation.

'And you don't mind he is to marry Merryem?' Lydia asked.

'No. I, too, am to marry, a businessman named Samir. He is a good man, a kind man, but he is not Illy,' she said smiling up at him.

'Can you not marry each other?' I asked.

'Oh, no,' they laughed.

'Our families do the choosing. It is fine, really, but it is lovely to be able to see Aya one last time. She is very beautiful, isn't she?' Illy said.

'Yes,' we all stumbled, still in awe of her beauty. I wondered what this Merryem looked like, but imagined the poor girl would spend her whole life in the shadow of Aya.

Illy and Aya sat at the next table talking while Alana jumped back on the phone to find out where exactly Tom had used the card. Celine went to the counter to organise refreshments and Lydia raced for the bathroom.

I sat facing the window, watching the bustling street, my stomach filled with dread and anticipation, counting the minutes until Lydia would return, until Alana would enlighten us with more information, until we could go and get Tom from wherever he was, from whoever was holding him and using that card.

A kerfuffle erupted outside on the street. A group of men, two, large men laying into another. They were throwing punches. I could almost hear the crunching of bones. Then one of the burly blokes moved and I saw him. Tom! The men, burly blokes not too different from the Frenchmen had him bailed up against a wall across the street. His face had been hit, he was worried and afraid and they looked ready to give him another going over. He was clearly holding his own going by the blood dripping down his opponents face but he couldn't hold them both off for much longer on his own.

I raced outside, ignoring the sound of my name as Celine and Lydia and Illy all called to me. Nothing else mattered but getting to Tom. Car horns honked as I dodged cars as I crossed the street and without thinking I kicked one of the meatheads in the back of the knee as hard as I could and he crumbled to the ground. Tom took care of the other one who crumpled to the floor after barely a punch to the stomach.

While his assailants lay groaning, Tom doubled over, panting as though he'd just ran for his life. I watched him, my heart frozen, my breath caught in my chest as I stared, waiting for him to look up. Then he did and my heart restarted, skipped a beat and butterflies swam in my stomach as his face went from surprise, shock and then broke out in the hugest of grins before he stood, wrapping his arms around me as though they'd been made to do just that and I melted into him, never so glad to see a person in all my life.

'You're okay?' I whispered, tears in my eyes as we tried to get out of the fray before we got into trouble.

'I'm okay,' he said. 'I wasn't paying attention. I don't even know how they found me. What are you doing here,' he smiled, shaking his head.

'Looking for you,' I said, punching his shoulder. 'Where the bloody hell were you? You had us worried sick. We thought you were dead,' I cried.

'We?' he asked.

'We. Me and your sister. Your dad saw you'd used your credit card and she thought there was no way you'd do that, that you must have been in trouble. We imagined you chained up somewhere while someone else used your card. But you're not. Why aren't you?'

'I'm sorry. I couldn't find you,' he said, raising his eyebrows. 'I finally emailed you but you didn't reply and I called you and someone named Sophie picked up your phone but she wouldn't tell me where you were. Told me it was none of my business any-way but that she didn't know where you were. I was worried. I was terrified something had happened to you. I was coming home to find you.'

'To find me?' I whispered.

'Yes, Alex. I miss you. I can't breathe without you. I needed to know you were okay.'

Illy appeared beside me. 'Are you okay?'

'Yes. I am now. Illy, this is Tom,' I said making the introduc-tions and explaining how Papa G had sent me Illy.

Chapter 26

Just as Tom was thanking Illy, giving him some money for a night's rest before driving back to Tangier, Lydia came from nowhere, barrelling into his arms before punching him in the chest. 'Where were you?' she shouted punching him again. 'I thought you were dead!' she howled

'I'm sorry. I'm so sorry. My phone fell into the ocean when I climbed from one boat to the other. Then Moe busted his bung knee getting off the bloody boat, so Michael left me to stay put while he took Moe back to London for surgery. I was supposed to just stay in the hotel but Alex wasn't replying to emails and the person answering her phone didn't know where she was. I panicked. I left Tangier, to come here to get a flight home.'

'Why didn't someone call me?' Lydia asked.

'I tried, but it just kept going to voicemail.'

Lydia scrimmaged in her pack, unmentionables falling to the ground until she found her phone. She madly pressed buttons. 'It's dead. Its bloody dead,' she said, tears rolling down her face.

'Hey,' Tom soothed, gathering his sister into his arms. 'It's alright. I'm alright. It's all over Lids, we can go home now.'

'You're still going home?' she asked surprised.

'I thought it would be easier for everyone if I left, if I hid. But it's not. It's not better at all and I want a life. I want a life with Alex, to give us the chance to be normal, have a family or whatever else it is we decide we want. I deserve it, don't I? I didn't do anything wrong. But we can't do any of those things if we're running for the rest of our lives because it's not going to stop. They're not going to give up. They're not going away and this could go on forever.

'It's time I stood up and faced the music and sorted it all out once and for all. Because it can't go on forever. We can't keep living like this, Lids. It's not right. I'm not the same person I was when we left. They won't make me run this time. I called mum, warned her before buying my plane ticket so she would be safe, told her to tell no one, let it be a surprise for the old man but I wanted her to be prepared for the fallout, to be safe. For Jaz to be safe. Did you know Jaz was gone?'

'Gone? Gone where?'

'Just gone. Her and dad had a difference of opinion on how to manage her mental health after she hit rock bottom and she just left.'

'What about Jay? Where was he when all this happened?'

'Apparently driving the car,' he smirked, shaking his head. 'He was in love with her the second they met but she put him through the wringer. At least he'll make sure she's safe wherever they've gone.'

'Well good on Jaz,' grinned Lydia. 'At least I'll be able to check my emails now without the old man being able to trace our location and see what's going on. She better have emailed me.'

'But will you be safe if you go home?' I asked bringing them back to what was important right now, afraid there'd be a row of shotguns waiting for him as he stepped off the plane.

'George Cummins can't frighten me this time. As long as mum's safe, he can't get to me and I have Michael, he'll meet us when we land. If I stay at the country house and let the police sort it out like I should have done in the first place I'll be okay.'

'And you have me,' I told him.

'Exactly,' he smiled, pulling me to him. 'I have you and this is no way to live. We both deserve better. You deserve better too, Lids. Come home with us?'

She nodded apprehensively.

He smiled. 'Everything's going to be alright now. We're going home, we'll see mum, eat some of Margot's beef stew and everything will be alright,' he said, gathering his sister to him.

'Shit,' she said as though it suddenly hit her. 'We're going home.' She smiled so big I thought her face might split in two.

'Alright, we have to get you all off the street now,' insisted Celine bringing us all back to reality.

We were shuffled down the street and into one of the big hotels. We stood uncomfortably in the grand marble foyer while Alana handed out room keys before whisking Tom away so a doctor could look him over.

'I need a drink, or something,' I groaned to Lydia after Alana had dragged Tom away.

'Come,' said Celine, leading us to a courtyard full of sunshine and paved with orange Moroccan floor tiles.

We sat at some bistro tables, finally sighing with relief as Celine organised us bright orange cocktails.

The sun warmed our arms as we drank and caught up on the happenings of the last few weeks, my family, my confrontation with Billy, Lydia's visit with Andrea's family.

'I can't believe it's over, no more running,' Lydia grinned.

'Me either,' I smiled. I couldn't believe that somehow I was going to have everything, my family, Tom, a life together.

Lydia talked of all the things she couldn't wait to do when she got home, starting with a hug for her mum, her favourite chicken dish from Margot, the family's housekeeper and a walk through the orchards with the Australian sun beating on her shoulders. She was bubbling over with happiness and excitement. Once we'd finished our cocktails, all the excitement from the last few days began to take its toll.

'I need to sleep,' Lydia eventually gushed, the weariness taking hold as she ran out of words.

'Where's Tom?' I asked.

'Tom will be fine, go rest,' insisted Celine. 'We'll come and get you for your flights,' she insisted.

I followed Lydia to the elevator and we rode it together to the same floor and went into our rooms on opposite sides of the hallway.

Inside the room, I dropped my bag on the floor, kicked off my shoes and collapsed on the bed. I'd just turned on the television and was scanning the channels for something to watch when the door to the bathroom opened and Tom walked out.

I was speechless, frozen. It was still just sinking in that I'd found him and there he was, standing in the doorway looking at me, a towel gripping his hips, his chest bare, his jaw covered in a week or so's growth.

All those nights lying beside him came flooding back. All those weeks tending his broken body, the need, the desire, his breath on my neck, his beautiful hands on my body, between my legs, what his touch had done to my body. It was a sudden avalanche of emotion and desire and as I looked at him standing there in his towel, his beautiful, perfect body just begging to be touched, to be ravaged. I realised every one of those things I'd wished for all those days I couldn't touch him could now come true. He was here, right in front of me, nothing but a poorly secured towel covering him and I practically orgasmed from the anticipation, the knowing, the desperate, feral look of desire turning his beautiful eyes as dark as the ocean.

'Where have you been?' he asked, a smile crossing his face. 'I thought you were never coming back.'

I jumped of the bed and ran to him. His arms wrapped around me and held me tight. 'Geez, I missed you,' he whispered in to my ear.

He held me at arm's length, took a good look at me then his mouth was on mine and I melted into him, into the sweet perfection of the kiss.

We edged towards the bed, his hands holding my mouth to his as he took hungrily, as though he too had wondered if we'd ever be together again.

Then we were on the bed and he was pulling my t-shirt over my head.

'Wait, wait,' I breathlessly begged, my hand on his perfect chest.

'What exactly am I waiting for because I believe we've waited long enough? I believe I owe you some amazing,' he smirked.

I smiled. I wanted some amazing. I really wanted amazing, but not at the expense of his wellbeing. 'Are you okay?' I asked.

He smiled. 'Yes, Alex. I'm okay. I'm perfectly fine, see,' he said, sitting up so I could see his beautiful, perfect body was bruise free.

'Yes, well, we thought that once before, didn't we?' I challenged.

'I promise you, I'm okay. I just got a clean bill of health from the doctor downstairs and everything. And now that I'm here, with you, I'm perfect,' he told me.

'Good,' I smiled, bringing his mouth back to mine and throwing that cumbersome towel onto the floor.

It'd been so long coming, I thought being with Tom was only ever going to be a dream, a beautiful daydream that would forever tear at my heart and haunt my dreams because it would never come true. But it turns out some dreams do come true and not only do they come true but they go ahead and exceed every single one of your expectations.

He made me feel things they talked about in Nanna's romance novels. His hands did things, his body did things that there were no words for until my body exploded with exquisite pleasure that pulsed and pulsed through my body.

As we lay sweating and panting I couldn't believe my dream had become a reality, that Tom had elicited from me things I'd never thought I'd experience.

'I'm so in love with you,' he whispered into my ear and I knew no moment would ever be as perfect as that very one and grinned like a fool.

We spent the night in bed, making up for all those lost weeks. We ordered room service and we slept, sated and happy in each other's arms.

We lay that way until Alana eventually came knocking. It was time to go home.

We left Alana and Celine at the airport and boarded a plane with a very sombre Lydia who'd had a difficult farewell phone call with Andrea while Tom and I had been indulging in our hours of amazing. But she'd be okay. She was happy to be going home.

'So I found an email from Jaz,' Lydia interrupted the silence.

'Yeah?' asked Tom.

'Looks like it's from the day she left. She says, Hey Lids, don't know if you're checking your emails but I wanted you to know I'm okay. The old boy lost his shit, locked me up like a prisoner rather than discuss my mental health in public. The doctor says I have bi polar. I have pills and stuff and I'm doing better. But the old boy told Jay he couldn't come back and you know, Jay was all that was keeping me together. You know I love him, right? I know, don't laugh, I have a funny way of showing it but I do and he'll keep me safe, so don't worry. I haven't bothered emailing Tom because I know he won't check his emails but give him a big hug for me. I hope you guys are safe. Mum's stopped seeing Sue but dads still kissing George's fat arse, he's worried that all the strings that get pulled for him because of George will be cut if he stops but Mum will wear him down, I know she will. But I want a fresh start. I need it. I don't want to be who I am anymore. I don't want to be a Harrington. I just want to be me, whoever that is. I probably won't be able to email again because we all know Dad will be tracking our emails hoping to track me down and lock me back up but I promise I will be okay. Jay promises he'll make sure I'm okay. No more partying, no more craziness, I promise. I love you both. Take care and be safe. Love Jaz.'

'I'm glad she's okay,' Tom said. 'Jay will look after her but we'll find a way to get her back, even if it's just for dinner,' he said, pulling Lydia to him for a hug.

On the flight home we caught up on sleep and gossip until finally we were back on Australian soil. As we stepped off the plane, Lydia and Tom had the biggest grins, all their woes, Lydia's heartbreak, all forgotten in the familiarity of home.

We saw Michael as soon as we came through customs and lots of backslapping and hugging ensued before he guided us outside to a waiting car.

'You doing alright, Tom?' Michael asked concerned.

'I'm fine. How's Moe?'

'Feeling stupid, but he's fine, he's home with his sister now.'

I struggled to imagine Michael or Moe having families and wondered how they felt about them being away so long.

'You need anything?' Michael asked Tom

'No, we're all good, just get us back to Alex's.'

Michael nodded then spoke into his headset. 'Yes sir, we have him on board,' Michael said. 'Yes sir,' he agreed.

'You're not taking me to him. Not after everything, you're

not handing me over to him like a fucking Christmas present,' Tom told Michael.

Michael laughed. 'Tom, really, come on. But he'll know that and he'll be on his way to Alex's, so be prepared.'

Tom nodded.

'Tom?' I asked, wanting to know what he was thinking.

'It's fine. I should have known it would never be this easy, anyway,' he said.

There was a driver waiting for us when we got to the SUV, one of the burly guys from the Old Regent Hotel. We gave each other polite greetings before Tom and I climbed into the back of the van, Lydia in the next row and Michael sitting up front with the goon.

I heard Michael give instructions to drive us to my house.

The goon tried protesting, 'Mr Harrington said...'

'I don't care,' Michael said calmly. 'This Mr Harrington insists on going to the Deen house so that's where we're going.'

The goon shrugged.

'How far away is the other Mr Harrington?' Michael asked conversationally.

'Plane's bringing him in now,' he replied.

'You have about an hour,' Michael told us. 'I've had your car moved, Alex. It's now in front of your parent's house. Up to you how long you stay and what you do. We're dropping you off and going around the corner for some dinner.'

'No we're not,' the goon said. 'We're not to leave them unattended.'

I could feel Michael's exasperation. I didn't need to hear his stern tirade.

'We'll wait and see what's what when we get there, okay,' Tom insisted.

I nodded, thankful for his kindness but I knew, for him, I'd leave before the hour was up if he wanted to.

The house was quiet when we pulled up to the kerb.

'Go,' Michael said. 'Good luck.'

They were gone as soon as we closed the door. 'Come on, we don't have much time,' I said.

'Alex, it's okay. We'll stay as long as you need to. Don't worry about my dad. It's over, I'm not running anymore. I said I'm going to end it and I will. I'm going to face everything, go to the police, do all the things I should have done in the beginning.'

I kissed him softly.

He smiled. 'Go,' he said, indicating the front door.

I left them standing in the hallway to take care of themselves with my family and I went in to see Nanna. She looked pale and frail. I was surprised when she opened her eyes because she looked like death.

'Oh don't look at me like that,' she admonished. 'Sit,' she commanded, so I sat. 'Did you find him?' she asked, a little colour coming to her cheeks at the promise of an adventurous tale.

'I found him. He's here,' I told her.

'Well, why aren't I meeting him?' she demanded.

Lydia had been whisked into the kitchen where my mother was feeding her tea and cake but Tom was waiting in the hallway where I'd left him. He came in and took Nanna's hand when she offered it and sat when she told him to sit.

'It's alright Alexandra, go, your mother has cake. I want to talk to this beautiful man of yours,' Nanna grinned, a mischievous twinkle in her eye.

Tom nodded so I left them to talk, wishing I could be a fly on the wall. Poor Tom didn't know what he was in for.

The tears I'd been holding on to fell when I closed the door. Lydia wrapped me in her arms. 'She looks so sick,' I sobbed.

There was no way I could leave until it was over, not now, not now that I'd seen her looking so sick. I hoped Tom had meant it when he said he was happy to stay.

'Come, have some tea,' insisted Lydia, leading me into the kitchen where my family waited.

Lemon cakes lined the benches and my heart broke for my mum. I went and hugged her. 'Are you okay?' I asked.

'Oh,' she said, waving me off. 'I'm just glad you're okay,' she smiled.

Mum had just poured me some tea and passed me a plate of cake when we all startled at the sound of the front door slamming. Lydia and I raced towards the door, our only thoughts to protect Tom but we stopped short when we saw Mr Harrington standing in the doorway looking particularly uncomfortable.

'What are you doing here?' demanded Lydia.

'I've come to see my children seeing as they refuse to come home, to see their parents, their frightened mother.'

'Oh don't give me that. I've spoken to mum. She's fine.'

'She'll be better when you're home. Get in the car.'

'No.'

Tom came out of the hallway and calmly stood looking at his father with hatred. Tom was a few inches taller than his father and looked stronger. He stood to his full height, his face turning to steel and I thought for a second his father almost took a step back. 'Can you keep it down, there's a lady dying down there you arrogant pig,' he spat at his Dad as he came over and put his arm around me. 'She's okay, she wants to see you when we're done here,' he said, kissing my temple.

Mr Harrington scoffed as he watched the show of emotion.

'No,' spat Lydia. 'You don't get to do that. He's happy. She makes him happy. She's the only reason he's standing here. You have to fix this so he can stay. So we can both stay or we'll be gone before you can blink,' she said, pushing past him and outside.

Mr Harrington turned and followed her out. We could hear them shouting from inside but we pretended we couldn't.

'Go see your Nanna,' Tom told me as though the commotion outside wasn't occurring at all, that it wasn't about him.

I reluctantly left him to deal with his father and went into Nanna.

'Nan?'

She smiled. 'He's a keeper, Lex,' she told me.

'He is, isn't he?' I smiled.

'And handsome, too. Boy, won't you two make pretty babies,' she grinned. 'I'll be sad not to see them, but I'm hoping it's true what they say, that I can keep peeking at the goings on down here from up there,' she smiled.

'Yeah, well, just be careful, there's some things you mightn't want to see,' I grinned stupidly, thinking of all the amazing nights that awaited.

Chapter 27

We buried Nanna the following Saturday. The sun streamed across the cemetery, the blades of grass glistening like crystals as the ever so slight breeze made them dance a perfect recital in celebration of her life. She had been so much to so many people. The turnout confirmed she'd made the most amazing impact on everyone she met. It warmed Mum's broken heart to see so much love pour out for Nanna.

So many people returned to mum's for afternoon tea. Nanna would have been horrified at the fuss but chuffed all the same. Mum had done her usual and over catered to extremes. There were mornays and pastas and enough cake to fill a bakery in all different flavours and colours and sprinkles.

The day Nanna died, Mum's heart had broken into a billion pieces as had all of ours. But she was relieved too. Watching her mum in so much pain and caring for her as she had, had taken its toll and now Nanna was at peace, so was mum.

Nanna had spent time each day drinking tea with Tom. She

wanted to know him, know who'd made me as happy as Grandpa had made her. '*Not everyone gets as lucky as us, Lex,*' she'd told me. And on our last night of jelly beans and gossiping, she'd told me, '*He is just perfect, Lexi. He'll make you happy. He has love for you oozing out of him. No matter the obstacles to come, you'll make it through.*'

Tom and Lydia hid out at my parents for the duration. Mum had even made beds for them in my old bedroom while I remained on the couch. Word had it those that had hired the gunmen knew Tom and Lydia were out of hiding and they were hovering just outside the grounds of all the Harrington homes and hotels but they hadn't yet figured me into the equation. They knew I existed but didn't know my name but it was only a matter of time. Mr Harrington was due to have a press conference once Tom and Lydia returned to the safety of the country house so my family wouldn't be in danger and in the meantime Michael and Moe and an array of Harrington goons kept watch at my mother's kerb like sentinels.

Tom and Lydia supported me and my whole grateful family through the loss of Nanna, making tea, doing dishes, giving hugs and offering a ready shoulder. But as we stood outside, farewelling the last of the guests for Nanna's wake, Michael and Moe walked up the path with regretful looks on their faces.

Tom nodded. 'It's time, I suppose. It was nice of him to leave us alone as long as he has, really,' he said. Lydia nodding in agreement.

I wasn't ready. I tried offering food and coffee, leftover mornay, anything. I just didn't want Tom to leave yet. I never wanted to be apart again. I couldn't do it again. Never again.

Tom nodded. 'Time to face the music and sort this all out once and for all, so we can all move on with our lives, eh,' he said, far too brightly for my liking.

I couldn't believe it. I had to say goodbye again. I didn't think I could do it. Looking into his eyes, I tried smiling but my eyes filled with tears, my knees shaking, my hands trembling.

'Oh, Alex, you're coming too,' Tom smiled,

'Now? No, no, I can't go now... my family... we just buried Nanna,' I whimpered.

'Lexi, go, we're fine,' Mum said, actually smiling for the first time in a while as she stood on the front step, Dad's arm draped over her shoulder.

'I've got it, Lex,' Victoria insisted.

'See,' Tom smirked. 'Besides, I'm not leaving without you,' he said, leaning his forehead on mine, his forefinger trailing a path across my my collarbone, sending a sea of goose pimples all the way down my spine. Stopping just before I groaned, he whispered, his breath hot and moist on my ear, 'we have unfinished business. I owe you amazing, a whole life of amazing and it begins today.'

In actual fact it took a few weeks for the amazing to begin. We were holed up at the country house which was more like some holiday resort they should have been charging a nightly rate for. Out of consideration for Tom's mother, we were sleeping in separate rooms so amazing was on hold.

Tom spent some time with the police telling them everything and handing over footage of the night Lincoln Cummins went at it with Axl up against the lobby wall. From there they found enough information to piece together that Axl didn't really want to be going at it with Lincoln and Lincoln had been blackmailing him but Axl didn't have the family Lincoln had, Axl's family would have happily killed Lincoln if they found out so when he found out, Lincoln killed Axl first. There'd been security footage of Lincoln on the night Axl had died but no one was quite sure what he was doing or why until the missing pieces connected the dots.

George Cummins escaped investigation because he disappeared. Tom was sure there were no suspicious circumstances and that he'd just taken a private jet to somewhere no one would find him and was probably drinking cocktails on a beach. But Tom knew what it was like to be hiding every day and knew someday he'd slip up and pay the price.

'Alex!' Tom called from downstairs.

I jogged down to meet him in the living room. There were big doors that had been slid open, opening up the living room to the deck and giving a view of the resort style pool beyond glistening under the sun.

'Hey,' I said, letting him scoop me into a hug.

'I have a surprise for you,' he told me, unable to keep the stupid grin off his face. 'You know how I promised you some amazing but well we're still in my parent's house?'

'Ahuh.'

'Well,' he said, dangling a set of keys in the air. 'Linc's been arrested, Axl's dad has apologised and sent his men out to find George so we're free to go wherever we want. Live all the dreams you have in your head. So hopefully you'll be happy to start with a little place I've had tucked away on the water.'

'Really?' I asked, suddenly excited that we could actually get on with our lives now, do all the things I imagined, be purposeful and happy and together.

He jingled them for good measure. 'This time, a life of amazing really does start today,' he grinned before his mouth crashed into mine.

Acknowledgements

I t has been a long and arduous journey to publication as it often is for authors but I wouldn't have arrived here if it weren't for the amazing support of my family who don't always understand what I'm doing but support me anyway. To my extended family, a person would be blessed to have just one of you in their corner, I am beyond blessed to have all of you. And to the four angels I get to love as though they're my own, Patrick, Hamish, Bella-Rose and Serena, thank you for making the world a better place, giving the best hugs and always making me smile.

Unending thanks and eternal gratitude to the best friends a girl could have: To Amanda for never letting me give up, always making me laugh and for being one of the strongest, most inspiring women I know. To Kelly for reading everything from the beginning and championing everything I write. To Carly for always knowing when noodles and wine are needed and mid week visits to the Barossa. To Fiona for the long Sunday lunches and all the imparted wisdom. Thank you! To my friends who are still my friends even though I am so often distracted I forget to say hi for months, I really do love you. To my RWA family, some of the loveliest and most talented women I know, particularly Kaye and Brooke, my musketeers, I love you ladies. To my ASA family, thank you.

Enormous thanks must go to my brilliant editor, Carla Molino, this book is so much better for your input, thank you and to my talented cover designer, Kristyn McGuiggan from Drop Dead Deisgns, you are the very best, thank you.

And to all of you who have been so kind as to read Alex, thank you, she soothed my soul when it needed soothing. I hope you loved Alex, Tom and Lydia as much as I did, they were a pleasure to live with for the last eight years. To keep up with my releases, please go to my website at www.tamaramartinauthor.com and you'll find links to all the social media sites and we can keep in touch.

About the Author

Tamara lives and writes in Adelaide. She's lived many lives on this journey so far but her favourites are those of author and aunt. Like many writers, Tamara has written ever since she could hold a pencil and was telling stories even before then if you believe her parents. She always knew she would write a book someday but got a little distracted along the way until September 11, 2001 reminded her how short and unexpected life can be and she decided right then that doing work she didn't love wasn't good enough and so the journey began.

When she's not writing, she loves eating, movies and trips to the Barossa. She watches too much TV, travels as often as she can and of course owns a ridiculous amount of books and loves nothing more than curling up on her oversized couch for the afternoon and losing herself in the pages of a story.

If you would like to connect, talk TV, books, wine, anything, you'll find Tamara here https://www.facebook.com/tamarak-martinauthor